To anyone who was ever told they were *too much*
but wasn't willing to make themselves less

One

I cannot believe that Joshua Stallings has somehow managed to ruin school supplies for me.

Me, of all people. The girl whose divorced parents draw straws every year over who's stuck dragging her around for back-to-school shopping. It takes up at least half a day while I float down every single aisle and caress each paper clip and mechanical pencil like a benediction. I have a legitimate sticky-note addiction. I ask for gel pens in my Christmas stocking.

I grab a pack of highlighters like they're a life raft and squeeze my eyes shut. *See? This is still exciting! You can color-code your notes with this pastel multipack and the serotonin from that will practically drown you.*

"Momma, Marlowe's praying to some highlighters!"

Eyes are open and highlighters are back on the shelf before my very Methodist mother can round the corner and see another thing to be concerned about.

"I'm not praying, Blue," I say, asking God and the pristine

shelves of the Super Buy to find me a sliver of patience. "I was just testing something."

"You are so *weird*," she exhales through fourteen years of despair from having been saddled with me as an older sister. She's recently taken to correcting people with a quick "Marlowe is my half sister," as if that other set of genes made a world of difference. "Can't you just pick some notebooks like a normal person?"

Well, that's part of the problem, isn't it? At least for Josh.

We're all just clumps of stars and carbon, but my particular flavor of cosmic particles is not exactly popular. Almost as if there were a few substandard atoms tucked away in the curve of my clavicle, or the shell of my ear. A strangeness that poisons the whole batch.

I smile, my skin stretched so tight I could burst. "Why don't you just pick some out for me?" The entire experience is already ruined, and I need to pull the lever and eject myself from this day before it takes me down with it.

She perks up, blood in the water. "You've never let me do that before."

I shrug. "Surprise me."

She spins, her lime-green bodysuit twinkling. The lighting here would be unflattering on anyone else, but my baby sister shines. Even after an hour of gymnastics practice, she's glowing, and I have no concerns about her starting her first year of high school with anything less than complete adoration from everyone she meets. She's every inch our mother's daughter: a peacock, or a swan, or—a unicorn. Sunny blond hair, a golden Georgia tan, and a wall full of equestrian medals, pageant crowns, and cheerleading trophies. The perfect River Haven girl.

I, on the other hand, am solidly in badger territory. There's a lot to be said for that, though. I'm smart, efficient, and reliable.

Usually solitary but can work with a group in a pinch. The type of River Haven girl who was happily on the sidelines, quietly winning medals in math and spending all her time with her two badger best friends, until another peacock pulled her into the spotlight with him.

Blue grabs notebooks, pressing their covers tightly against her spandex so I can't see.

"Nothing too crazy," I tell her, already regretting this but desperate to get out of the store.

She laughs and twists away as I try to take a closer look.

"Not the pink one," I say, as she reaches for one that loudly declares I LOVE BOYS in a font that makes my skin crawl.

"No peeking!"

"Name two boys I love, and you can get it."

She scowls, stumped, and I grab my phone like it's an EpiPen and I need an injection of sanity stat.

I duck behind a pallet of binders while she's trying to scrounge up a single name and slide boneless to the linoleum. I don't even breathe until FaceTime connects and their faces fill the screen.

"I thought you were shopping with your mom today," Odette says, her eyes narrowing. "And where the hell are you? Is something behind you Saran Wrapped?"

"Is this some kind of murder-house-hostage situation?" Poppy asks, eating popcorn way too casually to be contemplating my imminent demise.

"Can't it be both?" I ask, ducking lower as Blue shouts to the surrounding aisles, "What about this one with two dolphins making out?"

Odette's eyebrows escape up into her beanie, and I decide silence is golden. "Dolphin erotica aside," she continues, "are you sure you're okay?"

My face, haunting this conversation from the upper corner of the screen, is pinched tight. Ghostly white, with auburn hair that topples forward into a red that's barely believable as natural. A joke, a self-deprecating comment, almost slips through my teeth but I think, *Why bother.*

"Not great," I say finally. "Momma's made me try on four pink dresses so far, as if a few ruffles will have Josh stampeding back to me."

Poppy coughs, popcorn catching in her throat. "Like you're a matador? That somehow seeing you in pink for once will whip him into enough of a frenzy to trample you with his love?"

"Nobody said it was a *good* plan."

Part of me wants to say that if a dress could put my life back together, I would clutch it with both hands, but it feels pathetic to admit it out loud.

"You are not a ruffled pink dress, Marlowe," Poppy says, making me suspect she's better at body language than she pretends to be.

And *I know* that. I do know that. I still can't explain it in a way that will make sense to them.

We'd found each other in kindergarten, and that was all she wrote. Gravitated to each other, like magnets who'd finally found a home after years of sliding off the surface of other kids. While our classmates filled recess with screeching and feats of bravery, we'd meticulously excavated a portion of the playground before we were forced to stop, but we walked away with sharp stones, muddy hands, and each other.

Not much has changed. Except I'm now older, none the wiser, and huddled behind school supplies while my kid sister shouts about flirty-poop-emoji notebooks.

"There you are." Blue rounds the corner, breathless. "Don't worry, I picked the horniest dolphins for you, specifically."

"Phenomenal," I manage, looking at the stack of notebooks in her arms, and knowing I only have myself to blame.

"Get off the floor, Marlowe," Odette says, her heart-shaped face filling the frame. "Take the flirty poop, the promiscuous dolphins, even the inevitable girl-power notebook, and get the hell out of there."

I wilt under the fluorescent lights and the mounting pressure of walking into school tomorrow. Of passing locker 118 and seeing all of *them* gathering as if I'd never even existed. But she's right, and I'm not going to collapse with a whimper on the floor of the Super Buy.

I get back on my feet, mostly to smooth the concern off their faces.

"I'm up, focused, and ready to truly disturb someone with my new school supplies."

"That's the spirit," Poppy says, sliding glittery purple frames up the bridge of her nose.

"Girls, can we please wrap this up?" Momma walks up, dumping ribbons and mason jars into the cart. I know she's going to fill them with cookies and have us give them to our teachers tomorrow with an equally sugary smile to remind them that they're appreciated. She's always being the *most*. The most thoughtful parent, the most doting mother, the most fashionably dressed in the early-morning drop-off line. Even here in the Super Buy, with her peony-pink sheath dress, pearls, and perfectly coiffed blond bob that hides any sign of the same burnished red erupting from my own scalp. She's Bunny Thompson, and she's made it her life's work to be perfect at being perfect.

"Gotta go," I mumble, and toss my phone back in the bag.

She turns forty-five years of patience and polish in my direction. "Did you get what you need? I told your father I would take care of this since he didn't have time while you were in Denver."

Perfectly polite, but always a small dig at Dad. That's the reason she divorced him back when I was a baby: *Time*. She couldn't excuse the time and attention he gave his patients as he provided them with new hearts, and so she found a tan, loud car dealership owner named Stuart who would give her every second he possessed. Then they had Bluebell, and the gangly, redheaded badger who will always be too much like her father became a little easier to ignore.

"Momma, I'll be fine. Blue is picking out some notebooks for me, and I have everything else."

She nods, already on to the next problem to solve, when Darleen Bridgers almost runs her over with her cart.

"Bunny!" she exclaims, with a heavy-handed sprinkle of delight that makes my teeth hurt. "Don't you look divine?"

Momma looks up, her photo-ready smile already in place. "Darleen! Why, it's been a dog's age. How are Carl and the girls?"

"Oh, they're just the best, and the girls can't wait for school tomorrow!" She turns to me and attempts to soften years of Botox into a sad face. "How are you, Marlowe? I was so sorry to hear about you and Josh. Imagine breaking up right before summer! Tiffany was disappointed to not see you at all the get-togethers over the break."

My Tiffany tolerance is about twelve minutes max, but I know my role in this conversation and smile. "It'll be nice to catch up with her tomorrow."

She gives me another attempt at a frown. *You poor thing.* "Girls have to stick together, right?"

"Why, Darleen, you know how teenagers are," Momma says. "Off one day, and on the next, who can keep up?"

Darleen's smile droops a little, and I know Tiffany has told her she likes Josh. A poorly kept secret among our friends. Well, *Josh's* friends.

"We'll see, won't we?" She gives us a small nod and wheels away.

"Are you really going to let Tiffany try to steal your boyfriend?" Blue drops the notebooks in the cart, face down.

"Josh should be allowed to decide who he does and doesn't date, don't you think?" I say, throwing in the highlighters to break the tension.

"Boys don't know what they want," she says, with a terrifying conviction that has me wondering exactly what she's been up to in junior high. She does a small pirouette, her interest already moving on to something else.

"I really don't see what the problem is," Momma says, inspecting me like I'm a dented package and she's looking for damage. "I never heard you two have a single argument."

"No, arguing was never the problem."

Josh had very set opinions, and when he explained them so passionately, sometimes they became my opinions too. He had a lot more data and experience to fall back on, at least from a romantic standpoint. It made *sense* that every Friday night should be reserved for date night, and it made sense that he felt it was lazy to say "I love you *too,*" so the correct response was always a definitive "I love you." An active declaration. A war of words back and forth, escalating in earnestness.

It wasn't unreasonable to accept that Robert trying out for quarterback was a betrayal to their friendship and should be repaid in kind, and that when standing in a group it was appropriate to always hold hands. It was so *easy*. I understood rules. I *loved* rules. For the first time, I didn't have to think about what the correct response to something, or somebody, was, and I could just float along in his wake.

"And it just came out of nowhere?" Momma asks, as if my answer will be different from the ten times she's asked prior. I could be honest. I could tell her that Josh had sat me down and let me know exactly where I fell short, and that it was terrifyingly similar to the complaints she'd had about Dad.

"Marlowe, you know you're really important to me, but I think we need to go ahead and take a break," Josh said, sitting next to me on the porch swing. I swayed, his words and weight knocking me off-balance.

We'd just come back from a day at the beach with his friends, and I was pink from the sun and from watching him, framed by sand and spray and everyone's attention. Golden-blond hair, a body whose dips and curves I'd carefully measured the angles of, and cerulean eyes that missed nothing.

Unlike me, who missed everything, and didn't see this coming until it was on top of me.

"What do you mean, I'm important to you? We're in love." I shied away from the word "break." It was too ugly to even look at. I knew we were in love. He'd told me.

His hand pressed mine, and I stilled.

"I'm going to be at our house in Hilton Head for most of the summer, you'll be with your dad in Denver, and we need to take some time to see if this is actually working." His fingers, still grainy with sand, scraped the inside of my wrist.

"But I love you," I said, the words falling out. No embellishments, no apologies. Just the facts as I knew them.

"Do you?" he asked kindly. "Marlowe, you say it, but I rarely feel

THE CALCULATION OF YOU AND ME   »   9

it. I don't think you've ever done anything romantic for me. Sometimes I wonder if you're even really that interested."

I sat there, frozen in place. My brain cataloguing two years of dates, football-game attendance, I-love-yous, and girlfriend tutelage under his careful expertise. I didn't know which assignment I'd failed. He gave my hand another squeeze.

"It's all right, Marlowe, not everyone's built for it."

I shake off the cobwebs of his pitying eyes, and the way he skipped down the steps of my house and didn't look back once. I dig deep and smile back at Momma, a photocopy of her own. "It's a mystery." I give her nothing but what she wants to hear. "You're right, these things are always on and off, and who knows what will happen tomorrow."

I say it with so much conviction I almost convince myself. After all, he just said a break. That he just needed some time. Maybe I'll walk in the door tomorrow and he'll appear next to me, his warm hand finding mine through the crowd.

Two

I lean into the dented burgundy locker and angle the handle up a few more degrees. I feel it give a little under my fingers, and shoulder-check the door to pop it open.

"The efficiency of that was extremely sexy."

My heart tugs a little as Odette arrives at my elbow. She has a very complicated relationship with punctuality. And alarm clocks. And other human beings. This combination results in her barreling into every class as the final bell rings, so I know she's here early for me. She stands almost a foot shorter than me, with pale blond hair and facial features that are ridiculous in their symmetry. A perfect little doll, if that doll was fifteen times smarter than you, routinely terrifying, and going through a jumpsuit phase.

"You're early," I say, hiding my smile.

"I couldn't wait another second before seeing the R-rated dolphins."

I pull out one of the cursed notebooks. "Well, you're going to be sorely disappointed, because this is barely PG-13." I hold up the two pink dolphins flying through space, their snouts meeting in a starburst of pink glitter.

"This was massively oversold," she says, wrinkling her nose. "Who exactly is the target market for this?"

"An excellent question," Poppy says, adjusting glasses fogged from the long walk from the parking lot. She's wearing a purple skirt with Cheshire cats dancing across the pleats, a pink blouse climbing with leopards, and a cardigan with rockets blasting toward her wrists. The most methodical and cautious of all of us, and her clothes are a level of chaos that's unmatched. Her brown skin is damp from the exertion, and her short curly hair holds three separate cat clips. She's Ms. Frizzle incarnate, and I couldn't adore her more.

"Poppy, doesn't your house have any mirrors?" Derrick Watts says, ambling past us and already laughing at his own joke.

"Yes, why do you ask?" She looks up with bland curiosity.

"Yeah, Derrick, why *do* you ask?" Odette shoots back. "Especially since you've dressed identical to Josh since fifth grade, and I'm pretty sure he told you to stop hiding in his bushes at night."

Derrick flushes as red as the polo that sits a little too starched on his shoulders. He doesn't nod at me, or say hello, or show any indication that we've spent countless hours in each other's company. The best friend and the girlfriend. Josh's bookends. He just murmurs "Freaks" under his breath and keeps walking down to where I've spent every school morning for the past two years. I've been thoroughly excommunicated.

"I guess we're not friends anymore," I say, one octave too high to pass for normal. "Now who will bore me with sports data I don't care about?"

"Maybe he has a newsletter you can subscribe to." Poppy wipes her lenses, completely unbothered.

"I could hack his laptop. He probably has a breathtaking amount of blackmail material on there." Odette nudges me until I give her the smile she's looking for.

"That's illegal," Poppy chides.

"I bet his password is literally 'password.' It's not illegal if it requires no special skill to do it. I would wager real money that he has folders of feet pics."

"*No,*" Poppy and I say in unison.

I track Derrick's progress down the hallway. I know I shouldn't stare, but I can't help it. I'm looking for *him*. It's been two months, and I don't know why I think his appearance will have all the answers. Will he look withdrawn and morose? Like he's also spent every day of the summer thinking about me and self-medicating with carbohydrates?

Would it be so bad to walk past rows of pitying glances and snide comments, and slide my arms around his neck until everything turns right side up again? Just for a moment, so my life, my routines, and my *boyfriend* can click back into place. All my particles solidified by the heat of his chest and his deep spicy scent that always burned a little before settling into my lungs with a sigh.

"Okay, I need some preparation on what today is going to be like," Poppy says, sliding rocket sleeves up to her elbows and pulling my brain back. "On a scale of fine to watching 2005 Keira Knightley *Pride & Prejudice* over and over again, where are we?"

"That was *one* week!"

"The Mr. Darcy binge was still better than the weird bread," Odette says. "Or the many PowerPoints I had to threaten you to not email him."

"Listen, Barbara the sourdough starter remains deeply beloved, and everyone loves a PowerPoint."

"Not when the topics include arguments like how his dog will miss you because he won't understand the breakup," Poppy says.

"The science behind pack dynamics is very well-researched." I clear my throat. "And I believe he used the word 'break,' not 'breakup.'"

"Marlowe." Her arms grip mine, anchoring me here in this deeply unpleasant reality.

I know what she's asking me. *Isn't it time you just got over all of this?*

The normal, cool-girl answer? Yes, it's time, but I'm not ready.

These two have walked with me from braces to Josh's backseat and every stop in between. They don't get it, though. They weren't there when a boy who gleamed so bright it was hard to look at him sometimes tucked my hair behind my ear and whispered into the darkness, *Let me teach you something for once, Marlowe.*

It's as if I made all of it up in my head, and I'm here alone in my detoxification and delusions. (That was one of the other PowerPoints—how love should be banned because it's a drug, and MRIs done on poor heartbroken losers like myself were similar to those of cocaine users in withdrawal.)

Most addicts require rehab. I got a summer in Denver to pretend it wasn't happening, but here in this ugly, familiar hallway, reality has me in a chokehold.

"Maybe it's just some sunk-cost fallacy I can't get through," I say, finally dragging the words out. A laugh bubbles up my throat, only a little more deranged than I'd planned.

Odette and Poppy move a little closer, and my poor heart rattles in its cage.

I hear the murmurs, but more than anything I feel the shift in the air. Like something heavy has moved into our space, and we're all just helpless to orbit. I brace myself for the impact, and there he is.

Joshua Shepherd Stallings.

His hair is a little longer than normal, and I know how much he hates it when it brushes across his ears like that. He's wearing a sky-blue button-down I don't recognize, and I immediately hate it more than any shirt I've ever seen. We'd been together for two years and I know the inside of his closet like my own, but I am not acquainted with this shirt. Me and this shirt have no core memories. He's out there laughing, and tanning, and shopping, and moving on, and I'm here. In *stasis*.

He looks up (likely scorched by my pitiful eyeballs) and I wait for it. For him to say, *Oh my God, Marlowe. It was just a joke, couldn't you tell? Come here and kiss me good morning.* For the roll of his eyes, and the stretch of his hand.

Reader, he does none of that. He smiles briefly, a nod in my direction, like you would give an acquaintance in the grocery store when you're hoping to God they don't stop to chat.

I sway a little, the cool bite of the lockers bracing me.

"Marlowe, what can we do?" Odette's voice is small and tense.

"Fix it." The words tumble out before I can swallow them back down. "Fix me."

"There is nothing to fix."

"I don't need the atta-girl bullshit talk. I'm standing here in the literal wreckage of my life, and I want it all back. I want *him* back."

"Okay," Poppy says, hands on her hips and over the small talk. "Let's be solution-oriented about this. What's the plan?"

"The plan?"

"Well, despite relatively decent grades, and a solid presence in AP classes, Josh is unfortunately a dumbass. But you're sad, and you miss him, so how do we help him realize how dumb he was to dump you?"

I laugh despite myself.

"I mean, I don't know if we can really support him as a part-ner after that staggeringly poor show of deductive abilities, but maybe you can tutor him," Odette says.

"I think all of this is a moot point." I pull out the dolphins to take with me to AP English. I simultaneously want to stop talking about this and never stop talking about it. Is it weird to want the world to be as obsessed as me over the implosion of my relationship? *Misery loves company, right?*

I shoulder-check my locker closed and feel five thousand years old. I don't want to make some plan to trick my boyfriend (sorry, ex-boyfriend) into *seeing* me. I don't want to stare too hard at the thought that maybe he didn't understand anything about me if he felt there was any part of me that was uninterested. That I loved wrong. This fear that I'm broken burrows down to my mitochondria. But I also don't want to spend the rest of the year wondering if I misunderstood the conversation, or the meaning of the word "break."

I bounce on the balls of my feet, adrenaline making me dizzy. "You know what? I'm going in."

Odette's head whips down to locker 118 and back to me. "Over *there?*"

I nod, my feet moving before the rest of me catches up. "Don't wait for me." My stomach twists as my Converse eat up the scuffed linoleum between us.

This is not the right response. Upon being dumped, you don't storm your ex like a castle in front of the entire school. You're supposed to act like the past doesn't exist and keep it civil. Give each other bland little smiles and well-wishes and keep the em-barrassment to a minimum.

Well, this isn't *The Crown,* and I want answers more than pride.

I ignore the fake coughs and sharp smiles surrounding him like a moat. Old habits briefly rise where I would usually remind myself to say good morning to everyone, ask people about their summers, or remember to smile.

Today, I go straight for the jugular.

"Josh." I stumble over his name, the syllable awkward with disuse. "Hi."

"What's up, Marlowe?" No preamble. He's forgoing the social niceties this morning too.

"Can we talk?" The words scrape coming out. "Please?"

His jaw tightens, and I know he doesn't want to. I also recognize the moment he decides to humor me over seeing whatever other unpredictable thing I might do this morning. He nods toward the classroom to his left, and I walk into the freshman chemistry lab before he changes his mind.

I move to the back of the room, hope fluttering against my ribs for the first time in months. I stop reflexively next to my old lab table and turn into the full force of him.

He raises an eyebrow and waits. Not a care in the world, not a single thing to get off his chest. I ignore that he has nothing he wants to discuss with me. I ignore that I have no plan, no Power-Point materials, and fully recognize that bleating *why* at him would not lead to anything productive.

"Hi," I repeat, stunned I finally have him to myself again. Every thought I've ever had evaporates into thin air.

"What's on your mind?" he asks, having apparently given up on me finding the point.

None of this is the same. I don't know this Josh. This one who makes no effort to pretend I'm more than a casual acquaintance. He's not going to slide his hands around my waist, outline all the ways he misses me, or ravish me next to my favorite Bunsen burner.

I curl my fingers around the edge of the table and lean back before I do something stupid like brush my fingers through damp, golden hair.

Focus.

Favorite burner.

Least favorite smile.

"Marlowe?" Impatience bleeds into Josh's voice. "You wanted to talk?"

This smile is not one that I see very often. I usually get the lazy, amused twist of his lips, or the laughing-with-friends dimple and flash of teeth, or, when we're alone—a slow curve at the corner of his mouth that makes my knees weak.

This is the one he uses when he blows off something his momma asks him to do, and he still expects love and forgiveness.

"Sorry." I shake my head, trying to clear out all the background noise.

"Did you take your meds this morning?"

I bristle, because I *always* take my meds. I have a vested interest in making my brain work at school, and I don't need anyone trying to take on the responsibility of reminding me.

"I'm focused" is all I say. I don't want to fight. I try to give him *his* favorite smile. The one that hints of secrets and promises passed between us.

"You said you wanted a break for the summer, but we're back at school now," I say, willfully ignoring all of his body language. I'm playing a game of autistic chicken and hoping that he won't call me out on it. That maybe, just maybe, he'll chime in with a *You're right! New year, new us, let's pick up where we left off.*

He stills as I dangle the unspoken question toward him.

"We're doing this here?" He sighs, the disappointment stealing the air out of the room. "All right. I think having some space this summer really gave me an opportunity to think about things."

Space. I hate that word. Not the space where we blast phallic-shaped rockets into the universe, nebulas collapse, and we're all made of stardust, but the space that has Josh inching farther and farther away from me.

"Me too. I think we should get back together."

"And I think we shouldn't." His tone is almost kind, and I hate that most of all. "Nothing lasts forever, Marlowe."

"Some things do," I say, desperation bleeding into my voice. I can't help myself, and the first example that comes to mind tumbles out. "The *Ganoderma* mushroom is supposed to be immortal."

"Jesus Christ," he says, brushing hair off his forehead. "Not mushrooms again." I know *this* expression too. It's the one after I say something that he would have preferred I kept to myself. "This is exactly what I'm talking about. We're talking about our breakup and instead of love, you bring up mushrooms."

My thoughts scatter into ten different directions. I swallow the urge to correct that we weren't talking about love, but about longevity. Another synapse sparks and tells me that if I explained the way the *Ganoderma* grows like curls of red parchment he would understand. I chase another brain cell that tells me to describe how the loss of him carved out an area of my chest that will likely always make me feel off-balance, but he beats me to it.

"It's not your fault, Marlowe. I know you tried your best."

My *best*. Like what you would tell a toddler holding up a sloppy art project, but instead it was my efforts to love him.

"You know Patrick and Brittany did long distance over the summer, and she made a Gabber post about how much she missed him every single day." He gives me a knowing look that skates the edge of accusatory. "I need something more like that in my life."

"You wanted me to make Gabber posts about you? While we were on a break?"

I feel the cold ledge of the lab table digging into my back and try not to make the scene I know he's hoping to avoid. He's cut me wide open, exposed all the wires, and now he's frowning at me like it was my hand wielding the knife all along.

He leans over and squeezes my shoulder. "Breakup," he corrects, gently.

Nope. I was wrong. There goes the knife.

I pull back as I'm summarily dismissed as defective.

I know I'm smart, I'm a good person, and I'm very careful about recycling and always using my turn signal. I have a great family, people who care about me and would likely help me hide a body, but sometimes I still feel like I'm performing well below average. Like the playground games I was expelled from because I just didn't get the rules. Teachers venting frustrations that my work doesn't look the same as my classmates', and why couldn't *I* read between the lines that they wanted *this* specific format? Boys who told me during spin the bottle at Marty Patrick's thirteenth-birthday party that nobody wanted to kiss a robot. And here. *Here*. On the first day of senior year, the boy who, two years ago, gave me a slow and careful smile that sank into my brain like honey, tells me he was wrong. That I was an investment that did not pay off.

He's looking at his watch, looking at the door, everywhere but me, and I nod. He needs a response, and I understand that there needs to be an end to this conversation before he feels he can leave.

He smiles softly, a shadow of what it used to be when he shined in my direction. There's a finality in the lines of his lips. No hint of regret in the easy slide of his shoulders. "I'm sorry, I didn't want to unload all of this on you before class. I really do care about you, Marlowe, but let's just call it, okay?" He tugs my braid, his touch lingering for a moment. He's comfortable again. Back on solid ground. A weight officially lifted. "See you in class?"

I don't respond, but he doesn't need it, and he's out the door before I can blink.

I continue to blink. And breathe. And tell myself that I am many things, but I am not a crier. It's an unnecessary expenditure of energy, and my cells need every scrap of ATP for me to remain standing. To not chase him and demand a better explanation. To insist on a detailed list of examples and evidence where I fell short.

Blink.

Breathe.

The first bell jangles, but I stay in place. I know I can't live here. This burner *is* my favorite, but freshman chemistry isn't going to be a class they let me take again for old times' sake.

The door bursts open, and unfamiliar faces pour in, scouting seats and making frantic game-time alliances for the semester.

Then a familiar face. Her long ponytail bounces over her shoulder and slides across a fuchsia-pink dress she modeled for us six times to make sure it was the perfect first-day outfit.

She pauses when she sees me, holding on to a lab table for dear life. Something in my expression has her flying past classmates and down the aisle until she's right in front of me. Synthetic vanilla floods my senses and reboots my brain.

"Marlowe?"

I blink harder. "Hey, Blue. You should pick this burner. The flame is the most consistent in the entire classroom."

"Okay." She nods slowly. "Anything else?"

"Well," I say, still selfishly hoarding ATP. "Josh is one hundred percent not interested in getting back together with me."

She exhales, the air hissing out of bubble-gum-pink lips. "Asshole."

"Language," I say, automatically, Momma's words rising to the surface like muscle memory.

"Marlowe, I think Momma would give me a pass."

I nod, because southern women know a thing or two about grudges.

"Well, are you going to prop up that table all day, or are we gonna go key his truck?"

"Are those really the only two options?"

"I'm calling Momma."

If there was one thing that would shake some sense into me, it would be having to explain to Bunny Thompson why I was making a scene at school and dragging Blue into it.

"No." I smile, hoping my face isn't as red as my hair. "I'm leaving, it's fine."

Blue clutches her phone, disbelief written into every feature.

"I'm good," I insist as I move toward the exit. One foot in front of the other. Away from this spot. I almost get to the door before turning around, but again—I really can't help myself.

"Blue, I *was* serious about the flame consistency."

Three

Back in the hall, Odette and Poppy huddle outside the door. They waited, of course. I answer their questioning looks with a shake of my head and follow the tide into first period on wobbly legs. I pack up the past ten minutes and lock them tightly into a box. I can pull out and analyze the contents later, but now is not that moment.

You did not just have your heart pulled apart (again) in a lab that smelled like ham sandwiches and cleaning supplies. You are not an emotionally crippled cyborg cosplaying as a human. You will pull it together and tackle one problem at a time.

AP English.

AP English with Josh.

I wouldn't say English and I have a tense relationship. I'm literate, and capable of stringing any number of sentences together. I can read articles and textbooks all day every day, but fiction and I have a shaky truce. I just don't *get* stories.

Is that a cyborg thing to say? I can't help it, it's true.

I watch Hallmark movies with Momma and Blue, but I'll

never understand, for example, the woman who gives up the career and life she's spent decades building just to become a gingerbread artisan.

I mean, that sounds like an amazing career! I love gingerbread! I would love to walk around in a cloud of allspice and desire, dizzy from the attentions of the handsome volunteer firefighter from next door.

For maybe a weekend.

Then I would go back to my actual day job of being a biomedical engineer, just like I've always planned, and nostalgically think of that firefighter around Christmastime when I bite into some perfectly spiced cookies. It isn't something you give up your life for.

God, maybe Josh is right—I don't have a romantic bone in my body.

I pause in the doorway, regretting my ancestors' decision to settle in this painfully small town so I have no escape from him all day. All year.

In the classes we've shared, Josh always preferred to sit in the second row, closest to the exit. I, on the other hand, am a solid front-row girl. My neurodivergent tendencies make sitting any ol' where not really an option. I have to be right at the front, practically straddling the teacher's lap, so their voice and materials are the only things that can catch my hyperfixation. I'd usually take the seat in front of him, so he could languidly slip my hair through his fingers and draw soft hearts on my neck with the pads of his fingers. I would sigh and shift with every touch—each micromovement a performance just for him.

Today, I almost trip over him on legs that are operating purely on muscle memory.

How's this for a performance?

I glance down, frozen in place, a possum that has reached its limit for the day. He clears his throat, eyes not meeting mine, and shifts under the desperate spotlight of my attention.

Making an executive decision, I bolt down the first aisle, power walking past him like I'm in my meemaw's fitness group. I blindly march to the back. To the darkest corner, where Josh couldn't see me even if he wanted to. (Spoiler: I am almost certain he doesn't want to.) I slide into a seat so far from the board I start to question my eyeglass prescription. Poppy and Odette close in on me as I white-knuckle the desk in front of me.

"Really, Marlowe?" Poppy asks. "The back row? Is any boy truly worth this?"

"You're both free to sit wherever you want."

Odette sighs, deflating into the seat next to me. "None of us are good enough at this subject to be sitting back this far."

Poppy fidgets with her book bag, front-row to her core, indecision written in the movement of her hands. Ms. Chris closes the door to the hallway, and the murmurs slide into silence. The decision made for her, Poppy slides into the desk in front of me.

"Good morning, my lovely new seniors!" Ms. Chris beams at us, like some beautiful, eclectic aunt who only shows up on holidays, with handmade presents and a mason jar full of martinis in her purse. She's draped in a fringed caftan, wearing earrings that I'm certain the art teacher sells out of the trunk of her car, and has laugh lines that spread like cracked glass across a face that knows what it's like to be delighted. Delighted with her life, with her job, and somehow even with us.

"I know you've all heard this is going to be your favorite class this year," she says, pausing dramatically. "I want you to know all the rumors are true."

Odette snorts, but I relax a little under her warmth. Like clay that finds itself next to an unexpected heat source.

"You're all on your victory lap this year." She weaves between the desks, dropping packets in front of each student. "You're looking at colleges, you're focusing on the subjects you think you're going to be pursuing when you graduate. You're worried about that upcoming football game." She moves past Josh and lays a deep brown hand on his shoulder. "But I want you to know that the skills you take from this class will help you in several ways after graduation. We'll learn to dissect many important works of literature."

Poppy slumps lower in her chair as Ms. Chris makes her way to the back row. She gives us a little smile as if to say *I see you, and am pleased to have you, my little wallflowers.*

"I'll grade you on all the usual—reading logs, unit tests and quizzes, your final exam—and also . . . the unusual." She spins around, a secret on her lips.

I rip into the packet, dreading the surprise. After the actual nausea that came with having to ingest *Tess of the d'Urbervilles* for the summer reading, I trust nothing.

"We're going to work on a group project that will span the entire semester."

I barely manage to hold in my groan, but other members of the class do not have the same reservations.

The clear negativity doesn't even dim her smile. She slips up on the edge of her desk, legs dangling. "You'll find our list of important works of literature on the back page of the syllabus. You'll be working in groups of two, and you'll select one of those works together to complete a project that is twenty-five percent of your grade."

Odette's hand shoots in the air, but she doesn't wait to be acknowledged. "Can we pick our own partners?"

My stomach twists a little. The problem with being part of a triangle is that sometimes one of the angles is left out. I know they both love me, but I'm also aware enough that the past two years have, if anything, helped move us solidly into isosceles-triangle territory. They have grown solidly more similar, and I'm just up there wavering at the top on my own.

"Not a chance, Ms. Norman. I'll be making my own random selections," Ms. Chris says, smiling.

Poppy sneezes four times in a row, shuddering.

"This is why I hate English," Odette mutters.

Ms. Chris looks out at us. "Oh, I know, you poor things. Working with people you wouldn't expect to? How on earth would that translate to real life?"

She pulls out a roster, and I remind myself that it truly couldn't get any worse. "You'll be responsible for writing a paper together." She adjusts her bedazzled glasses. "The criteria are listed in your syllabus, but you'll be analyzing the major themes and devices of one of these works. You'll also be responsible for a presentation to share with the class."

Cue the moans again.

"Y'all are so dramatic," she says, rolling her eyes. Her expression reminds me of my father trying to force cough syrup down my throat as a kid. *I know it's gross, but trust me, you'll thank me later.* "The paper will include the analytical techniques we'll be learning in this class, but the presentation can be as creative as you want it to be. You want to teach us the assembly dances that they may have done in *Pride and Prejudice*? I'm here for it! You want to flex those makeup-artist skills and become Frankenstein's monster? Let's go! You want to build a diorama of *The*

House on Mango Street? Well, I can't wait to see what you come up with!"

My thoughts are tumbling over one another, and I'm scribbling every word into the margins. The paper, I could handle. I could carefully lean over the words with a scalpel and slice out the plot, characters, themes, and literary motifs until nothing's left but my dull, organized little boxes. But any kind of spectacle is going to have to be up to a hopefully creative partner.

"Our groups will start formally meeting in class over the next few days, but feel free to check in with each other before that. We're not going to have any repeats, so if another group has already picked the book you want—well, that's just too bad."

She rambles off names and pairings, which display a complete disregard for personality and friend groups. Odette is paired with Tiffany, as in, Josh's-number-one-fan Tiffany. Poppy is grouped with a guy I know very little about, aside from the fact that he wears cowboy boots that cheerfully clack down the hallway.

"Marlowe Meadows—" She pauses to check her list. "—and Josh Stallings."

Whispers spread like wildfire, and my face is so hot I expect my clothes to start smoking.

"Dumbasses," Odette seethes.

Josh turns back to look at me, no sense of the same amusement on his face.

Ms. Chris crosses her arms. "I assume someone is going to let me in on the joke?"

Tiffany leans forward from her place of honor at the desk next to his. "Well, that might be a little awkward for Josh here," she says in a stage whisper I could hear from three counties over.

Yes, poor Josh. Josh who hasn't had to deal with any awkwardness. He was inconvenienced with one brief conversation in a chemistry lab and got to walk away without a care in the world.

And yet, a part of me wonders if this is my opportunity to show him he was *wrong*.

Ms. Chris looks back at me, and I hope she (I hope all of them) can see more determination than devastation on my face.

"I can switch," Tiffany offers. "I'll be Josh's partner, and Marlowe can work with her little friend."

My little friend, Odette, glares at Tiffany's perky ponytail with a vengeance that is palpable. As if we haven't all been in the same school system for a lifetime. She knows Odette's name, just like she knows she isn't fooling anybody.

Josh clears his throat, not turning to include me in any of this. But he's also not objecting. "It might be better for everyone." His voice is apologetic, as if he's so terribly sorry for this mess that he has no idea how he got involved in.

Ms. Chris is not impressed. "Tiffany, this is not an opportunity to try to keep your world as tiny as possible." She sighs. "I don't think—"

"I'll switch."

Twenty heads swivel to the other corner of the back row.

There, in unrelieved black, absorbing all the light and attention in the room, is Ashton Hayes.

He transferred here our junior year from someplace out west where people didn't believe in pastels or saying hello when they passed you in the street. He's held strong to those principles since his arrival, and most of his clothes have weird straps or spikes that I don't understand the functional necessity of.

When he first showed up, I remember Josh walking over to introduce himself. He's on almost every social committee and has

been in student government since they let us start voting on popularity contests dressed up as offices. "Welcome to River Haven
High," he'd said, with a blinding smile and a hand thrust out for
a shake. Ash had looked him over, taking every ounce of his measure, and promptly walked away.

"Sometimes trash just takes itself out," Josh had said later as I
kissed the frown off his lips, his biceps stiff under my hands.

Ash had fallen in with some other kids who also wore a little
too much black, and I heard something about a band at one point,
but he'd faded into the background of my attention.

Until now.

Now he's staring at Ms. Chris, as if they were casually discussing the ownership of some wayward item nobody wanted
to claim.

"You'll switch with Josh?" she asks, looking for the catch.
The part of the deal where this was the worse arrangement.

"What's going *on*?" Odette hisses.

I have no answer, and Ash still isn't looking at me, but he nods
once in Ms. Chris's direction. His ink-black hair is pushed back,
the long ends curling over one ear like a question mark. Several
small gold hoops in varying degrees of spikiness cascade up his
ear, matching the thin gold circle interrupting the middle of his
bottom lip.

"Marlowe," Poppy whispers, turning back to me. "Why's Josh
staring at you?"

I look up, torn between two ridiculous outcomes. Josh *is*
looking at me, as if affronted that there's something about me
that's surprised him.

"Well, Marlowe, is that all right?" Ms. Chris puts me on the
spot, and I use every remaining brain cell to keep myself in my
seat. I want to say *No, let me work with Josh*. Let me show him that

there's still so much left between us. That he just needs to hear me out. To give me a chance.

I say none of that, though, because I can't always read a room, but this is clear. He doesn't want to hear that from me. He doesn't want any more declarations from me today.

"The switch sounds fine," I say, my voice surprisingly level. Am I sure? Not about anything. Do I think it's a better solution than trying to pretend to be normal under Josh's knowing gaze, or letting the class witness the flaming dumpster fire of my relationship in a public forum? Absolutely.

"Well, that's settled. Ashton and Marlowe, and Josh and Beth," she says, nodding at a supremely unbothered softball player who shrugs as if she couldn't care less.

Tiffany puffs up in irritation, and I try to breathe without looking like I've forgotten basic brain-stem reflexes.

"All right, maybe now we can finally get to some English," Ms. Chris says, walking to the board. "Everyone open your books to page eighty-one."

I put my brain on autopilot, dutifully writing out notes, looking up when it feels appropriate, and smiling when Ms. Chris says something that I can tell she thinks is a joke. On the surface, I'm sure it all looks business-as-usual, but inside I'm one big crime board, full of red threads and unknown motives. Why did Ash step in? Is this some sort of attack on Josh? Did he not understand they were talking about me?

I close my notebook with the bell, the dolphins offering sympathetic looks, and struggle to follow the last few threads.

I know my reputation in this school. You win a few math medals and have questionable social skills, and people assume school is your life. That you'd be happy to do the majority of the work because you have nothing better to do. Well, not this time.

I grab my bag and march over to Ash's desk with my head held high. He's scribbling the last of his notes in elegant cursive when I clear my throat. He tilts his face up, almost resigned.

"I'm not doing this project alone."

A single eyebrow bisected by a shaved line creeps up his forehead.

I put my hands on my hips. Nope, too aggressive. I pull them across my chest, before finally dropping them and trying to hold eye contact.

"I know it might seem like I would do something like that," I start again. "But English is not my strongest subject, and . . . I'm not going to do it all." He doesn't move. "So, you can just forget that now."

He stands up, and he's taller than I remember. Josh didn't love it when I wore heels, because it would make us the same height, but I feel my neck craning up, up, *up,* as Ash stares at a spot over my head.

"Are we . . . clear?" I ask, despite desperately needing some clarification myself.

He gives me one last look, worrying the ring in his lip with his teeth, before stepping around me and marching out the door.

I look from his desk to the doorway, trying to calculate what just happened.

"Now, *this* is interesting," Poppy says, grinning as wide as the cats on her skirt.

Four

I sink deeper into the couch and pull the fleece blanket over my head. Today? Today calls for burrito mode. I deserve this. I've *earned* it.

I want to tunnel into fabric like the Nile crocodile. Not really the poster child for animals that like to dig or hide from the world, but their dens can be up to forty feet deep. Forty feet of dirt between you and the world, and a cold-blooded crocodile heart that doesn't care that it's Friday night and you have no plans.

I used to have plans. Friday night was always date night, and date night was nonnegotiable. A concept I'd struggled with a few times, when things had come up with friends or family, but Josh was clear. If we didn't prioritize our relationship, who would?

Now, after all the prioritizing my brain and heart were capable of, I'm sitting here, smothered in fleece and feeling my lack of plans like a wound.

It's been weeks since he verified in the chemistry lab that this was more than a temporary break. Four entire Friday nights when I've had no idea what he's replaced me with.

I pull out my phone, the screen casting a dim light in my little cave, and I go right to the message thread. The same texts I've pulled up several times a day since he cut me loose like deadweight. To convince myself we were real. That I didn't imagine it. That I wasn't alone in it.

> Rise and shine, beautiful girl. Let me know your plans for the day.
> Lying here in bed, wish I had my girl here with me.

I scroll, almost frantic.

> I love you, Lo.
> Are you really going to make your boyfriend go to this party by himself?

The fight from that one had been memorable. I ended up canceling on Odette and Poppy to keep the peace, but the soft slide of his hand in my hair later that night—the gentle kisses until I melted like spring snow—had almost made it feel like I made the right choice.

I scroll back down and start to type out Not our usual Friday night, huh? I'm trying for glib, but I know I've fallen far from the mark.

We're not exes who've reached a cautious peace, or a comfortable indifference. I'm actively bleeding, and it's messy and unpleasant to witness.

I carefully push the backspace key until it's gone. He's not the one to commiserate with. He's the one who set fire to all of this. He's the instrument of this destruction.

But I still want him, my heart thumps pathetically.

The past few weeks have been clear, my brain replies. *He's made it clear he doesn't want you back.*

"It's all right, Marlowe, not everyone's built for it."

I huff, my breath warming the air under the blanket, and pull myself free. I'm not some shameful, sordid secret, like when we found out our postmaster was sticking letters in his pants prior to deliveries. I refuse to be an awkward memory. I'm going to *make* him look at me. I'm going to show him that all this time wasn't for nothing.

I can be romantic. How hard could it be? I turn the phone back on, the cursor blinking at me in pity.

Your hair is as gold as . . . gold. I wince, deleting the last word.

Your hair is as gold as pyrite. How is that worse?

Your hair shines like neon in a light-emitting diode. *Ugh, why am I fixated on the periodic table? Gold like Momma's favorite hoops?*

I close the message thread before any of my pitiful attempts spill into the ether.

I wince into the darkness of my crocodile cave. Just because I don't have the words doesn't mean I don't have the feelings.

I open a browser and pull up my new favorite website and distraction, burying sickly feelings of failure down deep. I refuse to feel guilty about searching for information about Ashton Hayes after the way he spoke up in class. What if he'd murdered someone in the past with one of his spiked ear cuffs? Or was a secret Transylvanian prince? Both would be important pieces of information to have, but the only thing that popped up was that band he seems to have started shortly after moving here.

The Never Mind the Monsters website leaves a lot to be desired. Now, I'm not a website purist, but nothing could have prepared me for the blinding neon-green background or the Papyrus font. There are only a few grainy pictures, and one video where you can barely hear the music over the videographer's talking. But what I could hear has crawled into my brain. I know the words, I know the moments where Ash grabs the microphone as if steadying himself, and I find myself humming the melody throughout the day.

A throat clears and I kill the video. My stepdad, Stu, leans against the doorway to the dining room. "Hey, Lo," he says, salt-and-pepper hair tousled, with a smile that shines from half a dozen billboards in our town. Most people I know have bought their cars from his dealership. Once a River Haven High football star, he stayed in this tiny little town and now sells Cadillacs at a rate that makes it seem like everything he touches does indeed turn to gold.

He came into my life when I was three, still reeling from my parents' divorce the year before. Dad still lived in town, and the back-and-forth between houses was giving me whiplash. I couldn't figure out a schedule or a rhythm. He showed up one afternoon, leaned down, stuck out a hand, and seriously introduced himself as Stu. I sometimes wonder if it hurt him that it never once occurred to me to call him anything else.

He gleams, just like Josh does. A sense of self that I look on with envy. Tan skin, and shining white teeth that he protects by drinking red wine through a straw.

"Our appearances are our first impression, Lo," he'll tell me, as if it's not ridiculous, swirling Merlot with a pink silicone tube. I'll nod sagely, because he's probably not wrong, but also because he's *kind*.

He's always been kind, and though his booming voice and even louder personality tend to take up every square inch of a room, he's always tried to make space for me too.

"Hey," I say now, pulling the blanket farther down from my face. "Was just a little cold." No Nile crocodiles here. I'm using this blanket for completely normal reasons.

"Sure, those brisk September nights in Georgia will do that to you."

"Exactly," I say, ignoring the smile in his voice.

"I'm driving Blue to a sleepover, and then me and Mom are off to dinner. Do you need me to drop you anywhere?"

See? *Kind*. His tone is light, and he knows as well as I do that my old but sturdy Volvo is poorly parked in the driveway, but he's just trying to check in.

"Nope," I say, with more emphasis than the room can bear. "I'm in for the night." I smooth the blanket across my legs.

"Are you sure? You're always out on Fridays," he says, not taking the hint.

Yes. Yes, I was. I will Stu all the emotional intelligence I can spare and pray he won't make me say it. *Again*. Yes, Friday nights were always date night, when there was someone who wanted to date me.

He finds a clue in my silence, and realization blooms across his face. A rosy hue rises to the deep tan that remains in place year-round thanks to the methodical application of Sun Bunny Self-Tanner.

"Oh, gotcha. Sorry, kiddo." There's so much remorse in those words I almost feel worse for him.

"Yeah, well, things are a little different now."

He wilts a little more, his big personality shrinking in real time. He liked Josh. He *was* Josh, at one point. But I think he liked me *with* Josh most of all, because we finally found some common ground. He understood parties, football games, and homecoming dances. I still had math club, science projects that spilled out and took over our dining table for weeks at a time, academic award ceremonies, but now I was also a "normal" high school kid. I don't even think he thought of me as a real teenager until the fateful weekend Momma found condoms in my room.

He turns his salesman shine my way. "Well, you should come to dinner with me and your mom, then. We're heading to the steakhouse, and I won't even try to steal some of your dessert."

I smile and infuse as much gratitude as I can into it. "That's a really nice offer, Stu, but a crowbar couldn't get me off this couch right now."

He laughs, and it's filled with both guilt and relief. I know neither one of them know what to do with me right now. I was the stability in this house. Reliable. Unflappable. A steady presence in the face of Blue's daily hurricane. Sad me has cast a pall through every hallway.

"I'm ready, can we *go* already?" Blue crashes through the kitchen door in a cloud of body spray. She drops her overstuffed duffel bag at Stu's feet.

"Don't do anything I wouldn't do," I say, just to see her roll her eyes, and she doesn't disappoint.

"Are you just going to sit there all weekend?" The words are sharp, thrown carelessly over her shoulder, but I see the stalling. The slow shuffle of her feet as she waits for my answer.

"I'm fine, Bluebell. Promise." I hide a smile. "You better not have left that duck wandering around this house."

"I will have you know that duck is better behaved than most of the other occupants of this house." Her cheeks pink, she folds her arms tightly. "But Snow White is in her hutch since you're too mean to want to hang out with her."

"She's a farm animal."

"She's *family*."

"All right, girls, let's table this old argument for the night." Stu picks up Blue's bag and gently tugs on her ponytail. "Go tell your momma to come on."

Blue walks to the doorway and yells up to the second story. "Momma, let's go! Night, Meemaw!"

Coming, baby drifts down to us, but I can't resist one more poke. "Meemaw can't hear you from this part of the house."

"Yes, she can! You don't know *everything*, Marlowe."

"I know it's my room she's haunting, and you would have needed to yell from the kitchen doorway."

"She haunts my room sometimes too!"

"Girls, *girls*. Meemaw is haunting all of us, okay? Marlowe, quit teasing your sister, I'm trying to get my steak this century."

My heart tugs fondly as Momma races down the stairs with a kiss in my direction and they finally pour out the front door.

And then the house is mine, and quiet. I flip through channels, but nothing can capture my attention for more than a second. I feel like static is buzzing under my skin, keeping me constantly alert and uncomfortable. Waiting for the last shoe to drop. For the next explosion in my life. I shove the blanket to the floor and try to shake off the jitters.

The house creaks beneath me, and I move my heavy limbs into the kitchen and put my brain to work. We're solidly an in-gredient house—Momma doesn't believe in snacks or a messy pantry, and we work for every guilty pleasure here. I pull out a sturdy mug and start measuring.

Flour. Cocoa powder, oil, milk. Sugar.

Ninety seconds later, the microwave beeps with my salvation. I choke a little on its density. It's less the cake of my dreams and more a heavy concoction that will sit in my gut like a brick.

I try again, adding chips and espresso powder for a mocha vibe. Again, close, but just this edge of bitter.

I put specimen two aside and try another version with some vanilla, brown sugar, and butter. Sweeter, but still flat and dense.

I move on to specimen four and add baking powder and cinnamon. This one fluffs up very satisfyingly, but the cinnamon falls a little flat. It's too quiet a cake for heartbreak. I need sprinkles.

The fifth version boosts my spirits enough to get halfway through it before the doorbell rings and the front door crashes open at the same time.

"We're here, where are you?!" Odette yells.

I choke around a bite a little too big. "Here" creaks out of me.

They push through the swinging door and pause at the cake mug sentinels surrounding me.

"You okay there, buddy?" Odette asks. Poppy follows close behind, her lips forming a silent O.

I straighten, pulling up Josh's old River Haven football sweatpants. "Never better, why do you ask?"

"Oh, no reason," Odette says, moving forward and picking up specimen one before wrinkling her nose and putting it down.

"The original was not my best effort."

Poppy opens the silverware drawer and snags a spoon and specimen three. She takes a bite before pushing it away.

"The vanilla ratio on that one might be a little heavy-handed." I grimace.

"So, just casually making an excessive amount of cake for no reason?" Odette asks, inspecting me for cracks.

"Well, that's better than going to his house, right?"

She covers her face. "Tell me you didn't."

"Or texting him everything I'm remotely feeling?"

"I truly cannot tell if you're joking or not, and I'm going to need a hard yes or no."

Poppy holds up specimen two. "This one isn't good either, Marlowe."

We pause to look at her. She grabs specimen four.

Odette shrugs. "Ignore Pops. This is me again asking if you're okay."

"I'm fine," I say softly, just to make the tension bleed out of her shoulders. I bury the instinct to ask why they're here. I know why. They always know where my mind is at.

"This one's much better," Poppy says, holding up the snick-erdoodle attempt.

I nod. "Yeah, that one was less hot, solid pudding, and more cake."

"It's the baking powder, the carbon dioxide makes it spongier."

I swallow around the lump in my throat. "Thanks, Pops." She slides number five, the one I ate the most of, closer to me.

"What can we do?" she asks, examining me behind green leopard-print glasses.

I half-heartedly lift a shoulder, my hands curling around the warm mug.

"I know you dismissed us creating a plan before, but we have the next valedictorian, a state champion science fair winner, and the captain of the math club all in this one room. You know there isn't a single problem we can't solve," Odette says, tilting her chin up, and I can't help laughing.

"Fine, what do you have in mind?"

"I mean, what exactly did he *say*?" Poppy jumps in, pulling out a slim notepad from her bag. "That you didn't act romantic enough? That's easy, what are some romantic acts you can display to show your expertise?"

The silence hangs heavy between us.

"Why are you asking me? I was literally dumped over this." I rub my eyes as a dull ache grows behind them. "Josh was always the grand-gestures guy. The flowers, the songs he would AirDrop me if they reminded him of us. I never realized it was a contest."

"Were you supposed to keep buying each other carnations until you were both smothered under their weight?" Odette asks.

Poppy frowns at us. "I refuse to believe that we can't figure this out."

I sigh, committing to the process. "Okay, well he said I didn't seem that interested." The shame bubbles up again. "That I never did anything romantic. I doubt he would have considered copying him very romantic either." I shrug like it's nothing. Silly Josh and his silly words. No Chernobyl-level emotional wasteland here!

Odette doesn't bat an eye. "Okay, fine, what romantic behaviors or acts have we witnessed between people?"

"Well, remember when Brad let his cousin give him a homemade tattoo with Jennifer's name across his bicep?" Poppy starts to scribble.

"Yeah, and I remember her leaving him for that same cousin the next week. Can we maybe avoid any body modification?"

Odette steps closer and leans over Poppy's shoulder. "What about when Tiffany was dating Marcus and shoved paper hearts and confetti in his locker?"

I frown. "Confetti is terrible for the environment."

"Also, for the wildlife. It's not biodegradable, Odette," Poppy says, mouth twisting in judgment.

"I wasn't endorsing it! I was just mentioning it!"

I set my mug down, mulling it over. "Marcus couldn't stop talking about it, though."

"For you, I would build a confetti cannon that would shove both plastic and your love down Josh's throat until he tastes them both for weeks," Poppy says, closing the notepad with a snap. "Despite the repercussions for the fish."

"That's a horrifying mental image, but I love you too." I smile, and this one is just for them. No sadness, no thoughts of Josh haunting the corners of my mouth or the shape of my eyes. "Why don't we turn all of this impressive brain power toward something else for a while."

Odette opens the silverware drawer again and slides my phone inside it. "You're right. Let's stop wasting time with these half-assed mug cakes. Let's whole-ass a plate of brownies."

We measure out ingredients as methodically as chemists and gather around the oven with cold glasses of milk already in our hands.

I use pot holders to pull our masterpiece out while they hover at my elbows, then carry the tray into the living room. We pile blankets and throw pillows on the floor. I find a documentary on fungi, destroying angels and false death caps unfurling across the screen while we grab brownie squares that burn our fingers.

"Look at that one," I say as a lace dress explodes out of the mushroom like a lady doing a curtsy.

"Ten out of ten," Odette says, licking her fingers.

"I'm going seven out of ten and deducting points for color and consistency," Poppy says.

"Come on, Pops! You have to at least throw it a bone for razzle-dazzle."

"I do not use razzle-dazzle in my scoring system."

I smile, melted chocolate and gratitude sticking in my throat.

Poppy yawns, her warm limbs leaning heavily against me. "What's that one's name, Marlowe?"

"*Phallus indusiatus,*" I say into the darkness, the light from the TV playing over our sprawled bodies.

Odette hums her acknowledgment, stretching out like a cat.

The documentary goes deeper into the forest, and the mushroom rankings fade into heavy, even breathing. I roll Poppy over, unable to fall headfirst into sleep with them.

I snatch a paperback off the coffee table, and a lady with a gown slipping off her shoulders stares back. Her hair is in a curly updo, and she's gazing up at a muscular man in a kilt as if he's the only steady thing she's ever seen. He's grasping her bare shoulders like he's going to devour her.

Momma's had books like these lying around my entire life. They've blended into the background like lamps and the cream baroque wallpaper that has hung on these walls since before I was retaining permanent memories.

They always felt a little . . . frivolous? Like, compared to Dad's autobiographies and sturdy leather-bound books, they've always seemed like less.

I pick it up and tilt it into the light of the TV. The cover is worn, and the pages soft and curled in the corners. You know, I don't think I can ever remember seeing one of those beautifully leather-bound books in my dad's hands, but this? This is loved. *Lady Jessica Conquers a Duke* has been read more than once, and obviously with devotion.

Maybe just a few pages and I can relax enough to sleep.

I flip the page. And then another. And then another. Next thing I know, it's two A.M. and I've moved to the couch, found a book light, and am knee-deep in Jessica and Collin's bullshit instead of my own.

I laugh as Jessica gives Collin every scrap of attitude right back to him. I groan when they have their fifth misunderstanding, and when they fall into each other I start to question whether those hushed and hurried moments in Josh's bedroom had actually been sex.

Jessica and I aren't too different, actually. She's a quiet wall-flower who ends up married to a duke after being accidentally compromised in his presence. None of that may mimic my own life, but she *does* start to fall in love with him, and then set about making him love her in return. Maybe I don't need grand gestures; maybe I just need Jessica's solid advice.

I burrow deeper into the couch, reading the sex part a second time, *for research purposes only,* and let myself fall into their happily ever after.

Five

After Prince Albert died, Queen Victoria wore black for forty years mourning the love of her life. Not to be dramatic, but it's been more than a month and I'm already thoroughly sick of myself.

Sure, if you're going to split hairs, it's *technically* been several months, but it was harder to stress about this when I was hundreds of miles away in Denver. At the time, I was just glad there were fewer people I had to talk to on the phone.

Now Josh is shoved in my face on the daily, and I'm not handling it with any degree of grace. He's all the way near the front of the class, gold hair glinting under fluorescent lights, and I can still feel his murmurs in my toes. His dimple is in my soul. I lean forward across my desk, as if being a few inches nearer to his warmth will fix any of this.

"And that's a wrap on chapter three," Ms. Chris says, clapping her hands. "I'm going to give you the last twenty minutes to check in with your group project partner. I've only received three book selections and the rest of you need to make some big decisions. These next three months are going to disappear before you know it."

"If Tiffany thinks I'm going over to her first, she's even dumber than any of us have guessed," Odette says, sinking lower into her chair.

"We're in an AP class," Poppy says, shaking her head. A sparkly parrot barrette falls out of her curls.

"AP doesn't preclude you from dumbassery."

Poppy doesn't bother to respond and pulls out her physics book.

"Are you also making a stand with Billy over there?" I ask her, when she makes no move to get out of her seat.

"Of course not. We've already decided on our book."

"What? When?" How is it the beginning of the semester and I already feel hopelessly behind?

"I don't know, within a day of becoming partners, I suppose. He had strong feelings, I didn't." She casually turns a page.

"Well?" Odette asks.

Poppy looks up, remembering we're still here. "*Cyrano de Bergerac,* by Edmond Rostand."

"Is that the catfishing book?" Odette says, taking a second look at Billy.

"It's an allegory on inner versus outer beauty," Poppy says, closing her book with a roll of her eyes.

"So . . . the catfishing book."

"Where does the catfishing come into play?" I'm dragging my feet, but it's not like Ash is rushing over here either.

"Cyrano is a talented soldier with a big nose, and despite his many talents he thinks he's too ugly to be loved."

"People were dicks in the 1800s." Odette shrugs.

"He falls in love with this woman named Roxane, but realizes she's into this other guy, Christian. Cyrano finds out that Christian loves her back but thinks he's not smart or witty enough to date her."

"But he was a total smoke show."

"Real helpful, Odette," Poppy says. "Anyway, Cyrano offers to write these extremely romantic letters for Christian, and Roxane falls in love with the faker and marries *him* instead."

"Got to say, not really loving this so far." I chew on the end of my braid, wondering how long I can realistically stay over here. Nobody said we had to work with our partners in person. Maybe I could just email Ash from right here.

Poppy shrugs. "Christian dies in battle not too long after the marriage, and Cyrano refuses to ruin her memory of her husband by confessing it was him all along. She goes into a nunnery and fifteen years later Cyrano gets into an accident and is brought there on his deathbed. He confesses, she tells him she loves him, and then he dies."

"He *what*?"

"Dies," Odette says, about ten times too loud.

Heads turn in our direction, and I frown at them both. "He dies? Just like that?"

"If I remember correctly, it's not just like that, and actually takes him several speeches to get on with it." Odette rolls her eyes and opens her laptop.

"That's a little dark." I flip through the syllabus. "Nothing with Disney vibes on this book list?"

"It's kind of a garbage story," Odette agrees.

"I mean, I *am* paraphrasing," Poppy says.

"Are you paraphrasing the part where everyone is a shallow, narcissistic liar?" Odette's typing her usual million words a minute, and I know we're close to losing her interest.

"Billy's thesis is that it was romantic how Cyrano was willing to sacrifice his own feelings to make sure the woman he loved was happy."

I snort. "Happy to marry a secret himbo?"

She shrugs and returns to her textbook, but not before a pointed look between Odette and Tiffany.

"I mean it, Poppy. I'm not moving." Odette sinks even lower in her chair.

"Nobody is questioning your dedication to spite or power moves," I say, leaning forward to look around her. Ash is scribbling away in a black notebook and hasn't even glanced in my direction. We haven't spoken since my less-than-flattering accusation, so he's either deeply insulted or couldn't care less about my continued existence.

Can it be both? I'm going with both.

"Good luck trying to out-Tiffany Tiffany," I tell Odette, pulling myself to my feet.

It's just one stupid project. Maybe we can start over and find a good balance. He can keep his weird reasoning for being my partner a mystery, and it won't kill me to not know the answer to everything.

I stop right in front of his desk and wait for him to acknowledge me. The collar of his black jean jacket brushes against the stray wisps of hair that have escaped from the knot on top of his head. The lines of his shoulders tense, and he slowly puts his pen down and closes the notebook with a sigh.

There are plenty of places to sit, as if there's a force field around him that repels anyone else who might get too close. I slip into the desk on his right and quietly unpack my stuff. I boot up my laptop, pull up the syllabus, and wait for some cue. That I'm welcome? That he remembers he (very publicly) made me his partner? That he's going to tell me what to do next? He gives me nothing but silence.

"Look—" I begin, not even sure where this sentence is going to take me.

"Have you gone through the list?" He steamrolls ahead, shifting his body and words slightly in my direction. "We should start there. I'll pick what I'm interested in, you do the same, and we'll see if anything matches." He nods in the direction of my syllabus and opens a new document on his laptop.

Why, so happy to have you join me, Marlowe! I hope you're having a good day as well. You're not a burden at all. You're not some piece of baggage that people are annoyed at being saddled with. I clear my throat, the words clamoring to spill past clenched teeth.

"Did you say something?" His voice is low and gruff and does not contain an iota of inflection.

"Nope," I say curtly, scanning the list. Some of them I have a passing familiarity with, but nothing jumps out at me. He punches keys methodically, the sound hammering away at my skull and reminding me that he's either way better at this than me, or he's playing computer games and waiting for me to get on with it.

He finally pauses long enough to slip out of his seat, grab the bathroom pass, and disappear out the door without a single acknowledgment in my direction.

Tiffany's shrill laugh surges above the murmurs, and every tangled feeling in my brain swells to a crescendo of awfulness. I'm so sick of group projects, Ash's stupid typing, and having excellent seats to the Tiffany-and-Josh show every day in first period. I just need one thing to not be difficult in here. One task I can focus on until all of this fades into the background.

A noisy exhale rattles out of me, and my greedy little fingers slide Ash's laptop toward me before I can talk myself out of it. He has a document open on *Wuthering Heights,* with bullet points on theme, setting, and characters.

Fine, so it's not computer games. I cycle through the tabs and similar breakdowns on *King Lear* and *Invisible Man.* The words blur together until the last window pops up.

This document is different, and stanzas float down the page. I lean closer, scrolling over words that I'm pretty sure aren't Shakespeare.

> *Frozen fingers, frozen heart,*
> *it's not this cold where I come from.*
> *You dull the chill, and warm my side,*
> *I know it's wrong, we still collide.*
>
> *Cross my heart and say goodbye,*
> *keep your words to justify.*
> *I'd rather stay outside than burn,*
> *I'm no longer your concern.*
>
> *Why are you the only one*
> *that brings me back to life?*
> *Why are you the only one*
> *that brings me back to life?*

A part of my brain turns on enough to say *Hey, cool, this is a song! Or a poem! Or a curse!* Another part perks up and says *This . . . this is personal.* His syllabus is on the desk in front of me, doodles spilling into the margins. Curling loops of forest green that yell *NEVER MIND THE MONSTERS* in different fonts. Sketches of hands, gravestones, and a perky little cat pepper the sheet. The synapses in my brain finally find the connection.

This is more music for his band. I go back to the document, scrolling through with new, hungry eyes.

The laptop snaps shut, almost catching my fingertips, and I shrink as it's yanked from my grasp.

A shadow looms over me, as a low "Are you lost?" falls between us like a stone, and I recognize how badly I've fumbled this entire thing.

Sure, the autism makes me different, but not an asshole. I know I crossed a line with his privacy. I saw almost immediately it wasn't schoolwork, and I kept going. I recognize boundaries, as people usually have no issue stampeding past mine.

I force myself to tilt up into the full force of his feelings. "I'm sorry. I wasn't sure I was doing what you wanted me to do and I was too nervous to ask you. I thought I could figure it out if I could *see* what you were doing, and I overstepped before I realized." His eyes are dark and distrustful, but I don't look away. I'm sorry, and I want him to know I mean it.

His mouth snaps shut, and he sits down, angling his computer away from me.

The shame smothers me like a blanket. "I really *am* sorry. If you'd like to look through my computer, it's only fair."

He starts typing again, determined to ignore me.

I'm more determined. "I don't have any secret documents on mine, but I do have a folder with my school pictures from middle school."

His fingers pause over the keys.

"There were braces, and a brief bowl-cut phase."

"Fine." He leans back, expectant. His eyebrows tell me he doesn't believe me. "Let's see it."

"Seriously?"

"I thought you were sorry."

I pull up fourth-grade Marlowe, her smile a grimace. Bright turquoise orthodontic bands clash painfully against a lime-green sweater vest.

"Wow." His consonants are crisp, without the meandering that comes with being born south of the Mason-Dixon Line.

"I know." I turn the laptop away, and close the folder my grandpa insists I email him every few years when he buys a new computer and doesn't know how to transfer anything over.

"Was this a Velma from Scooby-Doo phase?"

"More like an I-was-scared-of-hair-salons phase, and my aunt Birdie slapped a cake-mixing bowl on my head and cut away while she tossed back a few whiskey Cheerwines."

"And is this your normal currency for apologies?"

"Well, the home videos are all at my house."

Down south, we're people pleasers at heart. Our entire life's purpose is to make each other more comfortable. A soft smile here, a pat on the back there. We're hospitality to our core. A person could run over my hamster on the street, and through my tears I would beg them not to think anything of it.

Ash does not struggle with this.

I fidget while he stares, as if he's still trying to decide whether to forgive me.

"Fine." My shoulders sag as I turn my computer back around. "I'll show you the second grade, but I will *not* enjoy it."

The corner of his mouth twitches, and I pause. Was that an almost smile? It feels thrilling, that flutter of muscle. Somehow hard-won.

I want to do it again.

"Just forget it," he says, opening another browser and shrugging out of his jacket. "All I want you to do is look through the list and help me pick a book."

I nod a little too quickly. I can do that. I can focus and pick out the best book on this list. He will be *staggered* by my ability to pick books.

I scroll through the list again. And again. I open a tab and find the Wikipedia entry for *Robinson Crusoe*. I scroll some more.

I try to hold it in as long as I can before it slips out. "Was that a song?"

His typing falters, and he punches the backspace key pointedly several times before answering. "What do you think?"

"I think I would like to hear that song."

"I don't play that one." I can hear the hard stop in his voice. He's done talking about this, and I swallow the next question back down.

I comb through what I know about him. That song hinted at a heart broken, and although he looks like nothing in the world could touch him, someone clearly did.

I remember hearing about him dating Brandon Stewart shortly after getting to town last year. I think that might have gone on for a few months. I didn't hear much about a breakup, but there were whispers of him and Rebecca Marson being off and on toward the end of junior year. Pretty sure she literally wrapped herself like a present and parked her butt on the hood of his car for his birthday.

I cock my head. I wonder if Rebecca is the *only one who brings him back to life*. I wonder what Josh would say if I ever said something like that to him. He'd probably fall over in shock. I shiver, imagining the delicious look of surprise on his face.

I narrow my eyes at the laptop, now protectively close to Ash. What if I *did* say something like that to Josh?

"Ash, would you consider yourself a romantic?"

His fingers jerk, and again with the backspace key. Tap. Tap. Tap. "I'm having trouble following your train of thought."

"Just a question. Would you consider yourself romantic? That song seemed pretty romantic." The almost smile has made me bold.

"Which is none of your business." He draws the barriers between us again.

I cautiously poke them. "I'll answer it for you. You clearly know what you're doing, and I'm hoping you can help me."

"Help you?" he asks, his stormy face lightening, like confusion has made him forget to keep glowering.

"Yes," I say, scooting my desk closer. "I don't know if you've heard, but I used to date Josh."

"I know," he says flatly, pulling the clouds back in place, too polite to drop the "no shit" I know is lurking behind his teeth.

I clear my throat. "I think our breakup was a poor decision, and you might be able to help me get things back to normal."

He closes his laptop, turning all his attention to me. "How so?" Disbelief drips off each word.

I focus on a spot over his head, the newly forming plan feeling shakier under his microscopic gaze. "It seems Josh did not feel like I was very romantic or that I really knew how to be as loving as a girlfriend should be." I smile, like it's the easiest, breeziest thing in the world. Just your normal little relationship hiccup. "And that's where you come in!"

He pinches his nose. "He said *what* to you?" I fixate on the skull ring staring at me from his middle finger. It looks sympathetic.

"Of course, it's just a huge misunderstanding." The idea is building rapidly in my brain, and I feel like I've jumped off the high dive without holding my nose. This could actually work. "You can help me Cyrano him."

"Cyrano him?"

I take a deep breath. "You see, Cyrano was a soldier who had a lot of gifts—"

"I'm familiar with the story, Marlowe."

"Okay, so *you* could write some letters, or songs about him, and I can give them to him, and prove I'm romantic, and everything will go back to normal." My chest loosens a little. The sun has finally come out from behind weeks of smothering skies.

"I have so many problems with this, I don't even know where to begin."

I frown and pull open my notebook to draw out a plan of action for him. I must not be explaining myself well.

"Actually, I do know where to begin. He's an absolute dipshit."

His voice carries to the front of the room, and he punctuates his words by pointing in Josh's direction. I see golden hair turn toward us, and I snatch his hand out of the air, curling black-painted nails back into his palm.

Ms. Chris moves toward us, sensing drama she needs to squash before it blossoms. "Everything okay over here?"

"Everything is perfect!" I say, overly bright. "We were just finalizing our choice." Ash yanks his hand back.

She raises an eyebrow, waiting.

"In fact, we'd like to pick now." I smile at Ash's impassive face. "Umm . . . we're going to go with *Wuthering Heights*."

She smiles. "A tortured gothic tale about revenge and the nature of love. Quite a bit to sink your teeth into there."

I perk up, feeling like I've passed a particularly challenging test.

"I'll make a note of it," she says as she turns away from us. "Odette Norman and Tiffany Bridgers, y'all better be done with this project if you've got this much time to *not* sit together."

Ash at least waits until she marches away before pouncing. "Do you even know anything about *Wuthering Heights*?"

"Sure, it's a tortured gothic tale about revenge and the nature of love."

He groans, and I almost feel sorry for him.

"Oh *relax,* I'll read everything I need to know about it later." I wave off his concern and pour every ounce of energy into a smile I aim at him like a laser beam. It promises best friendship, my undying devotion, and a framed picture of my second-grade school photo. He just has to help me with this one little thing. "So, do we have a deal? You'll help?"

He shakes his head. "Just be glad you're done with him."

I'm surprised, but not discouraged. "It's not like I expect something for nothing! I'm fully prepared to make an even trade."

"I don't want anything from you," he says, packing up.

I blink, ignoring the sting of his words. "You don't even know what I have to offer."

"I know everything I need to know. You have a shitty ex-boyfriend and he's done you the favor of removing himself from your life. Consider it a win."

The bell rings and he eases out of his seat.

"Ash," I say, my voice catching on his name and keeping him in place.

He doesn't know me. He doesn't know what this breakup has done to me. He doesn't know how much this matters. If he did, how could he say no?

"I love him." My voice is as small as I feel.

He pauses for just a moment. "It'll pass."

Six

We pull up at the edge of the field, and Odette wedges her white Jeep between a lifted truck that I would break my neck trying to descend from and a Honda covered with decals detailing what southern girls are made of.

"Wait, so Lady Jessica *didn't* want to marry him, or did she?" Odette asks, killing the lights. That inky darkness you can only find deep in the country floods every available space.

"She *didn't,* but then she *did.*"

"I'm confused," Poppy says.

I step out into smothering air that has only lessened slightly in intensity with the dusk. A deep earthy smell rises from the ground as my sneakers break the soft crust of earth. "They had to get married for societal reasons, and hated each other, but *then* Lady Jessica fell in love with him and wanted him to love her in return, so she concocted a plan to *make* him fall in love with her. All the while not realizing that he secretly loved her too."

They blink at me for a moment.

"It's hard to explain."

"Obviously," Odette says, sighing deeply. "And we're show-ing up to one of these ridiculous parties to do what, exactly?"

I pull out a small notebook full of my very careful notes. En-couraging cats in disco attire boogie across the hard cover. "We're winning back Josh! Despite my excellent Cyrano plan, Ash re-fuses to help, so I'm on my own. Luckily, Lady Jessica seems to have some solid ideas for landing a duke, and I think some of her moves can easily translate to real life."

"Into real life, and two hundred or so years in the future?"

"These concepts are timeless," I say primly.

"And that's the reason you're dressed like a tomato?"

I spread my hands wide. "Lady Jessica wore a shocking red dress to capture the Duke's attention." I spin in a circle so they can take in the red fitted T-shirt, red denim shorts, and red Con-verse. "Obviously I had to improvise."

Poppy raises her hand. "And *we're* here for what reason, ex-actly?"

"For backup! You have to tell me what Josh is doing while I'm ignoring him."

She shrugs. "I need to scope out some uneven terrain for my maze-finding robot anyway."

I turn to Odette, the unspoken concern pulsing between us. "Do not let her get trampled by cows."

"I don't know enough about cows to know if they're a trampling sort, but you worry about your own shit show, I've got this one."

Poppy straps on a belt bag over a jumpsuit covered in dancing broccoli. "All right, what are we waiting for?"

Farther up ahead, the warm glow of a bonfire lights up the weathered face of a dilapidated barn that's a wolf's breath away from total collapse, and a rusted-out tractor embraced by waist-high weeds. The Bridgers farm is now a sprawling and modern affair, with shiny lemon-lime combines maintaining pristine fields of cotton and corn, but this corner of the property is just for River Haven High. This little postscript of the original barn and the farm's more modest past has been overrun with teenagers every Saturday night since Tiffany's older brother christened it "the place to be" almost eight years ago.

"You know you don't have to do this," Odette murmurs as Poppy pulls ahead.

Her words seep into my skin.

"I feel like I do." My voice seems insignificant as we're both swallowed up by the night and farmland sprawling in every direction.

"Then it will work. If he has a single ounce of sense, it will work."

Though I can barely see her in the dark, I feel buoyed. A laugh spirals out of me, and my neck loosens with the strain of carrying around my own failures for the past few weeks. The weight recedes a little with her words. With the crystalline night and her unwavering belief that I will turn this around. That I will make the most sugary lemonade out of the mess that Josh has left behind. I breathe in the earthy air, deep enough that I almost believe it too.

"Okay," I say. "Step one, identify the target and environment to figure out which of Jessica's moves might be best in that scenario."

Odette trips in the dark, and her hand shoots out and grabs my arm. "You did not just say target."

"Victim?" Poppy suggests, turning back toward our voices.

"Love interest," I say firmly.

We step around puddles and soft mounds that hint of moles until the faint strains of music reach us. It's always the same song about back roads, a pretty girl, and a boy with nothing else on his brain. Tonight, I don't even mind, and Odette starts moving her hips before the fire-bright glow reaches us.

"Try to act like we thought this would be a totally normal, casual thing to do," I say, forcing my mouth into what I hope is an excited expression.

Poppy adjusts her utility belt and smiles uncertainly. Odette does a two-step around her and past a stack of hay bales into the crackling-warm circle of the best River Haven has to offer.

The party extends into the barn, where more hay bales are arranged in half circles around a keg. Roy Holder's F-150 is backed up to the edge of the circle and all the doors are open, spilling honeyed words and twanging guitar solos into the night. I pick at my shirt as the fire sends a wave of warmth to my bones.

Tiffany saunters over, content in the fact that this is her place, and she reigns here just like she does at school. She presses a Solo cup into my hand, and the smell of cheap beer mixes with ash and fertilizer.

"Fancy seeing you here, Marlowe," she says, drawling out the word "you" in a way that makes me want to pour the beer right back on her.

I smile and tip the cup in her direction. "I can't imagine why. Where else would I be on a Saturday night?"

"Didn't think any of this was your scene now that you're single again," she says, dismissing Odette and Poppy with a glance. "In fact, I'd say you were our most unusual guest tonight, if Ash Hayes hadn't also decided to make an appearance. Any coincidence there?" An overlaminated eyebrow slides up her forehead.

I see what this is now. A recon mission.

"The Prince of Darkness is here? No offense, Tiffany, but I doubt he finds your barn that exciting." Odette laughs, stepping around her.

"That's how much you know," she says, hands on her hips, but we're already moving past.

I can't imagine Ash Hayes here any more than I can imagine myself hanging in one of his crypts, or secret poetry-writing caves, or wherever else he hangs out. Somewhere everyone dresses in black and refuses to do any favors for others.

My face flushes, and my glasses slide down as sweat beads at my hairline. Ash fits in here about as well as I do.

Poppy nods toward the left of the fire. "That field looks half plowed. I'm going to check it out."

Poppy pulls a headlamp out of the belt bag and puts it on, and Odette squeezes my arm as she follows Poppy into the darkness. I track their progress as they move farther and farther away from me, a little reluctant to be on my own already. *This is fine.* I used to come here all the time. Groups of familiar faces fan out around me in short shorts, ball caps, and school jerseys. I smile at a group to my left and pretend I don't see their eyes skate over me and away.

Meredith Wilson and Wesley Capps start slow dancing, even though the tempo is way too fast for that, but they've been dating since seventh grade and are going to fall into marriage the second they graduate.

It's so familiar, it *aches*.

I spin in a circle, alcohol-laced breath puffing like clouds around me, and it hits me like a punch to the stomach. I kind of miss this. I hated some of the forced socializations that came along with being Josh's girlfriend, but I miss being a part of something big. A big group of people who would laugh with you, tell you stories they knew would make you smile, and spin you around as a new favorite song bled into the night. That meant something to me, and as I stand here surrounded by people, but still alone, I feel it to my core. They *forgot* me.

And that *sucks*.

I take a drink, the trickle of light beer moving into my blood. I miss Josh. For a lot of reasons, but right now I miss the easy comfort of someone's arms around me on a clear, balmy night that feels like it could last forever.

"Penny for your thoughts?"

I swallow hard as the boy in question slides into my orbit. His face as familiar as my own, the swoop of his hair falling carelessly over his forehead. I clench my fist as he moves closer, until I can feel half-moons carve into my palms. *You don't get to touch him whenever you want anymore.*

My notebook in my back pocket, my plans, my brain cells all evaporate. All I can do is stand there and breathe *Josh* into the night.

"Just wanted to see if you needed anything," he says, and I hear the unspoken question in the air. He's being gentle with me, but he wants to know why I'm here. This is his place. His friends. And I'm ruining it. He shoves hands into jeans worn paper-smooth, and I recognize them as his second-favorite pair. There's a spot of motor oil on the left leg that he's never been able to get rid of.

"I'm doing great," I say, a little too loud. The sense that I've made a mistake grates along my brain. I've run out of words, so I toss the rest of my cup back, and the sour taste floods my tongue.

His mouth tightens; he doesn't believe me. I wonder if it's hard for him to be near me too. If he's holding back from falling into old habits and sliding his hand into mine.

I finally have all his attention. It's shining in my direction, and I hate that I'm going to throw it all away. My brain screams *remember the plan,* and Jessica's first step toward making a duke overwhelmingly decide that he's in love with you. That he can't live without you.

Ignore him.

Ignore.

Him.

I shrug, my small smile stretched so tight I could snap. I take a jerky step backward. And then another, and a rushed *bye* falls from my stiff lips as his own part in surprise. I dart away from him, around the other side of the fire, and duck behind the rusted-out old tractor. I lean my back into warm metal, a shaky laugh bubbling out of me.

His face as I dismissed him felt incredible. Jessica's advice is golden, and this was all I needed. A little guidance from the world of romance to get this train back on the rails.

I fill my lungs to the brink with smoky air and courage, and pull out the disco cats. Step one is complete, and now it gets trickier.

Step Two: Drop a favor for him to pick up for you.

A bit dated, and handkerchiefs are objectively disgusting, but I can substitute something else in a pinch.

Step Three: Flirt with someone else.

My stomach pitches like I'm riding the Blazing Fury at Dollywood. *You can do this.*

Step Four: If all else fails, pretend to faint near him and he'll catch you and realize what you've meant to him all along.

It would have been more effective if I could've arranged to be kidnapped by a deranged half-sister desperate for my dowry, but I'll work with what I've got. I step back into the crowd.

Josh hasn't gone far; he and Derrick are locked in a heated debate on the far side of the fire. I should probably space things out, but I don't have all night. I'm one more beer away from weeping on somebody's shoulder if my and Josh's song comes on.

Not that "Your Love Is Whiskey Neat" is a *good* song. I hate its dull melody and slow-as-molasses words about tradition and finding *the one* when you're young. But I loved the way Josh would look at me as he sang along, and that's just as good, right?

I pull the pencil out of my bun, and my hair tumbles down my back. I feel it expanding in the heat, and I clutch the pencil tight as I walk toward him.

His back is turned to me, and I bite my lip. I can't just yell *Hey, I'm dropping a favor here,* and chuck it at his head.

Jessica didn't have to work this hard, her handkerchief fluttering onto a polished dance floor for all the world to see.

I would just have to be creative.

I straighten my T-shirt, the lumpy cotton molding to me in the heat. I have to create a diversion.

I move closer, and snippets of conversation trickle in my direction.

"Who were they supposed to trade instead? Matthews?" Derrick is saying.

"Exactly," Josh says, derision in his voice. "What has he done for them lately?"

Now's my moment. I adjust my angle, and my pencil falls to the ground near Josh's feet as I pass by. I bump into Derrick's shoulder. *Bingo.*

I smile, slow my steps and wait for the inevitable. *One, two—*

"What the hell, Marlowe?"

I spin, and Derrick is scowling at me like I'm personally responsible for trading Matthews in whatever sports game he's talking about.

"Oh, sorry—"

"Look where you're going." He turns, his wide back dismissing me, and I see Josh's foot shift slightly. My pencil disappears under his boots and burrows deep into soft mud.

Well, shit.

Jessica didn't include a troubleshooting guide, and now I'm out of accessories to throw.

Pressure builds behind my eyes, and I press my palms into them until the sting lessens. It's just the smoke. This is only a minor setback, and I still have two more tricks up my sleeve.

I fetch another cup of watery beer, my eyes still burning with ash and malt and failure. My gaze sweeps past the groups circling the bonfire and snags on a splotch of black piled onto some hay bales.

Wait.

I cannot believe Tiffany was right.

I creep up, moving behind Hannah Whitely as she pulls up into a keg stand with lousy form, and there he is.

Ashton freaking Hayes.

I've never seen him outside of school, and it feels unnatural to see him here in Tiffany's barn. He's brought a girl I don't recognize from school, and the abundance of black was almost enough for me to miss them in the dark corner they're perched in. Ash's hair is loose from the little tie he uses at school, fanning across his shoulders with soft curling ends. His black shirt is bunched up over previously unseen biceps, and his boots look mean enough to make it across any of Tiffany's cow pastures. Five freshly painted midnight-black nails curl around his own Solo cup, and the idea of him drinking Montgomery Beast just seems plain wrong.

You shouldn't.

He's made it clear that he doesn't have any interest in helping you.

"It'll pass."

Move on.

I inch closer. He's even smiling a little at the girl with the stop-sign-red streaks through her hair. That small twist of his mouth in the classroom rises like an unwelcome ghost. I wonder if she makes him laugh. I wonder what that sounds like.

I shake my head, those thoughts scattering like starlight. I should go back to the party. He doesn't want to help, and I have flirting and maybe some fainting to do. My stomach bottoms out and my brain screams that an anonymous letter would be a gift in comparison.

It's the small smile tugging on his lips that does it. He looks relaxed, and if he was ever going to say yes, it would be now. I lock in on his location like a targeted missile.

Thirty feet. I slap on a smile that's set to stun. *Twenty feet.* The girl looks up and a scowl settles on her pierced lips. Too late. *Ten feet.* He looks up as I come to a stop, and I dial up the enthusiasm level to student bake sale.

"Ash!" I say, as if we hadn't mutually decided not to speak to each other for weeks. "I had no idea you were going to be here tonight! What an excellent coincidence."

He looks at me, swirling the liquid in his cup, with not a flicker of expression or a single word.

"Excellent," I say again, echoing into the silence.

Light dances off a jawline that could slice me to ribbons.

"Look, Ash," I continue. "If you're overcome by emotion, or nursing an infected tongue piercing, we can simply have this conversation on Monday. I just wanted to revisit some aspects of—" I glance at the girl, who's looking way too interested in our conversation. "—of our *project*." I pause another beat under his unblinking evaluation, but he's content to just watch me from his hay bale.

"Great talk," I say into the continued silence, while the girl giggles.

I drop the smile, and the pretense, and swear on my great-aunt Louise, *bless her soul,* that I will do this entire project by myself before I ever speak to him again. My face feels like a furnace, and he's so *rude* I can barely wrap my mind around it. I spin on my heel, back to the party and people with manners. I can handle the paper, and for the presentation I will dress up as a sheep and pretend I am lost on the moors if I have to, but I will *never*—

"The answer is still no." His voice snakes around me, and I stop in my tracks. His accent is like a black hole of accents—no twang, no lilt, no drawl of any kind. It's flat and perfectly legible. Crystal clear.

His rejection sticks in my brain like a splinter, and it hurts the way he just tosses it onto the grass between us. Indignation chokes me, and I slowly spin and give him a smile I reserve for senile meemaws. "I don't remember asking you a question?"

"We both know what you were asking."

I shake my head, still planning out my sheep costume. Ash and I weren't friends, but just because he saw me in my braces era and I've played his music more times than I care to count, I felt for a moment that we were closer than we are. I let it confuse me, blind me to the fact that we've had approximately two conversations and he's made it clear he doesn't want to be friendly with me.

"You know, you made this much easier, Ash," I say, blinking back that familiar sting. "As it turns out, I don't want anything from you either."

He frowns again.

I don't stop this time. I don't need his help. He's surly and rude, and I am *fine* on my own. I will stick to the original plan. *Jessica's* plan.

Rip it off like a Band-Aid.

Fast.

Make him jealous.

It's a solid enough concept, but I'm a little shaky on the details. In the book, Jessica let the Earl of Northam waltz her across the dance floor, which is unlikely to be on the agenda tonight. I can improvise, though. All I need to do is find somebody to flirt with.

I squint at the crowd, little pockets of cliques separating like oil and water. I need someone Josh likes enough that he would care if I was flirting with them, but also someone who isn't a complete tool like Derrick.

There.

There, near the keg. Ryan Michaels. He's all brown skin, black boots, and the same burgundy and gold school colors splashed across every boy here tonight. *Go Rabbits!* He's also nice. Nice in a way that many of Josh's friends aren't. He'd always smile at me, a fist-bump greeting at the ready, and ask me about myself. He's perfect.

I walk toward him, and he doesn't disappoint. He grins and raises a Solo cup in an unspoken question.

I nod, grateful for the excuse, and he fills another cup before passing it my way.

"Well, if it isn't the marvelous Marlowe Meadows. Having fun out there, killer?" His drawl is so smooth, it's practically candy.

I lick my lips. No time like the present. "Much better now."

Hi eyebrows shoot up under his baseball cap, and I'm not sure I did it right.

"What's that now?"

"That's a great shirt, Ryan. It really highlights your . . . muscles."

He smiles, but it looks embarrassed, not sexy. "You might need to get those glasses checked, not that many muscles to speak of."

This feels so much more stilted than how things were with

Josh. I grasp for the next sentence. "Well, whatever you have, they seem perfect."

He chuckles, but not in the normal easy way I've come to associate with him. "If you say so."

I nod, because disbelief is written all over his face. "I really do."

I reach out, grasping both of his arms like a proud father on graduation day. It lasts a nanosecond before my brain says *NOPE* and I yank my hands back to my sides.

He's still as a rabbit that's been cornered (*Go Rabbits!*), and my body takes on a life of its own and jerks up both thumbs.

"Yep, feels great!"

I see Poppy and Odette standing behind him and eject myself from this conversation before the embarrassment strikes me dead.

"Okay, well, good talking to you! Bye!" I turn and bolt around him, not waiting for a response, and don't stop until I have Odette and Poppy on either side of me.

"Quick question, does Ryan look like he's not sure if he's been sexually harassed or not?"

Poppy coughs, but it doesn't hide the laugh. "Should he feel like that?"

"I may have been making several comments about his muscles."

"What muscles?" Odette asks, looking over my shoulder.

"He's a baseball player, they're there somewhere."

"It looks like he's making a beeline for Josh," Poppy says, pulling some small binoculars out of her belt bag.

I bat her hands down and freeze. "Josh? Why would he be talking to Josh?"

"Didn't you want him to tell Josh? So Josh gets jealous?" Odette asks.

"I don't *know*! It wasn't clear in the book! Word just somehow got out!"

"Well, Josh is now coming over here."

"*What?*"

"Do you want us to do something? Should we distract him?" Poppy asks, making me wonder what else she has in her belt bag.

I shake my head. No, this is fine. This is what's supposed to happen. I turn as his long strides eat up the ground between us.

"Having fun?" I ask when he gets close enough to hear.

"How many of those have you had?" he asks without preamble. He nods toward the still-full cup in my hand.

"Not many," I tell him, as the music and murmurs dim. "What's going on?"

"What's going on is that you're drunk and hitting on my friends. Not cool, Marlowe." He drops his voice, and the pity in his eyes threatens to undo me. "I think it's time to leave."

My throat clogs with tears, but I refuse to cry. None of this is going the way it's supposed to. The music officially stops, and everyone is looking. I feel a little lightheaded, and I'm moments away from deploying step four and fainting right into his arms.

"Marlowe and I were about to leave anyway."

I freeze, the words barely registering.

Josh scoffs, looking over my shoulder. "Why would she go anywhere with *you*?"

I turn and there he is—Ash Hayes, with a hand stretched in my direction. Inexplicably. But I know enough to recognize a life raft when I see it. I take his hand, his long, elegant fingers closing around mine, and my face feels as hot as his palm.

He pulls me toward the parked cars, and I nod when Odette mouths, *Are you okay?*

Josh produces one more irritated "Marlowe" before the night swallows him up behind us.

Seven

The silence is thick enough to chew and lodge in my throat. I shift on the warm black leather seat and can't wrap my brain around how I ended up here in Ash's pathologically clean 4Runner. I sneak a peek at him, but he's only got eyes for the road. His teeth worry the gold ring bisecting his lip.

He involved himself in this. You have every right to ask him why he stepped in. I squeeze my eyes shut hard enough to block out Josh's face. That sad, disappointed slant of his eyebrows. Him asking me to leave.

I can't take it anymore. Lady Jessica would ask.

"What was that about—"

"Marlowe, what the hell was that?"

We turn to each other at the same time, words and frustration tumbling over each other.

"I thought you didn't want to help!"

"He's such a *massive* dipshit."

I put my hands up. "Ash, stop. Me first. What was that? Why did you step in?"

His hands grip the steering wheel until his knuckles blanch. "Why? Would you rather go back there? To where he was kicking you out?"

His words are sharp, but he stumbles over each one. I raise an eyebrow, almost positive that he's as clueless about how we ended up in this car as I am.

"Of course not," I say, rolling my eyes. "I just don't get it, and I like to understand things. First, the project? And now this? All the while being very rude to me, and growling about how you don't want to help me?"

"I don't growl."

I wait him out.

He groans, exasperation written into every feature. "Can't I just be doing a nice thing?"

"Nope," I say, mentally calculating that probability at a robust 7 percent. "Mainly because I'm pretty sure you dislike me."

The silence continues to crush me. I will be at least an inch shorter when I get out of this car. He lets it hang in the air long enough that I briefly reflect on the YouTube videos I used to watch about how to tuck and roll out of a moving car without hurting yourself.

Finally he cracks the tension, just as my hand is reaching for the door handle. "I don't *dislike* you, Marlowe." I shiver at his almost constant use of my name. Josh would always call me "girl" or "Lo," and it's strange to hear every vowel and consonant drop into the darkness. "It's just hard for me to reconcile a person who would love someone like Stallings with someone I would have anything in common with. Or *want* to have anything in common with."

I flinch, the words stinging. I know Josh can be demanding of his friends, and even those he doesn't consider friends. They don't see the real him, though. The soft, gentle boy who would thread his fingers through my hair and let me tell him all about my latest hyperfixation. *Truly, how amazing are mushrooms?*

I shake my head. *Focus.*

"But . . . you've still stepped in to help me. Twice, now."

"Because he's a massive asshole, and you shouldn't have needed saving in the first place."

His irritation bleeds into something a little more satisfied. I see the tug of his lips curve into the smallest of smiles under the passing streetlights. He turns to look at me, not even bothering to pretend he isn't enjoying it.

"Plus, he really, *really* hates it."

"Why, Ashton Octavius Hayes. You're trying to provoke him."

He shrugs, the elegant slant of his shoulder brushing off my surprise. "He deserves it, and my middle name isn't Octavius. Nobody's is."

"I imagine, statistically speaking, there is someone on this planet whose middle name is Octavius."

"Nope, sounds fake."

"What's your middle name, then?"

"I'm afraid that's a friend-level question, and you don't have access to that kind of information."

I lean back in the seat, off-kilter from the lilt in his voice that is almost teasing. "Do I get points for being a way for you to torture Josh?"

He hums, the low vibration filling the car and seeping into my skin. "I will give you two extra points, because that irritated '*Marlowe*' he yelled out when we left was very satisfying."

I cover my face with my hands. "Oh, God, I almost forgot about that." I check my phone. All that attention and still not a single text message.

"Imagine thinking he had the right to say anything to you after throwing you away."

I bristle. "I am not some old candy bar wrapper. He just doesn't understand that I'm very invested in our relationship, and willing to work to save it." I pull my lips into some semblance of a smile, refusing to let his words burrow under my skin. "Besides, you might not have been trying to purposefully help me, but you certainly helped me pull off Lady Jessica's tactics better than I could have done on my own." The look from Josh to me and then Ash's outstretched hand was thunderous. Just like I imagine the Duke must have felt seeing Jessica waltz with his rival.

We pull up to a stop sign. He turns and looks at me. "Lady Jessica?"

I wave him off. "It's a book, never mind."

A very undignified snort slips past his lips, and he pinches the bridge of his nose—his almost constant expression in my presence.

"I'm sorry," he says, "do you—do you mean from *Lady Jessica Conquers a Duke*?"

I gasp, sitting up. "You *know* it!"

He puts his forehead on the wheel, and the resounding silence throws me.

I bite my lip. Is he praying? I'm used to my meemaw breaking into prayer over the smallest detail, and I've been trained to be respectful in these moments. *Dear Jesus, please bless the workers here at the Super Buy to find your hand to discount the sirloins by Friday.* She would look to me for a loud "Amen" and we would carry on.

I put my hands together respectfully until his shoulders start to shake.

"Ash? Are you laughing at me?"

"I'm sorry," he says, not sounding sorry at all. "What was your plan, to tell him that it was your beloved guardian's dying wish that you two find a way to make it work?"

I almost lunge across the gear shift. "Oh my God, you *know* it know it."

His smile spreads, and I know it's one I'll remember.

"Yes, I know it. It's a classic, and my grandmother's favorite. Absolutely unhinged, but a classic." He leans back, in no hurry to move beyond this stop sign. "I can't believe I didn't see it before. The all-red outfit. Him accusing you of flirting with his friend."

I sigh. "Lot of good that did."

"What else did you do?" The smile is back, sharp and glittering in the dark.

I hesitate, but getting a response out of quiet, sullen Ash Hayes feels like earning a Girl Scout badge. Plus, the joy of talking about this book, unhinged or not, with someone who has read it is too much to resist.

"Okay," I say, leaning all the way in. "I dropped a favor near him to give him the opportunity to return it."

"Stop," he says, the deep, rich sound of his laughter filling the car and my lungs.

It's infectious, and I wipe the tears pooling at the corners of my eyes.

"*Well,* did he?"

"No, it was a pencil, and it got lost in the mud."

He puts his forehead back on the steering wheel, and it feels a little less like failure.

My phone goes off, shattering the moment.

He looks up, frowning. "Josh?"

I shake my head, still dazed in the aftermath of his delight. I answer the FaceTime and two worried faces pop up.

Odette speaks first. "Has Count Chocula drank your blood yet?"

"Really nice," Ash says dryly.

"You're clearly a spring palette, Ash, deal with it," she shoots back, not deterred in the slightest.

I zoom in on my unpunctured neck. "Ash has very kindly offered to take me home. You want to follow us back, and we can recap?"

"Sorry, I need to get home. Nonnegotiable family brunch in the morning," Odette says with a shrug.

"Ash, are you fine to drive?" Poppy asks primly.

Ash smiles as her disapproval crackles through the car. "Don't worry, my cup had water."

Poppy nods, mollified. "Call us tomorrow?"

I'm not sure I'll have many more answers for her, but I nod before signing off.

He finally eases away from the stop sign, and I direct him toward my house as we reach the outskirts of town. It's easier to see him as the glow of streetlights and flashes from the neon glare of the Piggly Wiggly slide over the sharp angle of his jaw.

"Your taste in friends seems pretty good, is it just your taste in guys that's terrible?"

"According to who?"

"Absolutely me, and anyone else who has ever spent a single minute in Josh's company."

"What's your evidence for this hypothesis?"

His mouth quirks again. "Well. For starters, he told you that you didn't love him correctly."

My gut twists. "You don't understand."

"I'm trying to." He's not teasing anymore. He's listening, and in a way that gives me stage fright.

I let the silence hang between us, filling every crevice and cup holder, and I realize I *want* to keep talking. There's no logical reason to share razor-sharp memories with someone who'll be out of my life with the conclusion of a project, but I still want to know him. I want to know the story behind all the rings on his fingers, and what shampoo he uses because there isn't a hint of frizz and the car smells like mint and sage.

You don't have to know everything, Marlowe Meadows. I try to bring myself back to reality. He's just a boy. A boy who is not my friend.

But he's listening, and he's driving me home, and I find myself answering anyway.

"Things were harder when I was a kid," I say, slowly, gauging his reaction with every word. "My differences were more noticeable, and while I've never tried to hide them, certain survival techniques kick in whether you want them to or not."

I clear my throat, realizing belatedly that maybe he just wanted me to say that Josh and I had the same taste in music, or that I was really into boys with blond hair. Too late.

"Anyway, needless to say, I wasn't very popular. I was weird Marlowe. Marlowe who was too honest, too literal, too dumb to realize that talking to someone every day in class didn't mean that you were friends and that you shouldn't try to give them a Christmas present in front of all of their actual friends." I want to use its name. I want to be clear with him. "Autism, amirite?"

We turn down my street, and Ash's silence fills my lungs until I'm dizzy. I keep talking, breathing uncomfortable words into the velvet dark. "I've known everyone in my class since pre-K, and a boy had never looked my way. But then two years ago, Joshua Shepherd Stallings *did*." I point to the pale blue Victorian house on the corner.

"No Octavius for him?"

"He couldn't pull off Octavius." I smile as he hugs the curb in front of my house. He turns off the engine and sits back, not a sliver of haste in his body language.

I shrug, trying to find my place in the story. "He looked my way and saw me. He saw what I was, who I was, and told me I was special. Then the rest of the student body believed it too, and it felt nice to be on the inside for once." I clear my throat. "So yeah, I relied on him, probably too much, to help me navigate uncertain waters. I thought he could help me understand how to be in a relationship, but now I'm here trying to understand and navigate the aftermath of him alone."

He makes an impatient noise in the back of his throat, and I find the courage to meet his eyes.

"Marlowe," he starts, before closing his mouth, his lips disappearing into a thin line that strings me tight as a bow. He clears his throat and starts again. "Do you know where Three Little Words is?"

I blink. Of all the things I'm expecting after baring my soul to him in the darkness, it's not this. "The bookstore?"

He nods, once. "Can you be there tomorrow at eleven?"

I pause, expecting more information or context to come, but it doesn't. "I think so," I say to fill the space.

"We'll start tomorrow."

My brain stutters over the sentence, and the way he turns and starts the engine again.

"Start tomorrow?" I unbuckle my seat belt and lean forward as the muscle in his jaw clenches. I've spilled all my secrets onto his floorboards, but he's keeping his close to the chest. "Does this mean you're going to help me?"

"Tomorrow, Marlowe," he says, nodding toward my house.

I scramble out of the car before he changes his mind.

Eight

Three Little Words opened about a year ago, and I remember some of the local buzz that came with the downtown finally getting a new store after at least ten years. I've never made it inside, and the cheerful window display has me immediately regretting that.

Tall, proud sunflowers with printed pages for leaves flourish in the bright morning light, and a tidy little sign at their base proudly reads NO BOOKS WERE HARMED IN THE MAKING OF THIS DISPLAY.

The same haphazard whimsy continues inside the store, with brightly colored bookshelves, every surface overflowing with Jenga towers of books, and a small café tucked into the corner. Sitting at one of the tables next to the counter is Ash. He's folded into a bright pink chair with teal polka dots, and his black jeans and black-and-white-striped button-down make him look like a lost crow. A fat tuxedo cat pumps biscuits into his leg.

I slide into a sunshine-lemon chair across from him, his companion taking me by surprise. "Who's your friend?"

The sonorous purring almost drowns out his reply.

"Marlowe, meet Darcy. Darcy, this is Marlowe."

Darcy keeps pumping, almost cross-eyed as Ash pats his rump.

"Aren't cats supposed to be named things like Buttons or Duchess?"

"Darcy, you know, like *Pride and Prejudice*?"

I nod, because I know all about Matthew Macfadyen. "I haven't read the book, but I have some passing familiarity with the movie." It's too early in the morning to admit to my sad-girl binges.

Ash stops petting, and Darcy meows in protest. "Don't let Sloane hear you say that, or I can't be held responsible if they drag you into the back and make you read it in front of them."

"And who's Sloane? If it's another cat, I'm going to say we should go to the sandwich place next door."

He grins, scooping a complaining Darcy to the floor. "They're the owner, and a bit of a superfan." He nods to a framed picture of a flexed hand propped up on the counter next to an espresso machine.

My stomach clenches, and I feel weirdly seen. That this scene from the movie that always made me breathless was more universal than I'd realized.

He stands, towering over me until I'm a little lightheaded. "Do you want a coffee?"

I perk up considerably. "A latte would be great." He waves off my money and steps behind the counter to wash his hands. When he starts grinding beans, I lean forward. "Ash, are you sure we're not supposed to wait for Sloane?"

He looks up, amused. "I work here, Marlowe."

"Oh," I say, taken aback. "*Oh*." I turn and see the space in a new light; one that has Ash as a permanent fixture. His moody presence alongside books suspended in flight from the ceiling, like seagulls.

He hands me my coffee, and I try not to jump right into business. People like small talk. They like to ease into these things.

I fumble for a topic. "Do you have to work today?"

He shrugs. "I might help out a little if it gets busy."

I nod, silence falling between us until my chest tightens enough to expel one burning question out of my lungs. "Ash, why are we *here*?"

I hate feeling lost or out of my depth. I want to insist that he pull out his calculus homework, so I can do it in front of him and prove that I'm at least good at something.

He frowns over the rim of his cup, which yells BOOKMARKS ARE FOR QUITTERS. "We have a few things to clear up." He sets down his coffee. "For starters, I'm not going to be writing love letters to that dipshit."

"Don't call him that," I say automatically. "Then what exactly are you proposing?"

"I am willing to be convinced to tutor you in romance." He gestures behind him. "And with books maybe a little better suited to the job than *Lady Jessica*. I'll help you find the words to describe your own feelings, and you can send those along to the jockstrap."

"Homework?" I ask, looking at the overwhelming selection of books popping up on every surface like weeds. "And these are *all* romance? That's going to take way too long. I was hoping to wrap this up by next week."

He picks his cup back up and breathes in the steam rising into the air between us. Not a care in the world. "That's all I'm willing to offer. You want a shortcut, but that would just be another guy *telling* you what love is. What you need are lessons from some of the masters and to make your own opinions."

I slouch back in my seat and sip my annoyingly tasty latte.

It isn't unreasonable, which is also deeply annoying. In fact, it's probably more time and effort on his part than simply slipping me a few songs from his top-secret stash.

"So, I read what you tell me, and suddenly I'm a romance expert crafting prose that will make Josh sit up and notice?"

"Are you always this moody in the morning?" he asks, falling short of accusatory and landing solidly in amusement. "I know you want specific parameters, so let's do this the right way." He pauses to think, but I have a feeling it's all for show. "Let's agree to four letters." I open my mouth to object, but he cuts me off. "Quality over quantity. Getting a good love letter from you is going to be noticeable enough."

"Anonymous letters," I clarify.

"I thought you were trying to win him back."

"I am," I hedge. "Like with most things, I assume I will get better with practice. I don't want him receiving one poor attempt and immediately discounting it." *Or for him to tell me to stop contacting him before I write one that can change his mind.*

He nods. "Okay, anonymous then."

I open my disco-cats notebook to the first blank page and make two columns, for *Marlowe Amelia Meadows* and *Ashton Napoleon Hayes*. His lips twitch.

"What's this?"

"A contract."

"What a shame, I left my notary seal at home." His posture is casual, but his attention is a high-beam spotlight and I'm melting under the intensity of his gaze.

"Your first mistake," I say, clearing my throat. "Because a notarized document could pop up at any time. I guess we'll just have to trust each other."

Under my name, I write:

FOUR <u>EXPERTLY</u> CRAFTED LETTERS

He pulls the notebook across the table and snatches the pen from my fingers. "How many romance novels can you commit to reading per week without it affecting your schoolwork?"

"Probably about one? I'm a fast reader, but it's usually interest that slows me down."

He doesn't seem bothered. "I don't think that will be a problem."

He writes next to my neat, cramped letters in swirls and flourishes:

One Ash-curated book a week for homework

I pull the notebook and pen out of his hands. "What do you want? A book report or something?"

He shrugs. "Not a bad idea. Let's say you keep track of them in this book. A quick synopsis, any tropes you identify and which ones you like best, and three things you learn from each novel."

"Like, this book taught me that if a duke doesn't offer to give up his title and lands for you at least once, you don't even want him?"

"Exactly."

I put pen to paper, feeling inspired.

FOUR ROMANCE FIELDWORK ACTIVITIES

"Now, what does *that* mean?"

"It means that I clearly need practical experience. You saw what a disaster that party was! I need real-time, boots-on-the-ground training."

"Fieldwork?" He slides the notebook toward himself, as if the shape of my letters will give him more of a clue.

"You can take me to possible date sites so I can scope out activities I need to incorporate into my own romantic practice. We can replicate some activities from the books, just *something*."

I pull the notebook back. "That's it. These are the things I need to be successful."

He exhales, leaning back. "All right, what are you offering in return?"

"Okay," I say, fighting the nervous energy bubbling under my skin. I smooth out the paper, giving myself some time to get my thoughts in order. "I thought we could do something about Never Mind the Monsters."

He stills, the coffee forgotten. "I'm listening."

I pull out my phone, and briefly tilt it away from him so he doesn't see I've bookmarked his website. "Your online presence is a mess. Who did this website?"

He looks at the blocky text and poor mobile format in front of us. "The bassist, Mateo's, little brother. He did it for fifty Pokémon cards and twenty rides to the mall."

I laugh and scroll down.

"Don't laugh, Mateo is still paying that off."

I hold up the grainy black-and-white photo, probably shot in someone's basement. "And how old is this picture?"

He shrugs. "Over a year? Right around the time we started the band."

I squint at the blurred blob that's supposed to be Ash. "I remember when you were blond." I look up at his hair, dark and loose. "This is better."

One single arched eyebrow is the only indicator he heard me. I pull up the band's two social media accounts. "Your last posts were almost a year ago. You have no presence on streaming services, and aside from this one video, I couldn't hear your music anywhere."

"Did you watch it?"

I stop scrolling, and again feel the physical weight of his gaze. "Yeah, I watched it."

His voice is softer. "Did you like it?"

I blush, but I don't know why. He sounds so earnest, my head swims. The question is careful, and I get a sense of something hanging in the balance. I worry often about giving the right response, of being too direct, or missing the mark. I want to be honest, though. I want him to know that I want to unravel all of the lyrics to all of his songs.

I look him full in the face and am simply myself. "I've watched it at least twenty times, and I would like to hear the rest."

He swallows and slowly picks up his cup. "Okay. You will."

I lean over the notebook and under his column I write:

REVAMP CRAPPY WEBSITE (SORRY MATEO'S BROTHER!)

He leans over. "Is that what you're going to study in college?"

I shake my head. "No, I'm going to be a biomedical engineer. I'm going to make synthetic organs, so nobody dies on a transplant list anymore."

He sits back. "That's extremely specific. How did you get into that?"

I pause, but I've known the answer to this question since I was seven. "My father is a cardiac transplant surgeon."

"Fancy. Is he over at the big hospital in Gardner?"

"No, he's in Denver. My parents split up when I was three." I smile brightly to dispel the awkward pity people usually aim in my direction when I say that. "He's unfortunately a little too much like me in this regard." I nod at the notebook between us.

"What does that mean?"

"Oh, you know. We're both a bit hopeless. Maybe if he'd had a tutorial like this, my parents would still be together."

Ash frowns, and I can see him weighing a response before he takes another sip and swallows those words down. "So, fake hearts aside, you know how to build a website."

"Anyone can build a website, Ash, which is how you were able to buy one for Pokémon cards and trips to Cinnabon. The neon-green background was a *choice,* though."

I move down the list and create a subsection:

UPDATED CONTENT

"This picture has to go. We need something recent and stylized. We can work out the details later, but updated photos of all of you."

He does smile now, and it breaks through like sunshine in February. "Are you a photographer now too, Marlowe?"

"Anybody holding a smart phone can be a photographer."

"Well? Do you have a portfolio I can browse?"

"You better be serious, because I have twelve albums of mushrooms that I will walk you through without a moment's hesitation. It will take the rest of this day, and all of your lunch period tomorrow."

He laughs, and goose bumps prickle across my skin.

"Okay, I believe you. What next?" he asks.

I write:

UPDATE SOCIALS AND STREAMING SERVICES

"You're literally nowhere online. What's the point of this band?"

He blinks. "Sorry, I blacked out for a moment and thought you were possessed by my grandmother." He pulls his hair up into a messy bun. "What's the point of it? I don't know. What's the point of any art? The love of it? Wanting to share it?"

I wave him off. "I didn't mean existentially. I mean, do you want to play local gigs? Record something? Hit it big?"

"Can we just go with 'all of the above' for now?"

"That's not going to happen if nobody can hear you. We can start inviting all of River Haven to whatever garage you practice out of, or we can bring it to them."

I look up, and his amused smile has me suddenly self-conscious.

Sometimes when I got too deep into a problem, Josh would tell me that the world wasn't math, and humanity did not need me to sink my teeth into figuring out which restaurant had the best cheeseburger based on a six-point scoring system. Or that I didn't have to go overboard with offering suggestions or research material to help Bo Dickerson train his new labradoodle when he just mentioned it in passing.

First off, the world *is* math. We're all just coefficients and reactions. But I got his point. That sometimes my enthusiasm was too much. A step too far. A knee squeezed under the table to let me know that nobody had asked for the deluge of my personality.

"I'm sorry," I say, sweating self-deprecation and embarrassment. "You probably know all of that."

"Don't apologize, Marlowe."

I look up again. His eyes are such a dark brown, they're almost black. Like *Craterellus cornucopioides*.

"I mean it," he says, and I can see he does. "I don't know much about a lot of this, and I feel a little put in my place by my own laziness. Everything you've said is true."

"Okay," I say, sitting up a little straighter.

His smile spreads, and it's startling. He's so much looser here. He still has the black clothes and the lip ring, but it's like he's cracked a window and I'm getting a glimpse of the rest of him.

I blush, feeling as exposed as if I'd forgotten to put on my skin suit this morning. "We'll use the updated pictures, and I'll post two times a week on these accounts. It'll be slightly different content, as it looks like the target market varies a bit across each platform."

He opens his notes app, and his fingers fly across the screen.

My confidence grows, and I keep going. *Why shouldn't he take me seriously?* "How often do you practice?"

"About three times a week."

I choke a little, my coffee going down the wrong pipe. "Oh! You're *serious* serious?"

He puts down his phone, and his mouth quirks a little. "I guess so. We love it, we're all best friends, so yeah, we like to practice."

I make my last bullet point under his name:

ATTEND FOUR BAND PRACTICES FOR CONTENT AND UPDATES

He sits back, and the expanse of this project stretches out in front of us.

"This is a lot of work, for both of us," he says, fidgeting with the silver rings on his left hand. "Are you sure you're up for it? I can just show you where the poetry section is, and you can copy a stanza or two and he'll never know."

"And then what?" I ask. "He leaves me again in two months because I'm still missing what everyone else just instinctively gets?"

"I don't think you miss much, Marlowe Amelia Meadows."

"Then prove me wrong. Are these terms acceptable? Do you feel like this is an even trade?" I slide the notebook closer to him, more forceful than I intend.

He holds my gaze for another moment and then nods. He grabs the pen and signs *Ashton Napoleon Hayes* at the bottom.

I take the pen and do the same, and he takes a picture with his phone. Relief bursts through me like fireworks, until it fizzles out just as fast. "We still have to fit in *Wuthering Heights* somewhere."

"Buck up, Marlowe. Based on this, it looks like we have plenty of time together to figure it out."

"I do have a futon; you could probably just move in." My face immediately catches fire, my filter gone with the wind. "I mean . . . you know what I mean."

"We'll call that plan B," he says, holding his hand out. "Give me your phone."

I hand it over, heat crawling up my neck as he programs in his number. It's practically a business arrangement, but not many guys have ever asked for my number. He opens a chat and sends himself a mushroom emoji, and his phone makes a little chirp.

"Now that that's settled." He stands up, and I'm craning my neck again. "Come on, I'll give you a tour."

I try to keep track of the organization, but there are so many subsections of subgenres. He moves me around tables toward the far wall. "You know we only carry romance, and there's just one rule: there must be a happy ending."

"Why must there be a happy ending?"

"Because shit out there is dark enough. Why *can't* there always be a happy ending?"

"Says the goth boy." I laugh. I pick a book up from a table

with a sign that reads MONSTER ROMANCE. "Is this man an octo-pus?"

He snatches the book out of my hand and points me toward the back. "We're going to ease you into this."

I follow him to the shelves where YOUNG ADULT is spelled out in pink neon lights. "We've got contemporary, historical, fantasy, sci-fi, and a trope for just about everyone." He turns to me. "I want you to pick out something that speaks to you. You reached for *Lady Jessica* for a reason. Let's see if we can re-create that."

I flush. "I have a confession to make. I only read *Lady Jessica* because I couldn't sleep and was a little raw at having just been told I sucked at love. I was hoping to learn something."

"Okay. Did you?"

My hands slide across glossy covers in all shades of the rain-bow. "I think so? She made me laugh, and she was so fearless about what she wanted. She made me wish I could grow up to be her—all bold speeches and refusing to compromise on what she wants."

"I guess you never forget your first."

"And what was yours?"

I swear he pinks up a little. "I was fourteen and staying with my grandmother for two weeks over the summer."

"The same one who possessed me earlier?"

"The very same," he says. "I was beyond bored. I didn't know any of the neighborhood kids and was too shy to really put myself out there. My Switch had died a terrible death when I dropped it in the bathtub, and my grandmother had very reasonably told me she was not going to be replacing it. Long story short, I was starved for stimuli, and she had a library of romance novels."

I pause over a book with a silver crown on the cover and pull it out.

"I found one with a pirate on the cover and decided *what the hell*. It was great. High stakes, sword fights, a beautiful woman he convinced to love him back. What's not to like?"

I put the crown fantasy back. "Was your grandmother upset that you were reading them?"

"No, she handed me the next one in the series." He grins, and that lone dimple feels shockingly indulgent among the black and spiky jewelry. "Love, human nature, grief, jealousy, all the sticky things that every one of us feel every day, they're universal. Now sprinkle that in among normal life, vampires, spaceships, even Regency England, *and* promise me the ending is going to be satisfying? Why are little old ladies the only ones allowed to enjoy that?"

My face burns, like I've been allowed to witness something personal. I like seeing him *like* things.

He nods at the wall. "See if any of these speak to you. I'm going to check on Sloane."

"Maybe an octopus man?" I ask, hoping to tug another laugh out of him.

He narrows his eyes, walking backward. "Try a second-chance romance. You're the one hoping to backslide. We'll see if the masters can show you something about what that looks like."

My insides feel like they're being pressure-cooked, and the sheer number of options are going to crush me. There are too many choices. There's too much to get through. I pass over one with a girl whose magical powers could either save the world or damn it. Then one that has a girl who captains her own ship on the high seas with a cast of mythical creatures. Next, there are two boys competing for the chance to be the world's next big pop star, but they find each other instead. I pull out one at random, pausing over the football uniform on the front cover.

First Down to First Love. The girl on the cover is smiling at this boy like he has the secrets to the universe. I skim the back: its protagonist swears she'll never date another football player after having her heart broken by one in the past. Can Chase Sawyer change her mind, or will he remain on the bench forever?

Ash appears at my elbow, and I show him. "This one might be helpful."

He's doing that thing again, where silence hangs between us because he refuses to say what he's thinking.

"Well, does it count or not?" I ask, needling him.

"It counts." His eyebrows bunch together and say otherwise.

"Ash, introduce me to my new favorite customer!" The person I'm assuming must be Ash's coworker walks up beside him. Their lilac hair is cut into a jagged pixie atop delicate bone structure with the finest dusting of freckles. Their forest-green blazer sports a bright orange pin announcing THEY/THEM, and by the time I get to the patent-leather oxfords, I'm smiling in delight.

"Hi," I say, my smile stretching a little wider. "I'm Marlowe."

"Sloane," they say, holding out a hand. "I hope we'll be seeing more of you around here."

Nine

"If they're awful, I'm not going to be able to hide my laughter."

"Odette!" I pause, my finger hovering over the doorbell. "You can't laugh!"

"Shame is an excellent motivator."

"I'm serious," I hiss, panic swelling like a tidal wave.

"Oh relax," she says. "I'm joking. I'll probably behave."

I'm considering blowing off this band practice completely when she snakes around me and presses the bell.

"Come on, it'll be fun! Plus, think how psyched your sexy and scary goth love professor will be with an audience of two instead of zero."

"He's not *my* goth anything," I say, wincing at the immaculate lawn of the sprawling brick house Ash gave me the address to. "And I don't know that I would put 'sexy' and 'scary' in the same sentence."

"Why? He's both. Exhibit A—" She holds one hand out. "You literally look at him and can see he's sexy." She holds out her other hand. "Exhibit B, he can be scary. Apparently, Devon

Black asked him to borrow a pen once, and Mary Beth swears he growled at him."

"I refuse to believe he growled over a pen."

"Oh, I believe it." Odette grins as Ash swings the door open.

"Odette," he says, both a declaration and a question.

I ignore it and smile up at him. He fills the doorway, as if someone just happened to forget a Dracula cosplayer in an elegant beige foyer.

I don't realize I say that last part out loud until Odette giggles.

"Gotta say, I kinda thought you at least lived in a creepy Victorian," she says, leaning around him. "Or a crumbling fortress?"

He sighs and swings the door wider.

"Marlowe! The throw pillows match the curtains!" she yells back as she walks right past him.

I want to apologize, but he looks so put out that I can't help being delighted. "I couldn't resist the opportunity for you to make another fan."

"Are there *three* robot vacuums?" Odette's voice is getting farther and farther away.

He reaches out and pulls me into the house by my bag strap. "Let's get on with it before she starts opening cabinets."

I leave my shoes by the pile near the front door and follow him across plush carpet to the stairs. Odette catches up, head swiveling at delicate sconces, pastoral landscapes with gilded frames, and a banister that curls down into a finished basement.

Overstuffed chairs and end tables have been shoved in the corner to make room for a drum kit, keyboard, and so many amps he could open his own pawnshop.

Ash pauses in the middle of the room, and I get my first look at the rest of Never Mind the Monsters.

"Everyone, this is Marlowe, like I told you about." He clears his throat, and I wonder exactly what he's said about me. "And her friend Odette."

I recognize two of them from school but am blanking on the others.

I smile and wave, my hand jerking up as if possessed. "Hi! I'm excited to hear you play today."

"I'm here, but not sure if excitement is on the table," Odette adds.

The girl I don't recognize chuckles a little and adjusts the black guitar against her body. Its jagged edges cut like a lightning bolt, clashing with the warm, comfortable room.

Ash follows my gaze. "This is Hazel, lead guitarist. She goes to Saint Mary's."

I haven't met many people from the Catholic school across town, as most of the people I know end up in a Southern Baptist or Methodist pew on Sundays, but her buzzed blond hair doesn't scream Catholic schoolgirl to me. It pops against her dark brown skin, and nothing about her leather pants or guitar-wielding-zombie T-shirt gives any indication she spends most of her time in knee socks. I smile, willfully holding back from waving a second time.

"Hey there, I'm Odette," my friend says, a little too loud. Hazel gives her a small nod of acknowledgment.

Ash continues down the row. "That's Spencer on drums, you probably know him from school." I do; he also played drums in band, and was football-adjacent enough to show up at a lot of the same parties I used to frequent. Something happened at the end of last year, and I heard he never showed up to another band practice. He looks at me, eyes wary, and doesn't say a word.

"Mateo's on bass, and also in our grade."

I shake off the chill of Spencer's gaze, and slowly thaw under the warm grin of River Haven's biggest flirt. I know Mateo Acosta better than Ash might realize. He dated Tiffany last year, and she's never had a kiss she didn't want to tell the entire lunch table about. I blush, and I swear Mateo can read my mind because his grin widens. "Long time no see, Marlowe."

"Last but not least we have Julian." I look up when Ash's voice softens. Julian stands quietly behind the keyboards in a starched polo and jeans that someone has definitely ironed. His baby face is hidden behind glasses that are a touch too big for him, but that he'll grow into in a few years. I put him at fourteen or maybe fifteen. A touch of pink blossoms under our attention on his light brown cheeks. "Julian's dad works with mine, and he's home-schooled. We're calling this a music extracurricular, right?"

"Something like that," Julian says, polishing a key with his finger.

"And then there's you," I say.

"Then there's me."

"And you're the singer?" I confirm.

"And guitar, although we could unplug me and Hazel's good enough to take the place of two people."

"I am," she says, looking up from her amp.

Odette makes a small sigh beside me.

"Okay," I say, feeling like I've caused enough of a disruption. "We don't want to interrupt. Please pretend we aren't here."

"And you're supposed to be what? An influencer or some-thing?" Hazel asks, a frown on her painted-black lips.

"Not really," I say, but the question is fair. "I'm just trying to help Ash with revamping the band's online presence."

"And what makes you think you can do better?" Her tone leaves no time for nonsense, and I deeply appreciate a person that says what they think.

"Well, since you currently have a neon-green website that nobody can read, and pictures so outdated I didn't even recognize you as the guitarist, I don't think I have to try very hard."

"The bar is in hell," Odette confirms.

"Hey, what's wrong with the website? I still owe twelve trips to the mall for that." Mateo frowns.

"You were overcharged, but I respect the hustler," I say, settling into one of the chairs shoved in the corner. Odette perches on the arm, and Hazel goes back to untangling pedals and cords.

Ash sheds his oversized black button-down and slides a white electric guitar across his body. He walks over to me and carefully drapes the shirt across the back of my chair, his black tank top riding up against the instrument. Deep riffs fill the air as Mateo warms up, and Ash leans in.

"Marlowe, I just wanted you to know that it can get a little loud in here."

I blink, waiting for the point. "This is a band practice, Ash. I'm aware."

He pauses and fidgets with the guitar strap. "I just wanted to make sure that was okay."

I've gotten lost in the conversation, and he's just hovering over me like I'm supposed to understand what he's saying.

Odette shifts next to me, before breaking the tension with a sharp "Not all autistic people have issues with loud noises."

I flush, and the meaning becomes clear. There it is again, rearing up like a scarlet *A* that brands me as different. I appreciate him trying to be thoughtful, but I would also like everyone to mind their own business and just let me navigate things by myself. Unless it's something surprising and overwhelming, in which case I would like a heads-up.

But also not, if that makes sense?

I want it both ways, *and* for them to read my mind so we can avoid these conversations. Or maybe a different brain. Or maybe for everybody else to have a brain like mine.

Josh would frequently ignore whatever he felt was not relevant to his plans or interests, and in a way, it was almost freeing that he never acknowledged my differences. Until he finally did, and decided he felt I was a little too broken to keep.

Ash is still hovering, so I nod once. "It's fine."

He looks like he wants to say something else, but he turns and walks back to the band without another word. They all move into position, and I pull up the camera on my phone. Hazel tests a few notes, and they fill the room while feedback buzzes through the amp. I try to frame some shots, but the composition feels off. The group looks the part—there are enough pieces of electronics here that speak to some level of competency—but the shots also include pictures on the wall of Ash and his parents at Disney World. They include the tub of summer clothes in the corner waiting for someone to store them in the attic. They still capture Ash's mother's dedication to beige linen drapes.

None of this screams rock band or big time. It all feels a little small.

But him . . . there's nothing small about Ashton Hayes. Not his giant-sized combat boots, or his towering body blocking out the light when he's looking down at me and trying to pretend like he's annoyed.

And not his voice. He leans forward toward a microphone that feels frankly unnecessary in this space, and every syllable winds around me.

Spencer's drums and the dissonant sounds Hazel is coaxing out of her guitar are almost too much, and the build to the bridge crashes all around me.

Odette moves a little closer, and her raised eyebrow tells me what I feel but wasn't sure wasn't biased by this deal we've worked out.

They're good. Like, *really* good.

Julian's fingers fly across the keyboard, and I doubt he's even aware any of us are still here. I lift my phone to try again. Hazel's bulky rings slide down the strings of her guitar. Ash's eyes close, and he leans into the mic, the strain of every note written across his neck and white knuckles. Spencer's arms rise higher and higher, as the beat climbs to something just out of reach. The sounds swell around me like a wave one last time, and the closing notes fade until all I have are ringing ears and a racing heart.

Ash's head snaps up, and there are too many threads of too many thoughts to give him anything coherent. I remember to smile, and when that doesn't feel like enough, I mouth the words *I like that one*. He ducks his head, the small twitch in the corner of his mouth almost lost in the movement, before he straightens and murmurs "again" into the mic.

They finish, and then they play it again. Then again. It gets a little smoother with each pass, and my foot starts tapping along with Spencer's beats. By the fifth attempt, I'm humming along with the chorus, and I can feel Odette swaying next to me.

I scroll through my pictures, but they don't capture that *thing* they have when they play. That spark. These pictures are all ordinary, and *they* are not ordinary. They're not perfect, and my nerves jangle with each wrong note, and the drum solo that's maybe a little too long, but the melody has found a way under my skin.

I can already tell I'm not going to get anything I need out of this practice. This dim, tastefully decorated basement is not going to impress anyone. I try again and again, each angle falling short.

"Did you get some good pictures, Marlowe? My right is my hot side," Mateo says on the next break.

"Well," I start, trying to find the best way to frame this information. Odette wrinkles her nose as I pull up my last attempt. "I'm not sure these are the pictures we're looking for."

"Are they blurry? Do you need a phone upgrade?" Spencer asks, his tone sharp.

"It's the space," I say, abandoning tact. "It's clear you're in a finished basement in the suburbs. It doesn't match anything about your band."

"It's not like we have anywhere else to practice," Ash says.

"Who says you have to be practicing to get your pictures taken?" Odette asks.

Hazel focuses all of her attention on Odette. "Do you have a better suggestion?"

"The world's your oyster," Odette says, her tone flirty enough for me to take a second look at Hazel. "Maybe the school after hours? Abandoned railroad tracks? The middle of an intersection?"

"A graveyard."

Every head turns to look at Julian. He shrugs. "It works with the imagery of this song."

Hazel smiles. "That's sick, I love it."

"Okay, but I'm not dragging the entire kit out there," Spencer says.

Ash smiles at me, and it's not even my idea, but I feel like I've somehow earned that dimple. "Oh, this is going to be good. Everyone free this weekend?"

"We're going to have to think of something to tell my mom," Julian says, sighing.

We agree on Saturday after next, and Odette smiles slyly between me and Ash as he walks us out. She holds her phone up to her ear. "Yes? Hello?"

"Your phone didn't ring." I squint at her as her expression melts into innocence.

"Yes, that's correct. Sexy *and* scary." She holds her hand over the microphone. "So sorry, I'm afraid it's urgent. I'll see you in the car, Marlowe."

She skips down the steps and I pray for Georgia to suddenly develop more fault lines and swallow me into the ground. "I'm going to smother her in her sleep one day."

"I assume she grows on you." The corner of his mouth quirks up, and blossoms into a smile (*with teeth!*) as my face burns like magma.

I slip on my shoes and hover on his stoop, not quite ready to go. "Will you have to come up with something to tell your mom too?"

The smile slips a little. "I'm good."

"Your parents already know graveyards are your natural habitat?" I desperately try to find the ease that just evaporated in front of me.

"Nah, they'd have to be here to notice." He leans against the doorjamb, his posture at odds with his words.

"Are they on a trip?"

"Usually." His eyebrows bunch together before relaxing into a bland expression that feels forced. Practiced. "They own a food-packaging company. Lots of traveling to different branches."

I look behind him at the pristine beige foyer. "And you're here all alone?"

He puts his hand on the doorknob, slowly moving the heavy door between us. "Come on, Marlowe," he says, his tone slightly mocking. "Dracula's always alone."

Ten

"Come on, Ash," I say. "It's time to pay up."

He wipes the café counter for a fifth time. "Aren't we supposed to be working on *Wuthering Heights*?"

"I'm only ten chapters in," I say. "I need to get at least one letter into Josh's hands. It's been too long already. What if he thinks I've forgotten him?"

"I thought you were going to send it anonymously?"

"I am, but he'll probably be suspicious, right?"

I *hope* he wants it to be me. Ash says nothing, and I recognize that as the gift it is.

"No more stalling, get over here and teach me your romantic secrets." I nudge the sunshine-yellow chair beside me with my foot.

He throws down the rag and eases into the chair as slowly and reluctantly as my grandpa joining my grandma's bridge group for tea.

He frowns at me across Formica. "Well?"

I flip open to a sparkly white page and look expectantly up at him.

He casually takes a sip of his Americano.

I fold first, patience being a virtue I do not possess. "*Ash!*"

"What?" His mouth quirks. "Marlowe, I already told you I wasn't going to feed you words to send him."

"How am I supposed to do this, then? I haven't had enough homework, and our first romance field trip isn't until this weekend."

He settles in, and I can feel the full force of Ash Hayes's attention.

"What do you want to say to him? What do you want, Marlowe?"

What do you want, Marlowe?

"I just want things to go back to normal." I can't keep the jagged edge out of my voice. As soon as the words come out of my mouth, I want to stuff them back inside. They sound pitiful. The countless YA heroines stacked on the back wall are having adventures and taking chances, and I just want my normal routine back?

And him, my brain yells, as I stumble over the sharp edges of our memories together. Every soft touch and tender word now stained with the fear that he was pressing his lips to mine and simultaneously thinking I was less than I should be.

My phone vibrates on the table, because someone upstairs has a terrible sense of humor. DAD pops up on the caller ID and I silence it, my heartbeat flooding my ears.

"We can take a break if you need to get that." Ash leans back, dark eyes missing nothing.

I shake my head. "He'll call back. We try to do a twice-a-week check-in. It's nothing that can't wait."

"That's nice that he calls so much." He slides a finger around the rim of his mug, his nails now a hunter green.

"Do your parents call often while they're away?" I trip over the words, and half expect him not to answer. But I want to ask just in case he needs someone to.

He keeps his eyes on his coffee. "Not really, no. I am neither a project that is going to make money, nor a problem that requires a lot of active troubleshooting."

My mouth snaps shut, and I use up every ounce of willpower to hold myself back from leaning over and hugging him. Or wrapping a blanket around him and tucking Darcy into his arms.

He finally pulls his attention away from his cup, and his eyes narrow. "Don't pity me, Meadows."

The words are out before I can screen them. "It's them that I pity."

He just *looks* at me, and I feel stripped bare. Like he's seeing more and more pieces, and I have no control over what final picture he's getting. I shove more words in front of him, to snap the tension.

"Dad's like me." I gesture wildly at the entirety of me. "Same brain. Same prickly grasp on emotions. Same spectrum."

"Same obsession with fungi?" He smiles, and it feels like a Friday.

"Mushrooms," I correct. "Fungi is the kingdom, and nobody loves mold." The blank page in front of me feels insurmountable. "And no, he has other interests."

"Like what?"

"Medicine." I shrug. "And me."

"Sounds like a pretty good dad." He brings the mug to his lips, and I listen for the soft clink of metal against porcelain.

"The best. He made sure I had an easier time of things than

he did growing up. Therapists, meds, and always looking up different strategies to help me navigate a world that was not made for me." I smile, Josh momentarily pushed to the back burner. "I went through this rough patch when I was seven. I was really struggling to put words to moments and feelings and was having these pretty bad meltdowns because I couldn't figure out how to categorize everything inside of me." Ash leans forward, and I feel the slide of his combat boot against my sneaker. I pretend I don't notice. "My dad's solution was these stacks of word-of-the-day calendars. I was *unbearable* for a long time after and sounded like this pretentious little know-it-all asking Momma to be less loquacious in the morning or asking her to expound on that night's dinner menu."

He laughs, and I blush at the ease of it. "Why is that not surprising at all?"

"It worked, though," I say, sliding him another piece of the puzzle. "I was finally in the club, I could put a name to all the feelings that were building up inside me. I could share them, commiserate, celebrate, and my grandpa stopped shaking his head and repeating 'Bless her heart' when I spent the afternoon with him."

"So, give me a word, Marlowe." His mouth curls around the letters of my name, and I blink at the flutter in my gut. "Since you're such a connoisseur."

"Fine," I say, pretending to think. "'Liberosis.' Happy?"

"Rarely. What does it mean?"

"The desire to care less about things." I tuck my hands under my thighs.

"Good, give me another one."

"'Collywobbles.'" It's ridiculous, and so is this game, but I'm most ridiculous of all, because I chose that word just to watch him pretend he's not amused.

I'm not disappointed.

"Let me guess, the trajectory of a hummingbird in flight." His hair is as messy and disordered as the inside of my skull.

"So close," I say, hiding my smile too. "It's butterflies in the stomach."

"That was my second guess." He takes a sip of coffee. "We have a word riddled with longing, and a word that describes how you feel when you're too close to someone you want. Sounds like you have all the tools you need." He nods down at my notebook, still open to a blank page.

I pick up my pen. "Excellent idea, Ash. I'll send him some definitions and wait for him to come running."

"Isn't that what you feel for him? You wish for liberosis because he gives you the collywobbles? Just put that in more words."

"I am eighty-five percent certain you did not use those in a sentence correctly."

"I'm feeling pretty good about those odds."

And was that even what I wanted to say? I missed Josh with a bone-deep ache, but so many bruised feelings have blossomed under his words that it's hard to think.

Sometimes I wonder if you're even really that interested. That one's a punch to the gut.

I think it's time to leave. There's a slap to the face.

It's all right, Marlowe, not everyone's built for it. That one? That's a mortal blow.

I droop, my forehead falling forward onto the page with a dull thunk. "Never mind, let's call it off. I'll just be alone forever."

The silence stretches long enough that I suspect he's left and gone back to scrubbing the counter.

"Do you want to go sit with Darcy and be in your feelings for a while?"

I huff some hair out of my face. "I just thought you'd be more helpful than this."

He rubs his eyes. "Marlowe, I'm not a magician. I can't just produce the perfect letter out of thin air. I still don't know what you even want to say to this jackass."

What do you want, Marlowe?

"Don't call him that," I say, barely registering the insult anymore. Looking too hard at the breakup was like probing a wound. I don't want to peel back those words and stare at the damage underneath, or unearth all of these moments that make me feel like I'm drowning.

"I want him to know how I feel about him in a way I clearly wasn't able to convey to him before," I say, finally. That's the right angle. Happy, loving, and moving forward to better and brighter times.

Ash looks like something he ate has disagreed with him, but he pries his lips open enough to mumble, "Okay, so just tell him exactly what he wants to hear."

I flinch, reeling from the vacillation between teasing smiles and sharp sentences. I don't always clock tone correctly, and I spend the majority of the time giving people the benefit of the doubt. But this? He's being rude and unhelpful. I've spent hours over the past few days looking at rock band photo shoots and poses, and I've already started overhauling his current website. If he isn't all in, neither am I.

I close my notebook and shove my emotional-support pens in my bag.

"Are you going somewhere?"

I ignore him and slip my cardigan back on, pushing my chair back.

He grabs my wrist, and I know my face is as stormy as his. "I'm sorry."

I pause. "For what?" Not to drag it out, but because I want to hear why.

He frowns but doesn't hesitate. "Because I don't like him, and I'm letting that affect our deal, which is unfair to you."

I put my bag back down. Only one question matters. "Can you do this?"

"Yes," he says, meeting my eyes. I believe him.

"I don't know what to ask you, and I'm sorry if this is annoying, but I don't know how to write something like this and I need a little more guidance."

He waves my words aside. "Don't apologize." His long fingers, decorated with calluses and small scars, flip my notebook open again. He pauses and I lean forward on the off chance his magic is contagious. He looks up with a small smile. A truce.

"You have four letters. Four letters, and you want him to know that you love him. That you know him. *All* the parts of him."

His pen dips down and he scrawls four words on the page before sliding it back to me.

Mind.

Heart.

Body.

Soul.

"That's it?" I ask, glancing down.

"It's a starting place," he says, rolling his eyes. "Each letter has a theme. Today's letter—" He stabs "mind" with a finger. "—is going to be what you love about his personality, his humor, his intelligence—what little he has."

He's trying, so I let it slide. "And 'heart'?"

"Kindness. Acts of service. The way he cares about the things that are important to him. The way he loves."

I flush, eyes skimming over "body." "I think I'm able to guess the next one. What about 'soul'?"

He shrugs, the movement jerky. "The whole picture. Who he is to his core, and the reason you're making deals with strangers to get him back."

"I like it," I say, looking up.

"Your surprise is immensely flattering."

I swat at his arm, jostling the Americano. "I mean it. This is helpful. Helpful, but familiar." I narrow my eyes, my brain snagging on the pattern. I pull my beat-up copy of *Wuthering Heights* out of my bag, and flip until I get to the chapter I read last night. "Wait, here it is!"

I slide it across the table, my finger finding the place for him. He lifts it up, and his voice finds the right cadence immediately. "'. . . *you love Edgar, and Edgar loves you. All seems smooth and easy: where is the obstacle?' 'Here! and here!' replied Catherine, striking one hand on her forehead, and the other on her breast: 'in whichever place the soul lives. In my soul and in my heart, I'm convinced I'm wrong!'*"

He looks up with my sigh. "You okay over there?"

"She knows Edgar is the safer choice, but her mind, heart, body, and soul tell her that she belongs with Heathcliff. It's just . . ." I trail off, my face flushing. "It's just romantic, the idea of this bond being more powerful than anything else."

I smile, waiting for him to agree with me, as we're surrounded by books built on the premise of love conquering all. Instead, he just closes the book and slides it back.

My smile wavers, but I busy myself with the soft edges of Momma's paperback copy. "Maybe we can do that as the central theme of our paper? All-consuming love, and the destruction that happened because two soul mates weren't allowed to be together."

A muscle in his jaw twitches. "How far along are you, again?"

I shrug. "Not much further than the part you just read."

He nods, pulling out his laptop. "We'll keep brainstorming."

I refuse to be disappointed that he didn't jump on my brilliant assessment of *Wuthering Heights,* and I focus every ounce of energy on not being intimidated by the large expanse of blank page.

Mind.

Josh's mind.

Josh's tidy, comfortingly predictable (except when he's dumping me) mind.

"It's hard to concentrate while you're thinking that loud." He pulls his hair out of its messy knot, and the scent of warm sage wraps around me.

I cough, eyes pinned to paper. "Nothing I'm thinking could possibly be louder than Darcy's snoring."

"He has sleep apnea, Marlowe. Have a little compassion."

I ignore him, chewing on the end of my pen.

"Just tell him his brilliant football strategies keep you up until midnight every night," he says dryly. I roll my eyes, but the easiness between us settles and I realize that at some point in this conversation, something has *shifted*.

I shake my head until there is room for thoughts that don't include boys who smell like herb gardens or what being friends with Ash would look like. "At midnight I'm solidly in bed, weighted eye mask in place, white-noise machine purring. I'm not thinking about Josh's *anything*."

But maybe that's what I'm supposed to be doing. Is this what dreamy girls who are good at love do? I look up at Ash, who's typing out a barrage of words like he's mad at them. I bet he would know. I bet he can't even go to sleep until midnight chimes on some creepy haunted clock and he does at least one ritual.

I go back to my letter, and finally I start, adding flourishes and curls to each letter in an attempt to disguise my own blocky hand.

> *I would like to know what was going through your mind when you first decided I wasn't enough—*

Nope, still the wrong tone. I cross it out.

> *Do you still even think of me? Seems like a lot of moments to throw away—*

I flip to another page and start again.

> *I love the way you look at the world. The way you approach a challenge. You don't do it by halves or sidle up to it with uncertainty. You attack it head-on. Unflinchingly.*

I wince and try not to think about the breakup. But this is better.

> *There's a beauty in that, and I can't help admiring it. A structure to the way your mind pulls apart obstacles that inspires me to be less of a pushover. That makes me want to be more honest about the things that I want.*
>
> *Your willpower, your strength, your jokes that coax a smile out of me when I'm at my lowest—it's no wonder I'm yours.*
>
> *Your secret admirer.*

It's not going to win a Pulitzer, but it's honest. It's an honest-to-God love letter.

I slide it across the table, my eyes gobbling up each microexpression as they flit across Ash's face.

"It's good," he says finally, the words raspy. He clears his throat, hands flying over the keyboard again. "You should send it."

I seal the letter, my heart threatening to hammer out of my chest, and check the time. We can make it if we hurry.

I throw my things in my bag. "Come on, let's go."

His eyes narrow, the paper forgotten. "Why? What's going on?"

"We have to deliver the letter."

"Absolutely not." He leans back, his expression shuttered.

"*Ash*." I drag his name out at least five extra syllables. "You're supposed to be helping me." I put my hands on my hips. "Football practice is almost over, I just need to stick it under his wiper blades."

He tries to ignore me, and I gently press the top of his laptop down until he looks at me. "Please? He doesn't know your car like mine."

He sighs, a deep, painful sound, as if I've asked him to carry me over the Alps piggyback-style. "In and out" is all he says, grabbing his bag and heading for the exit.

I swallow down my squeal, but happiness bleeds into the bounce in my step and a smile so wide I worry my face will crack.

This is *it*.

We drive the five minutes over to the football field in silence, but I'm vibrating in my seat. Ash parks a few rows away from Josh's black, oversized truck while I scan for witnesses.

"Keep an eye out," I say. I race between cars and shove the envelope under the wiper blade before I can stop to second-guess myself.

I climb back in the car, breathing like I've run a marathon. "Did anyone see me?"

"It was like watching a Mission: Impossible movie."

He grasps the gear shift, sliding it into reverse.

"Wait!" I still his hand with mine. "Five more minutes? I want to watch him open it."

Ash scowls, but I feel the gear shift move back into park. He's all bark and no bite, just like Biscuit—my neighbor's two-thousand-year-old decaying Maltese.

"Really, Marlowe?"

I shiver. I've never had someone use my name so often. No shortcuts. No hurry. Every vowel and consonant accounted for.

"Five minutes."

It only takes three.

The gates to the field swing open, and varsity and JV players slowly empty into the parking lot. I scan over burgundy-and-gray sweats, until finally he emerges at the end.

I slouch down a little, watching with hungry eyes. Josh slowly ambles through a crowd of back pats and high fives, throwing his bag in the back of his truck. He climbs up in it, and for a moment my stomach clenches as his engine roars to life.

But then he sees it. Pale pink and hanging on to his windshield for dear life.

He gets out, snatching it from its snare, and flips it over.

I lean forward, on the edge of my seat. He rips it open, and I watch his eyes fly over the page.

Then he grins, the smile expanding like a sunrise. Starting with a twitch of his lips, spreading up to his eyes, and not slowing until his entire face is shining.

There he is.

There's the guy I fell for.

He steps forward, eyes roving the parking lot, and I grab Ash's shirt and drag him down until we're practically kissing the emergency brake.

"I have so many regrets right now." His breath is warm against my ear.

"Shhh," I hiss, frozen in place. We can't spoil it now, not when we still have three letters to go.

"He's not Batman," Ash grumbles. "He can't hear me complain in my own car."

I'm not willing to take any chances. I give it a few minutes, the sound of our breathing roaring in my ears, before I release him. "Okay, see if the coast is clear."

"So he can think *I'm* his secret admirer?"

"Ash." I poke him in the ribs.

"*Fine*." He pops up, turning in all directions. "Romeo's gone. He certainly didn't try that hard to crack this mystery, did he?"

I spring up, but nothing can spoil my mood.

That *smile*.

This was the best plan. A brilliant plan. A Nobel Prize–worthy plan.

Ash drops me back at the bookstore, and I'm already preparing myself for when Josh texts me later. Of course, he will at least suspect me.

Should I do coy, but flirty?

Adamantly deny it, but then segue into a meaningful conversation about how much we've missed each other?

I pull open my car door, the options endless.

"Marlowe."

I look up in a daze, and Ash lifts one dark, no-nonsense eyebrow.

"We're still on for this weekend, right?"

"This weekend?" I echo dumbly.

"The Harvest Festival? Our field trip?" He's frowning again, and I shake my head free of cobwebs.

"Yeah, of course. See you then."

I barely register the drive home. I keep checking over and over that my ringer is turned all the way up.

I do a little homework, read some *Wuthering Heights,* and pick up my phone like a compulsion. I finally check his Gabber profile, and his latest photo is him standing next to his truck with a smug smile and a pink envelope. The caption reads: Dear secret admirer, you're the sweetest.

I text a screenshot to Odette and Poppy, swallowing my disappointment. He posted that two hours ago.

Odette responds immediately.

Plan Cyrano-Josh-the-douchebag is a go!

Don't call him that, I text back on autopilot. I shake it off, diving back into my English moors. There's still time.

Finally, around midnight, I accept that it's not happening. He's not reaching out. Even if he suspects it's me, he doesn't actually want to know.

I flop back against pillows as my disappointment drags me under. It's late, I'm sad, and right now would be the weirdest time to use the number Ash programmed in my phone. A small part of me wonders if he'd be amused, though.

That I'm here, staying up until midnight, thinking about love.

Eleven

We're a small town, but what we lack in population and industry, we make up for in sheer unbridled enthusiasm for celebrating every holiday possible. Santa's village in December. The Lovers Festival in February. A huge Easter celebration where the fountain in the town square usually still has green water from St. Patrick's Day. And tonight's the Harvest Festival.

It's exactly what it sounds like. The robust number of local farmers are about to harvest golden fields of corn, and we celebrate with carnival games, a corn maze that will be gone by next week, and whatever else we can set up under an inky October sky.

"Honey, you're going to freeze without your coat. What were you thinking?" Momma fusses over me, rubbing the thin material between her fingers. A cool wind whips through the square, and I deeply regret the very sensible jacket I left at home in favor of this thin cardigan.

I grab a handful of caramel corn from Blue's bag, ignoring the petulant "Hey" that was sure to follow. "I was thinking that this apple cardigan was the cutest possible thing to wear to a harvest festival, and that I don't trust our local meteorologist nearly enough." I stretch my arms out, the plump knitted fruit dancing down my arms.

Momma shakes her head, her hand tucked in the crook of Stu's arm. "Where did my sensible girl go? I never thought you'd be the one to suffer for fashion." We slowly walk down Main Street, the smell of pumpkin spice and funnel cake being the real indicator that fall has come to River Haven.

I throw a kernel of caramel corn in the air, catching it neatly in my mouth. "Well, I never intended to suffer, but that's rich coming from the woman who owns no shoes flatter than a kitten heel."

She picks a speck of lint off her wool trench coat. "That's completely different. I'll have you know that I have unnaturally high arches. Heels are *comfortable*."

"It's true," Stu says, his face grim. "I make her wear socks to bed." He leans closer to Blue. "Very unnatural."

Momma swats his arm, but Blue giggles—the sound making my chest ache a little. It wasn't too long ago she'd refuse to let go of my hand on a night like this. She hated the scarecrow decorations and would insist I point out every constellation I could remember and buy her no fewer than three candy apples.

I smile at her, inching closer, and she reluctantly holds out the caramel corn bag.

"Where's the sweater from, Lo? I don't recognize it." She reaches out, petting one of the apples.

"Uh-uh," I say, caramel coating my tongue. "Hands off."

"Sisters are supposed to share."

"I've shared plenty. I shared my family with you, my bathroom, and even my nose."

"I have my own nose," she says, eyes rolling.

I shrug. "It was mine first." The pointed little tip is practically a copy/paste from my face to hers.

"*Fine,* I'll let you borrow my new dress if I can wear that Monday."

I grimace, because she couldn't pay me to leave the house in cream-colored lace. She's trying, though. "I'll think about it."

She falls in step with Momma, curling into her side, eyelashes fluttering. "Momma, can I go hang out with Whitney? I know the squad is here somewhere."

"Go on." Momma smiles, her lipstick a perfect match for her scarf. "Remember curfew, and call us if you need a ride home."

She's off in a blur of blond curls, jogging deeper into the maze of festival stalls. Her puffy pink jacket marks her progress through the crowd.

We get closer to the town square, and I spot Poppy and Odette hovering near the corner by the fountain. Odette is drowning in layers, and a small robot rests at Poppy's feet.

"Happy reaping day!" Odette yells over the crowd. Heads swing in her direction.

"You know people get uncomfortable when you call it that!" I yell back.

"I suppose you're going to abandon us too?" Stu slings an arm across my shoulders, rubbing my arm vigorously.

"I'm not going to freeze to death," I say, smiling at his poor attempts to hide his concern. "And I promised Odette and Poppy we'd hang out tonight."

The smallest white lie.

I don't know what to call Ash. There is no title that would make sense, or at least that my parents would accept.

My professor in romance?

My life coach? I grin at the thought of calling him that to his face. Just to see his eyebrows bunch up in annoyance.

My *friend*? "Friend" is too loaded a word, and it would come with too many follow-up questions.

"Same rules," Momma says, brushing a kiss on my cheek. Her perfume wraps around me like a hug.

"Take these." Stu hands me oversized mittens. They're big, but they'll do the job. I put them on, because he's watching, and they hang off my hands like boxing gloves.

"Thanks, guys," I say, my voice soft. Ash's beautiful, empty living room pops into my brain without warning. "I'll see you at home."

I watch them melt into the crowd before crossing the square.

"What's the plan with Pumpkin?" I nod at the robot, shoving the mittens into my bag.

"It's her first night out, and she wants to see *everything*." Poppy's Day-Glo orange coat matches the racing stripes on Pumpkin's back.

"You fixed the steering issue?"

"Of course," she says, snorting.

"What's the plan with the Prince of Darkness?" Odette asks, sinking deeper into burgundy wool. The collar of her coat is popped up to her ears, and an oversized plaid scarf winds around half her face.

"I don't know about prince," I say, shrugging. "Maybe a duke at best."

"Elected Official of Darkness?" Poppy stuffs a slender screwdriver into her sock.

I snap my fingers. "That's the one."

She nods. "Royalty does imply a certain level of responsibility."

Odette sighs deeply. "Can you two focus?" She narrows her

eyes at me. "Is the plan to hide in a bushel of apples and spy on Josh?"

I straighten my sweater. I know he's going to be here. It'd be easier to count who *wouldn't* be here. What I don't know is whether he's here with the group, or with someone he's going to be winning some obscenely large stuffed animal for. My stomach revolts at the idea of him smiling softly at someone else under all the twinkle lights, or cuddling up to them on the hayride. He could be on a real date, and I'm probably going to freeze to death wearing an apple sweater because I thought my coat was puffy and yellow and made me look like one of those giant bumblebees that knock into things in confusion.

"Tonight isn't about Josh. I mean, it *is,* kind of, but it's also about me. *For* me."

Odette smiles slowly. "For you, huh? So, like, a date?"

"This is definitely not a date." I shake my head, stress hormones flooding my system and setting my face on fire.

"Maybe it should be." Her voice is so casual it takes me a second to register the words.

"What?"

"Me and Pops have been talking," she says. Poppy grimaces, guilt bleeding into every feature. "Ash seems pretty cool, and maybe it wouldn't be the worst thing if you kept yourself open to some possibilities?"

I snap my mouth shut. "I—I'm really surprised to hear you say that. You all were the ones who wanted me to make a plan to win back Josh." I wrap my arms around myself, chill seeping deeper into my skin.

"I understand he was your first real relationship, but things change."

"Not everything." I shake my head firmly. "I am knee-deep

in a very complicated romantic caper to win him back. I've committed to this course. I *committed* to Josh."

What do you want, Marlowe?

Odette bites her lip, her gaze unnerving. "I'm just saying you seem to be enjoying yourself . . ." She trails off, waiting for me to pick up the threads.

"It's a professional arrangement." I look at them both, so we're perfectly clear. "I asked for romance field trips, and this is our first attempt."

"What are you all whispering about?" Ash asks, arriving at my elbow without the slightest warning.

I crane my neck up as his lanky frame blocks out the harvest moon. His black peacoat flaps open and his mouth hitches into a crooked smile.

"What?" I ask. My blood is slowed to molasses by the cold and unable to perform the necessary connections. *How much did he hear?*

"An elaborate plan to make the cafeteria bring back Taco Tuesday?" One eyebrow floats upward. "Some mild world domination?"

"Ash!" Odette says loudly, bringing me back to Earth. "I have no idea what you're going to teach her at this festival that we've been going to our entire lives, but can't wait to see what you pull out of your ass."

"A pleasure, as always, Odette," he says. He frowns at Poppy's compact robot. "What's happening here?"

"Apologies," Poppy says. "Ash, please meet Pumpkin. Pumpkin, this is Ash, a boy who likes romance books."

Ash's stage whisper rises above the crowd. "Is that robot sentient?"

"Oh, for God's sake," Odette says, "of course not."

"Don't listen to them, Pumpkin," Poppy croons, bending down to pet the plastic body.

"Is Pumpkin here for the hayride?" Ash asks, the corner of his mouth twitching.

Poppy rises, the topic finally one of interest. "Pumpkin navigates mazes, and we're going to set her loose in the corn maze to see what happens."

"Besides terrifying the villagers," Odette says, delighted by this plan.

"What's terrifying about a maze-navigating robot?" Poppy asks, straightening her belt bag.

I smile at her offended tone. "Not a single thing, Pops. You and Pumpkin are going to have a blast."

"Are y'all sure you don't want to join us?" Odette asks, her eyes on me.

My head snaps toward her. I don't think she'd ever invited Josh anywhere. I had my best friends, and my boyfriend and his friends, and those groups had never wanted to intersect.

I cut my eyes to Ash, and he shrugs, leaving it up to me.

It's *still* not a date, but that doesn't mean that I don't want him to myself. He's supposed to be teaching me things tonight. This is an educational outing.

"Well," I say, filling the silence. "As much as I want to see Pumpkin in action, we have an important syllabus to work through. I'm supposed to be learning how to create some real-time rom-com moments."

"If there is really a syllabus, I would like to see it," Poppy says, her interest piqued again.

Ash coughs, and I think it might have been a laugh, but I haven't heard the entire spectrum of his amusement enough to be sure. "I'll work on that," he says, more to me than anyone else.

I pull the disco cats out of my bag, because this is sure to be gold and I'm going to need to save every single idea for Josh.

"Put that away, you're not going to forget anything."

"I would not trust anybody who ran an experiment and didn't take field notes," I say, but reluctantly follow his lead.

He shakes his head as we walk into the crowd.

"Bye, play nice!" I yell back to my friends as we walk toward the booths.

He slows, and I can tell he's trying to shorten his steps to match my stride. Josh always moved with such purpose, and sometimes my legs would burn as I power-walked after him toward whatever he was planning to conquer. A party. An errand his mother tasked him with. History class.

We move around people in tandem, and I can feel the carefully established boundaries that have him walking just a few inches farther away than necessary. The way he's frowning at my sweater, but his coat stays solidly around his own shoulders. We're cautiously friendly.

I'm so focused on his movements that I almost step in a container of nachos that someone left in the path. Ash's hand is warm on my elbow, and he guides me to the side of a booth where you can win a giant neon top hat if you knock over a pyramid of milk bottles with a softball.

"Do you want to wander around?" I ask, nerves creeping into my voice until he releases me. I don't know why Odette's questioning got under my skin. The brief touch marks my arm like a brand.

"Do you *want* an itinerary?" His voice is pitched low, and I lean in a little to hear him.

My brain feels itchy, but his question isn't harsh. "Ash, you should know that I always want an itinerary." I try to jam my hands into my corduroys for an extra carefree vibe, but the fashion industry doesn't care about female pockets.

"Do you prefer for all your dates to be planned out?"

Dates. My stomach twists at that word falling from his lips. Not that he was calling *this* a date. I hear the unspoken question, though. Am I this exhausting at all times? What accommodations are necessary for someone to date me? It stings a little, but it's an old ache. Like a sunburn that has gone through the scorch and has now sunk deep into the skin.

"No," I say, finally. "But they've never required much planning. Josh had a very specific way of doing things, and we live in River Haven." I look around at the same exact vendors, games, and people that I have seen every year, every day of my life. "There are rarely surprises."

I start walking because I want him to look at something else.

"Besides, you're trying to teach me something different. I'm a much more diligent student than I am a girlfriend."

"Are all the teachers at school terrified of you?"

"No," I say stubbornly as he falls into step beside me. "I'm a delight to have in class."

"Oh, I'm sure," he says, his amusement warming me up by several degrees. "A delight, but intense in a way that somehow makes me feel like *I'm* the one who's forgotten his homework."

"Well, maybe you should be more prepared when we hang out." We move closer to the food stalls; the aroma of burnt popcorn and corn dogs is thick in the air.

"I'll take that under advisement." The rumble of a laugh he's buried deep fills the space between us.

I clear my throat. "Are you regretting your plan to take me here, this pinnacle of romance? I've got to admit, I don't think you're going to have a lot of material."

"Are you kidding?" He stops, eyes roving the crowd. "This is a hotbed of yearning, first love, and sexual tension."

"Unless you're referring to those two mustachioed gentlemen

selling hot beverages, I'm not seeing a lot of any of that." I tip my head toward the stalls up ahead.

"I'm absolutely referring to them. One serving hot chocolate, the other serving cider, destined to spend their days so close, yet so far."

"Ash, be serious."

"Soon," he says, chewing on his lip ring. "First, let's get something to keep us going. Chocolate or cider?" he asks, but he's already in the first mustache's line.

"Ash, there's nobody in the cider man's line."

"For obvious reasons."

"Do you think he feels bad? I'm sure he worked so hard on all of this." I look up at him, and he studies my face. "Will you get something from him?"

"You want me to trade chocolate for cider?" The overhead lights strung from booth to booth slip off the slant of his cheekbones.

"Look, I think his mustache is drooping a little."

Ash sighs. He moves to the other booth and soon we're on our way with two steaming cups. My fingers start to thaw.

"Okay, back to our plan," I start again.

"You're relentless," he says, wrinkling his nose near his cup. "You've been here before?" He pauses. "With Josh?"

I nod, busying myself with my drink.

"What sort of things did you do?"

"The usual, I guess." I shrug as we walk closer to the corn maze. Josh and I went every year, as part of a group. He played every marksmanship game or anything involving feats of strength. I would dutifully cheer him on and be forced to drag home whatever creepy creature he won. Honestly, this might be my chance to finally get rid of the pink panda that takes up forty percent of my closet.

"The usual," he parrots back to me. "Sounds like a dream."

I jostle his arm a little, and he leans back to avoid the splash of cider. The movement feels natural, as the required personal space between us rapidly continues to shrink.

"Who says it wasn't *my* fault our Harvest Festival moments weren't romantic?" Thick chocolate slides down my throat and floods every sense. I bite back the sigh that wants to escape my mouth.

"Good?" Ash asks, eyeing my cup.

"Brain-altering good," I say. "Seriously. There's an amino acid called tryptophan, which is found in chocolate, and it's the precursor for serotonin." He smirks as I take another gulp. "Chocolate *wants* us to be happy. How can we not adore a food that cares so much about our well-being?"

"What do you know about apples?" he asks, looking down at his drink.

"Only that they look very cute on my sweater."

"Okay, switch," Ash says, holding out his cup.

"Switch?"

"Yeah, we're doing cute rom-com things. Sharing like this is cute."

"Are you sure about that? I want references. I'm pretty sure you just realized you ordered hot apple juice over chocolate."

"Because you *made* me, and I've got plenty of references."

"Okay, let's hear them." Satisfaction races to my toes, and I try to tell myself it's silly to be so pleased that he agreed to something just because I asked.

He plucks the hot chocolate out of my hands, and the sour smell of apples travels up to my sinuses. "This is gross. Are we cute yet?"

He snorts into my cup and doesn't even hide that he takes a third sip.

This is why I'm not a romantic heroine. I never laughed prettily and offered to share my hot chocolate with Josh. I hoarded it like a dragon and devoured it enthusiastically while he poisoned his with someone's dad's whiskey. He'd pour a splash of spirits into the thick chocolate and say "Now we're having fun"— loosening in front of me, and I would tell myself it was special when he leaned heavily against me later that night.

Tonight, it feels *different*.

"Want to try funnel cake next?" Ash leans close, a smudge of chocolate lingering on lips pulled into a smirk. "You can practice wiping loose sugar off my chin in a romantic way."

"Again, you're going to need to provide those references."

. . .

We do the entire circuit—the best River Haven has to offer. Ash sits next to me on the hayride, perched on a hay bale like a giant crow. We're seated next to a couple who've been married for sixty-four years. They cuddle together, hands clasped tight, and answer Ash's question with a laugh.

"The secret to a successful relationship is different hobbies." The woman leans forward, her hand on my knee. "Make sure you keep something for yourself."

I drag Ash through the corn maze—no sign of Pumpkin or Pumpkin-related screams, but we see at least two first kisses, as junior high couples lean in hesitantly and take advantage of the moon and the moment.

Our own awkwardness dissolves, and we both pretend nothing is happening when he swears under his breath and drapes his thick wool coat across my shoulders.

"I can't even concentrate with your teeth chattering that loud."

"I don't know what you're talking about," I say, sniffing as I pull the collar close. It smells like him. Like a fancy French kitchen with lemons and herbs hanging in sunshine.

We thread through the crowd, and I feel half drunk.

"Where were we?" Ash asks, zipping his hoodie to his throat.

"Okay, romance lightning round," I say. "Sexiest fruit?"

"That's easy, pineapple."

"How is a pineapple sexy?"

"Easy. I'm allergic, so it makes my lips tingle."

"There is nothing sexy about having to give someone an EpiPen."

"You better write that in your little notebook, it's sure to come up at some point."

"That isn't notebook-worthy," I say, his mood making me giddy. "Has the tryptophan addled your brain? I told you three cups of hot chocolate was too many."

"Three cups is the perfect amount, and I will not be taking additional questions on the matter."

I dig my hands into the pockets of his coat. "Okay, let's try another one. What is the most romantic song?"

He shrugs. "The one I'm writing now."

"Sing it for me."

"Nope," he says, but he smiles.

"Most romantic car?"

"Anything with a bench front seat," he says, not even hesitating.

"Most romantic historical figure?"

He thinks for a minute. "Napoleon."

I frown.

"Don't wrinkle your face until you read some of his letters to his wife."

"Really?"

"Yeah, then you'll actually have a reason to make that face. He had some questionable hygiene practices."

"Hard pass," I say. "Okay, what is the least romantic school subject?"

"Math."

I gasp. "Ash Augustus Hayes! How *dare* you say that to my face."

"I refuse to believe I'm the first person to have said that to you." My outrage has given me another smile with teeth.

"You are, because math is *universally* beloved."

"You asked, and I'm the expert." He shrugs, hands buried deep in his pockets.

"Nope, I've lost all faith in your credentials. Math is the most beautiful thing on this planet."

He stops, and I have one thousand percent of his attention. He leans against the back of a booth, and my limbs feel tingly, like they've all fallen asleep at once.

"Educate me." The words are crisp, and my confidence flees. But he doesn't budge, so I search for the words.

"Math is perfect, by nature," I start slowly. "And it *is* nature. It's the building blocks of the universe."

"How so?"

"Do you know that a Venus flytrap can count to two? When a poor little fly lands in its mouth, it prepares to close, but it only snaps shut if a *second* contact occurs within approximately twenty seconds of the first touch."

"Keep going," he says, the words warmer than his coat.

"You can see perfect mathematical fractals in the leaves of a fern, the branching neurons in our brains. Honeycomb and snowflakes make hexagons just as well as any computer. Math is elegant, beautiful in its complexity, and it doesn't matter if you take a million different approaches, there's a finite answer. No gray zone or wiggle room."

"You like having a set answer."

I shrug, the movement lost under his coat. "I like knowing where I stand."

"You make a compelling argument." He pushes himself off the booth and nods back in the direction we came from.

"I also refuse to believe that gym class is more romantic than math." I want him to concede the point. I want another dimple sighting.

He shakes his head. "I don't know, there's a lot of contact and sweating in gym."

"I've smelled the locker room."

"It wouldn't have deterred Napoleon."

I laugh, because he's ridiculous and he's loose with his smiles tonight.

An explosion of noise and congratulations erupts behind us. Loud laughter that sounds competitive, a few feminine squeals, and a name I would recognize at any decibel: *Josh*.

Ash straightens, and all the languid lines of his posture disappear. The easy conversation dries to dust, and I move around him toward the front of the booth.

And there it is. My old life staring back at me, and I'm Ebenezer Scrooge haunting these moments, trying to find where it all went wrong.

Tiffany holds an overstuffed killer whale, and Josh winds up to throw another fastball at a stack of cans. My heart stutters a little as I recognize Blue's pink jacket hanging on the periphery of the group. The smile slides off her face when she sees me. Then Josh sees me too, and his next throw goes wide.

"Damn, son, you didn't even get *one* this time," Derrick says, slapping him on the back.

I feel Ash's warmth behind me, and Josh's face clouds over as he registers the two of us. Tiffany tugs on his arm until his attention is back on them, and he doesn't turn in my direction again. Blue refuses to meet my eye, her face pointed down at her shoes. I spin and plunge into the crowd, so I no longer have to look at all of them not looking at me.

"Marlowe!"

I slow for a moment but leave the rows of booths behind. I feel suffocated by it all—the candied apples, the stale popcorn, and the evidence that Josh was having the same Harvest Festival experience that he always does, and my presence didn't disrupt the plan at all. The main square opens up in front of me, empty except for a small stage where a band composed of several old men is setting up.

"Marlowe," Ash calls again, catching up.

"Sorry," I say, leaving it open to cover any number of wrongs.

"Don't apologize," he says, his voice rough. The band slowly fills the air with banjo twangs and a lively fiddle.

I focus on the divot between his clavicles as I wrangle my thoughts in order. Josh's face. Blue's face. The way nobody said a word.

"I can't remember if I promised to stop calling him a jackass or not, and I don't want to go back on my word." His throat bobs.

"You didn't promise that."

"Good, he's a jack—"

"Ash!"

My pocket vibrates, and I pull out my phone to see a text from Blue.

Don't be mad.

I sigh, and I'm not, really. Not at her. She only sees the glittering polish of that crowd and is blinded to anybody or anything else.

Do not drink out of Josh's hot chocolate cup is all I respond with, but it's still a peace offering of sorts.

That whole five-second interaction with Josh still *stung,* and I know I'll feel it later, alone in the dark with nothing but my thoughts and that look on his face. But for now, my poor bruised heart wants to laugh again. Just for a little while longer.

"Most romantic baked goods?" I pull my eyes up to Ash's and will him to let it go.

He looks at me for a long moment, and I cannot take another rejection. He glances away, jaw tightening, but finally he says, "Ice cream sandwich."

I blink. "That's not a baked good."

"It has 'sandwich' in the title, Marlowe."

"And why is it so romantic?" I ask, eyes narrowed.

"Because it's my favorite." He glances back, his small smile tipping into smug.

"Are you really refusing to play me the song you're working on? If it's the most romantic song ever, I think I should be allowed to review it for science."

The edge of his mouth curls up, like the edges of *Cantharellus cibarius* as it dances across a log. "Well, if it's for *science.*"

"Absolutely, I'll be doing a case study."

He nods toward the band as couples move toward the makeshift dance floor. They're twirling and moving like Momma and Stu practice in the kitchen. "Come dance with me, I'll hum you a few bars."

I shake my head. "No, thanks."

"I thought it was important for science?"

"I'm not a dancing girl."

"A dancing girl?" Ash repeats, like he doesn't know exactly what I'm talking about.

"You know what I mean."

"I don't." He raises my least favorite eyebrow.

I take a deep breath. "My momma knows the moves to all of these dances. My baby sister is the same way." I clear my throat, her guilty face tattooed on my brain. "They know all the right moves and footwork, and I grew up in the same house and don't even know how that happened. I don't know if it was passed in the blood, or only some girls are blessed with it, but it skipped me."

Ash steps a little closer and pulls the heavy weight of his coat off my shoulders. I nod, recognizing the cue to call it a night.

He folds the thick wool neatly, and places it on top of a bench. Then he holds out a hand.

"Ash," I say, panic bleeding into my lizard brain. "Did you not get any of that?"

"Marlowe, do you honestly think I know the steps they're doing?"

"What?"

"I'm from San Diego, and I have no intention of boot-scooting across this square."

"Ash, there are *steps* to this dance."

"So?" His warm hand grabs mine, and he pulls me onto the dance floor.

I freeze as the weight of his fingers settles solidly against the small of my back. He turns my other hand in his, and slowly starts moving.

I shuffle awkwardly until he huffs a laugh into my hair. "Quit overthinking it, Meadows."

"Stop telling me what to do," I say, relaxing a fraction and finding the sequence. The pattern of his movement. A pause, a two-count, a sway, a squeeze of his hand.

I feel too warm, despite the loss of his coat, and he hums little snippets of melody up into the atmosphere and the twinkle lights above.

"I don't believe you, you know," he says.

I resist the urge to lay my head against his chest. *This is not Josh. He is not your boyfriend. He is barely even your friend.* "Hmmm?" I say, trying to keep the movement going as the thoughts creep in.

"Everything in the universe is math, right?"

"Yes . . ."

"I have no doubt you could learn a repeating-pattern dance based on actual counts in a song." I look up, ready to protest, but he keeps going. "I believe you could, but if you never cared to I don't see why you should have to. We seem to be doing just fine."

I can't hold on to a single brain cell or thought other than the one that has been bubbling to the surface all night: What is this? None of those word-a-day calendars prepared me for this moment. For the ease I feel as we disrupt the flow of every other couple on the dance floor.

"Ash, are we friends?" It feels very important right now, and I learned a long time ago that if you're not sure, it's best to just ask.

His expression is unreadable, but his hand is warm, and he doesn't stop moving. "Sure, Marlowe. We're friends."

I nod, and I'm glad we established that. I needed us to establish that.

My phone releases a series of meows, and I fumble for my back pocket. My fingers are clumsy with shock, and the phone slips between them and lands on a hay-dusted dance floor.

Ash crouches down, and hands it back to me, a text from Josh flashing across the screen.

I pull open the chat, and a single sentence stares up at me.

That sweater looks good on you.

My heart thunders in my chest. This is it. This is what I've been waiting for. My fingers are flying and I send back: You looked really good too.

The notification pops up that he's read it, but he doesn't respond. I wait another minute, before reassuring myself that a single step is still progress.

I smile up at Ash, showing him the thread. "Everything's falling into place, right?"

His face is still unreadable. "If you say so."

Twelve

"You know, Marlowe, I have to say, things have certainly gotten more interesting around here lately. Maybe Josh did us all a favor."

"Hush," I say, ignoring Odette as we navigate through rows and rows of headstones. The sky turns a bruised purple as the day fades into dusk.

"I don't think we're supposed to be here," Poppy says. She pulls her bag closer, as if afraid of contamination.

"It's a public space, and the band thought it was a good idea." I stop abruptly, the path splitting in front of me.

"Left," Odette says with conviction.

Poppy bumps into my back and stays there, her hand curling around the strap of my messenger bag. "How do you know it's left?"

"Because right takes us back to the entrance, and we're trying to get deep into the graveyard. Nothing but the band and all their ghostly friends, right?"

Poppy groans. "And you're sure you have to do this?" She breathes the words into the collar of my jacket, and I turn to her.

"Ash and I have an agreement. He's already helped me write a letter, and we did the Harvest Festival. It's time for me to hold up my end of the bargain."

"That contract would never hold up in a court of law."

I smile, her earnest defense warming me against the cold snap of fall. "It doesn't have to. I *want* to do this. He's helping me get Josh back."

I resolutely ignore Odette's snort, and warm Poppy's hands between mine as she eases into the knowledge that we're going deeper into the graveyard.

"Speaking of Josh, he won't stop replying in the comments to his post about the letter. Are you sure you want to keep them anonymous? Don't you want him to be bragging about a letter from *you*? Or thinking of you when he reads it?" Odette asks, before adding, "He did send you that text message, maybe he's ready to patch things up."

It's a fair question. The answer sits heavy in my gut: I'm not sure he's ready to know it's from me. If he'd continued to message me, *maybe,* but he's been radio silent since the festival. My brain still has a hard time reconciling these two Joshes and my place in his heart. He *loved* me. From the three romance books I've made it through, it seems like all the signs were there. But his cold expression at the bonfire? The annoyance on his face at the festival when he saw me and Ash? I don't really know that person, and it's turning my brain into a pretzel.

I settle on "I want to give him the opportunity to fall in love with the new me too. The romantically aware me. He was always bringing me a flower before class, or slipping doodles in my locker and sending these grandiose text declarations." I throw my hands out helplessly. "I didn't even think to do the same at the time, but I'm learning."

Odette's expression is so stony it could break glass. "And these romance novels are supposed to change your personality?" She tugs us both toward the left branch of the path.

"Not change, expand," I say, desperate to break the tension. "I just finished a new one last night and it was pretty great." I don't say that I stayed up until four in the morning to finish it because I couldn't untangle myself from the story. "This woman's fiancé cheats on her, so she leaves him and goes back to her hometown to clean out and sell this cottage her great-aunt left her. She decides to stay and work on her dream of becoming a children's author and falls in love with the man who broke her heart back when they were teenagers."

"That sounds okay, I guess," Odette says.

"You don't understand. Her life was in ruins, and this coastal town, the community, and Eric Sinclair helped her figure out how she wanted to put herself back together. It was—" I blank on the words. "It was *so* good."

Odette smirks. "Were there spicy parts?"

I blush. "Maybe."

"Do you have it on you?" Poppy asks hesitantly.

I blink in surprise before digging into my bag and handing it over.

"Let me know when you get to a good part, so I can jump in," Odette tells her.

We come around the bend, and there they are, parked on the path in front of a lichen-covered mausoleum. Never Mind the Monsters.

They're just missing the mountains of cords and speakers and pedals that make it look like they're going to launch a spaceship instead of sing about angry heartbreak.

Hazel bends down to unpack her guitar. She's wearing dark green plaid pants with a black bralette and mesh shirt that I would never be able to pull off. I could barely pull off standing next to her. A spiky gold metal collar curls around her neck, and Odette slams to a stop, her mouth wide open.

"Marlowe!" Mateo grins, looking like he does every other day of the year. A brown flannel is tied messily around his waist, and his Iron Maiden T-shirt is cracked and faded from overuse.

Spencer is already sitting down behind a single snare, his long-sleeved black turtleneck still with crispy lines folded into it. He frowns and waves a drumstick over his setup. "Does this look dumb?"

Mateo rolls his eyes. "Spence, unless you wanted to wheelbarrow your entire kit out here, this is literally the best we can do."

"You look great," I tell him, smiling, but he doesn't return it.

"Hey," Ash says, looking up from helping Julian set up the stand for the keyboard.

"Hey," I say, feeling self-conscious. His peacoat swallows up his lean frame, and I can't see what he's got on underneath. His hair hangs loose, and black liner is smudged around his eyes.

I put down my bag and pull out my phone as my hands start to sweat. They've gone to so much trouble; I wish I had lighting or a real camera, or a single clue how I'm supposed to pull this off. I take pictures for myself, but I have no training or sense of photo composition.

I pull up a browser and search How to take good pictures.

"Don't worry," Odette says beside me. I look up, panic rising in my throat. She smiles, the weight of her hand on my elbow grounding me. "You saw the pictures on their crazy old website. This is already ten times better."

Poppy sits on a stone bench and opens my book, like she's in a park and this is any old day. A lamppost along the path shines above her, and she angles the pages as the sky continues to darken.

I clear my throat. "Are y'all almost ready? We're losing the light."

"See, you already sound like a photographer," Odette says, laughing.

"Just about," Ash says, pulling his guitar out of his case. He slings off his peacoat and stands in front of his band in dark black dress pants, combat boots, and a white button-down under a black leather harness.

He looks at me expectantly, and I raise my phone just as Odette says, "No."

I pause.

"No, it's wrong." She walks up to Hazel. "Give me the collar." Hazel hesitates for only a moment before unhooking the spiked collar from her neck. Odette walks over to Julian. "Do you mind?"

He fastens it around his neck, blushing when Odette undoes the top button of his black polo, which is obviously brand new. "And untuck your shirt," she says, before walking over to Mateo. She pauses briefly over the Iron Maiden shirt and shrugs. "This works, I guess."

Mateo grins. "That means she thinks I'm perfect."

Ash meets my eyes over her busy little frame, but she's not wrong. The band already looks more cohesive.

She stops in front of Spencer and frowns.

"What?" he asks, more than a little defensive.

"You look like you're working backstage at a high school musical."

"It's just black clothing," he complains.

"Exactly, and everyone can tell you never wear it. Mateo, give him the flannel."

"Aye, aye, Captain."

Mateo throws the shirt at his head and Spencer faux-gags as he shoves his arms into it. "Ugh, it smells like him."

"Does this mean we're dating now?"

"You wish."

Odette comes full circle, back to Ash.

"It's okay," she admits. "Something is off, though."

He allows the scrutiny, and she finally snaps her fingers. "Okay, I've got it. Shirt off, Harness back on, and then let the shirt billow around you."

"You want me to take off my shirt?"

"Ash, if you're going to be the lead singer, you're going to have to try a little harder to be eye candy."

He turns to me, and I valiantly try not to laugh, with mixed results.

He swears, but puts down his guitar, and the harness and shirt come off. Hazel helps him strap the leather back onto his bare chest, and I look everywhere else but at him. He slings the open shirt over his shoulder and drapes the guitar back across his body.

"Okay," Odette says. "Now we're ready."

You're going to have to look. You can't take pictures by just pointing randomly in their direction and hoping for the best. I center them and tap the screen to focus. Shadows creep in at the edges as night starts to fall. They all look in my direction like they're taking school photos.

I put down my camera. "Can y'all not look like we're posing for the yearbook? Start playing a song or something."

Ash clears his throat. "Good idea. Let's do 'The Crash of Summer' on three, two, one."

Then they move. The electric guitars leak little bursts of sounds, Julian's keyboard isn't turned on, and Spencer is softly tapping his single snare. You can tell they can hear the music, though, even if we can't. Hazel sways, her fingers flying, and the muscles in Ash's arms bunch as he plays and softly sings words that I don't know but want to.

"Are we absolutely, positively certain we want Josh back?" Odette murmurs.

Heat floods my face as I take picture after picture: Julian leaning forward over the keys, Spencer's arms swinging higher and higher, Mateo rocking back and forth. I capture the satisfied joy on Hazel's face as she and Ash grin at each other over a melody we can barely hear.

And Ash. Ash backlit under a lamppost, his hair and his shirt flowing around him, silver rings dotting his fingers and ears. I step closer and *click*. I crouch a little, his torso stretching taller, the light washing over him like a halo. There. That's the one.

Click.

I straighten, pulling up the photo, and it looks as if the marketing gods took it themselves. It's perfect—moody and sexy. Sexier than it has any right to be.

"Oh, damn," Odette breathes, pulling my phone out of my hand. "I'm officially Team Ash."

"Shh," I say, as my face, skin, and brain continue a steady burn. I get in a few more photos as night fully falls. I try to take snapshots of each member that they can use for themselves, but something tells me that Julian will never be using his outside of the website.

As they all pack up, Odette is complimenting Hazel on all her jewelry, her face, and every aspect of her personality. Soon they're exchanging numbers, and I'm only surprised it took this long. I stand off to the side, trying to stay out of the way, and re-sist the urge to scroll through the photos on a never-ending loop.

I don't have to wait long before Ash appears at my side, nudg-ing my arm with his. "What do you think? Anything usable?"

His chest is covered again, and I find myself able to string together a sentence. "I think so," I manage to force out.

"Can I see?"

I swipe through them and pull up my favorite. Ash in the spotlight.

His lips curl into his almost smile. "Looks like we've gradu-ated from my parents' basement."

"Do you like it?" I ask, trying not to sound needy or like his answer will matter at all.

He shifts, swaying into my side, and the contact bolsters me. I suppress the urge to fix the eyeliner smudge under his left eye.

"Yeah, Marlowe. I like it."

Thirteen

Poppy's pen thwacks against her notebook, the staccato beat never varying in tempo as she stims her way through a history assignment.

Three Little Words is in that dreamy after-school-but-before-work-ends lull. Only a few customers mill around the stacks, and Poppy and I are sprawled out at a table in the corner of the café.

Sloane came over briefly after we first arrived and stayed long enough to give me a latte that tasted like the inside of a drain before wandering off, clipboard in hand.

The silence hangs between us comfortably. There's no anxiety over entertaining each other or trying to force a conversation. The three of us have a connection that is impossible to disrupt. A *history*. A bond that is built on a decade of books, video games, TV shows, and an entire language of inside jokes based on all of the above.

Odette will never live down her Kim Possible cosplay photo shoot, and how the ancient old dragon who runs the one-hour photo in the Quickie-Mart thought the photos were too scandalous and called her mother and preacher.

We'll forever tease Poppy over her favorite Doctor (Peter Capaldi), and we'll never let a distinguished older gentleman walk by without enough winks or nudges to turn her scarlet red.

Or me, and my serious Sims addiction in fifth grade. Odette and Poppy staged a surprisingly formal intervention, and a banner that shouts COME BACK TO REAL LIFE, MARLOWE has hung above my bed ever since. Odette *still* yells that in my direction when I space out.

The point is, we've amassed stories and secrets like collectibles acquired by an exclusive club, and it's easy by now. There's nothing to maintain, and I'm too deeply out of practice to add anyone new.

Especially if that someone new is a moody romance nerd who's allergic to color. Finding a way to be his friend in a way that isn't too clingy or too distant is *hard*. The neurodivergence doesn't help either.

I glare at my phone as if it's solely responsible for me being too chicken to text him. I finished the second letter last night, but is that a notification worthy of crossing that bridge? Of sending that first message?

I pull the pink envelope out. I should just send a picture of it. That feels more casual. A little FYI. He doesn't have to read it, and I've already sealed it, because Josh's *heart* felt a little more personal to me. I didn't want to see the smirk or eye roll that I knew Ash wouldn't be able to hide.

Josh is complicated, and his cool absence in the wake of our breakup has made him even more so, but when Josh really wants to be sweet, there's nobody more thoughtful.

I wrote about his grandparents' fiftieth wedding anniversary. They'd met at a community center in the 1950s, and his grandma has Alzheimer's now. They live in an assisted-living facility, and his grandpa lovingly cares for her every single day.

Josh's parents were just going to do a small party, but Josh re-created the night they met. He found pictures of the center and made decorations. He had everyone dress in costumes from that time period, and Momma helped me pin up my hair and let me wear one of my meemaw's old dresses. When his grandma walked in and saw it all, she looked over at his grandpa and said "Fred" for the first time in three years.

I was so proud of him. Of his *heart*.

"Did you put the graveyard pictures online yet?"

I look up, blinking back the water pooling in the corner of my eyes. Poppy sets down her pen and measures me over her textbook.

"I did." I clear my throat. "Yes, last night."

"Well? Are they viral yet?"

She pulls a laugh out of me. "I don't think so, not yet. Fingers crossed there's a good response, though."

"I've seen the pictures, I doubt it will be a problem," she says dryly. "What's your plan?"

"I've built a little army of Gabber bots." I blush as her eyebrow shoots up. The success of this is important to me, and I've been working nonstop for more than a week. "My army of little monsters will be reposting five of my favorite pictures, along with their songs, and some band-member profiles I've put together. They're keyed to certain hashtags and trends, and then it's just a matter of numbers and exponential growth."

She's fully grinning, and my face flames. I don't know what's causing the delight written all over her features, but I want her attention focused on something else.

"Tell me about Pumpkin?" I ask, aiming for casual. "Is the science fair looking like a slam dunk?"

Her lips twist in amusement, but she allows it. "I think she's almost ready. Her primary function is to navigate mazes and collect samples, but I've programmed her to hand me a can of Diet Dr Pepper too."

"And the goal is to shoot her off to faraway planets? Or sell copies of her to men who need something to beer them during sports games?"

"I like to be versatile. The possibilities are endless."

She's not even bragging, and she has every right to. Especially since the possibilities *are* endless, and she built this in her childhood bedroom, surrounded by posters of the Jonas Brothers and Katherine Johnson.

"How's the competition looking?"

She bites her lip, and I nudge her feet with mine.

"That bad?"

"No," she hedges. "Just different. There're rumors of a water-filtration system, and Vignesh is doing something with corn, and you *know* how that's always a crowd-pleaser."

"Nothing can touch Pumpkin," I say, squeezing her wrist until she looks up and I think she believes me. "MIT is going to knock down your door like the Kool-Aid Man."

"That's horrifying," she says, blinking rapidly.

"And what are you doing while you're not working on her? Are you managing three separate farms on your Switch? Joining your mom in her evening karaoke set?"

"I liked the book you lent me," she says, leaning forward. Her focus feels like a weighted blanket that kills the rest of my jokes.

"Really?"

"Yes, really."

"What did you like?"

"Literally all of it," she says, laughing. "I liked the small town that reminded me of this one. I liked that Sydney and Eric argued a lot at first, but slowly grew to like each other. I liked that we thought they had gotten together, but then they split up again, and then got together for good. I liked all the feelings, and stress, and physical bits."

I'm dazed by the dreamy expression on her face. I say the only thing I can think of. "I have more."

"Tell me about them," she says, scooting closer.

"Well, my book this week is about these two scientists. They're supposed to be working on this project together, but they don't like each other and don't trust each other, so it's going disastrously." I grin. "God, I hope they kiss soon."

Poppy grins back. "Are you almost done?"

"Almost!" Her face falls, and I try not to laugh. "Don't worry, there's plenty more where that came from. I'll have to ask Ash to really give me a syllabus so you can skip ahead."

"Okay," she says, brightening. "And things are still going well? With Ash?"

"I think so?" I pull out the disco cats, flipping through pages and pages of scrawled notes. Tropes, sweet nothings, questions for Ash on why a protagonist did this versus that, and one NSFW drawing of a scene from the last book, involving a staircase that I could not wrap my mind around the logistics of. I skip ahead to a blank page. "I've just finished the second letter, and hopefully I'm one step closer to patching things up with Josh."

She makes a noncommittal noise, and I look up. "And you're sure that's what you want?"

I lean back in my chair. "Why does everyone keep asking me that?"

It feels like a constant refrain these days. What do you want? Are you sure that's what you want?

What do you want, Marlowe?

Sometimes it takes everything I have not to stand on the table and scream *I don't know* as the constant refrain fills every crevice of my brain. Doubt, shame, anger, fear, and love just folded over and over into white matter until I can't tell one from the other.

Poppy leans forward, her hand catching mine as my fingernails tap an allegro beat into the Formica. "Are you at least having fun? The books are great, and Ash is kind of hot, right?"

I'm stunned into silence.

Odette breezes through the door, a carefully controlled tornado, and slings her bag onto the table. I narrowly save my latte from shooting off the edge.

She grins. "What are we talking about?"

"About how hot Ash is or isn't," Poppy says, shoving Odette's bag off her textbook.

Odette slides into the chair on my left, her grin widening. "Well, well, well, that's an interesting turn of events."

"No, it's not," I say. I'm firm, unyielding. I don't need this growing beyond this moment right here. I especially don't need Odette even whispering a hint of this to Hazel and it getting anywhere near Ash's ears. "Also, how can you talk about anybody else being hot when you have Hazel's handiwork all over your neck?"

"Please, I'm sure she'd agree with me." She takes out her phone and opens the camera to inspect the damage. "What do you think? Think Mom will believe they're curling-iron burns?"

"Maybe if you'd ever worn curls in your life," Poppy says.

"Maybe tomorrow I will. Ringlets cascading down my back just like the cover of one of Lo's books." She grins at me, chin in hand. "But only if she quits trying to change the subject and admits that Ash could also easily be on one of these covers. Especially from the graveyard. Shirt open and billowing in the wind, ghosts ruffling his hair—"

"Ghosts?" Poppy laughs, and it pulls a tiny smile out of me.

"*Fine,* he's very tall and symmetrical," I say, rolling my eyes. "Happy?"

"For now," she says, shrugging. She slides my notebook across the table and flips through the pages. She holds up the NSFW drawing. "Lots of surprises in here."

I flush. "I just wanted to prove it defied the laws of physics."

She snaps a picture with her phone. "Okay, back to Ash the hottie."

I choke as the boy in question walks through the front door, and I give Odette my pleading eyes. "Please, drop it."

She holds up her hands in surrender as he tosses his bag on the floor and fills the remaining seat.

Odette slides the notebook back across the table. It's open to my latest report, on *Luck Be a Lady,* an enthusiastic summary with a couple too many exclamation points to be truly academic. The page is littered with the three things I learned, five of my favorite words from the book ("ineffable," "propinquity," "sumptuous," "scintilla," "anorak"), and all the page numbers with kissing in case I want to read them a second time.

I smile at Ash, glad to have my texting issue solved. "Hey, you."

His hair looks like he's used his fingers as a brush. "You'll never believe this." He laughs a little, breathless. "The band videos you posted, and some of the pictures from the graveyard? This really big account reposted them."

"Which one?" Odette leans forward.

"Their handle is @TheAxeMan, it's this guitar company that makes these incredible custom pieces. They have over a million followers and they liked our sound." He leans back, the smile opening up his entire face. "This might really turn into something."

"I hope so," I say, internally rooting for my little monsters. "I have news too."

He looks up, still dazed, and his lopsided smile jolts through my system. "If it's about that third Chicken Shack opening soon, I already know."

"Not that."

"A *fourth*?"

I roll my eyes and slide the second envelope toward him. He studies it like a snake before flipping it over.

"You already sealed it?"

I nod, my smile breezy. "It felt right."

He slides it back to me, and Odette knocks her knees into mine under the table. I jump in before he has time to unpack anything. "Will you come with me to school? I want to put it in his locker."

He shrugs. "Just do it before school tomorrow."

I shake my head. "He has student government after school today, and he'll go to his locker before he goes home." It's burning a hole in my bag, and maybe this one will make him think of me. Miss me. Maybe it will remind him of how we held hands tightly under the table as his grandparents slow-danced.

He wants to protest, I can see it, so I sweeten the deal. "Just think, the sooner this is done, the sooner you get rid of me."

I meant it as a joke, sort of, but his expression is so flat it makes my stomach ache.

"Okay, let's do it," he says finally.

"Oh, I'm coming too." Odette shoves her phone in her bag.

"Poppy?" Might as well drag the entire crew along.

She shakes her head.

Sloane chooses this moment to walk up to us, smiling like the sun. "Anything I can grab any of y'all?"

Poppy's hand shoots into the air.

Sloane blinks for a moment. "Yes, Poppy?"

"Can you help me find a book?"

"Well, that's exactly the reason I exist on this planet. Which book are you looking for?"

"I don't know. A romance novel."

"No shortage of that around here. Any more information you can give me?"

"Can you just show me everything?"

We pack up, leaving Poppy in good hands, and head back to the school. Odette fills the heavy silence with anecdotes from her and Hazel's car ride, and I'm grateful for the buffer.

We race across the parking lot, and by the time we get to the seniors' hallway I'm sweating. I ease around the corner, and it's still clear.

I thrust the letter at Ash. "Locker 118."

"Why do I have to do it?"

"Because they get out any second, and he can't see *me* lurking around."

He nods at Odette. "Odette can deliver it."

She snorts. "He'll think it's a prank."

Ash looks up, bargaining with his higher power, before grabbing the envelope and storming down the hall. He shoves it through the slats of the locker, none too gently, and is walking back when Josh rounds the opposite corner.

I yank my head back, my heart thundering against my ribs.

"*Hayes.*" Josh's voice ricochets down the hall.

Odette goes still next to me.

The silence is crushing, but I don't dare look.

"What?" Ash's voice is crisp and filled to the brim with derision.

Odette mouths *What is going on?* I shrug helplessly.

"I want you to stay away from Lo."

Odette's fingers dig deeper into my arm, and my brain short-circuits at his demand.

Ash's laugh is low and humorless. "And why is that?"

Josh scoffs. "I don't have to explain myself to you."

"No, you never do have a good explanation, do you?"

"What the hell is that supposed to mean?"

"The marching band is kind of struggling this year, isn't it? If only they had a drum major who had a clue about what he was doing." Ash's voice cracks like a whip.

"You *know* none of that was my fault." Josh's voice is dismissive, and goose bumps prickle down my arms.

"What are they talking about?" Odette whispers next to my ear, and I shake my head.

"You keep telling yourself that." I hear Ash's heavy tread down the hallway, and Josh's next words come out rushed.

"You're just going to hurt her."

The steps slow. "Of the two of us, I'm not the one with the track record of hurting Marlowe."

Josh's laugh is ugly and sharp. "Oh, *please*. She's a good girl, from a good family. She deserves someone a lot better than *you*."

Ash's silence is deafening, but Josh keeps going. I feel like I've stepped outside my body. "You think her parents will accept someone like you, after me? Some *freak*? With your creepy clothes and death music?"

"Careful, Josh." Ash's voice is mocking. "The mask is slipping. Discovering for the first time you can't have your cake and eat it too?"

"You're wasting your time. I know she still loves me. Do you really think you have a shot?"

I can't breathe. His words crash over me, pulling me under, and I focus on Odette's fingertips anchoring me in place.

What do you want, Marlowe?

Ash's voice snaps through the haze. "Two whole years, and you never pulled your head out of your ass once."

Odette and I clutch each other, waiting for more, but then Ash turns the corner and brushes past us.

I swallow the lump in my throat and peel myself off the wall.

"We should . . ." Odette nods toward Ash, already on his way back to the parking lot. She looks as dazed as I feel.

I didn't recognize that Josh, or those elitist, ugly words. *Careful, Josh, the mask is slipping.* A band of pressure wraps around my chest, and I feel lightheaded.

"The audacity," Odette seethes.

I jog to catch up, tugging on Ash's arm. "Hey, are you okay?" I choke on the words a little. "He's not normally—"

"I swear to God, Marlowe, if you defend him right now I'm calling the whole thing off." His jaw is clenched, and he won't look at me.

I don't want to defend Josh. I can't even process the words I heard him say with my own ears. I just want to remove this expression from Ash's face, but I don't have the slightest idea how. I drop my hand.

"Okay. Let's get out of here," I say instead.

He drives us back, shoulders hunched, hair hanging forward like a barrier between us. Every inch of him radiating *leave me alone,* but I only last about half a mile before I cave.

"What were you talking about?" My voice sounds shockingly loud in the silence. I half expect him not to answer, but he glances over at me. "What does Josh have to do with the drum majors?"

He's quiet for a moment, but he can't help himself either. "You remember Spencer was in band?"

"Sure." I shrug. "I saw him with the band at games, and then I *didn't* see him around."

"That stupid team." Ash's hands tightened around the wheel. "He was one of my first friends here. Did you know that? He's cool, would give you the shirt off his back if you needed it and can play the drums like he's possessed." He exhales loudly. "But then your precious Josh and his little cronies decide they want to show him who's in charge."

My stomach clenches and I don't know where this is going, but it's not going to be good.

"They thought this cheerleader that Derrick liked was smiling in Spencer's direction a little too long, and they felt that their significantly less talented friend should get to be drum major this year."

"Jesus," Odette murmurs from the backseat. "Spencer would have gotten that with his eyes closed."

"They were coming back from an away game in Jackson last year, and Spence fell asleep on the bus. One of the football players had a pocketknife and they used it to cut up the hat and jacket of his uniform."

I'm rooted to my seat, and all I can manage is one question. "*Josh* did that?"

Ash scoffs like my surprise is personally offensive. "Was he wielding the knife? I don't know, but it doesn't matter. He watched it, he laughed at it, he did nothing to discourage it. There was an investigation and nobody on that bus admitted to seeing a thing. He was the team captain, and when Spence came to him for help, he told him that maybe he did it himself in his sleep."

I feel like I've stepped outside my body. Like all of this is happening to someone else, or on some angsty teen soap opera that Odette tells us is worth the hype. How had I heard *none* of this? Was I just walking around with my eyes and ears closed to anything and everything that didn't impact me directly?

Ash keeps going, each new detail turning my blood to ice. "The investigation eventually ruled that they couldn't prove foul play, and Spence would just have to replace the uniform." He pulls up in front of the bookstore, but none of us move. "His family . . ." He takes a deep breath. "They don't have a lot of money, and it was about five hundred dollars. He's been trying to pay it back little by little, but they won't let him back in the band until the debt is settled. He can't even graduate if it's not paid back by then."

"Maybe we could raise the money—" Odette leans forward.

Ash shakes his head, and her words die out. "We've all offered, but he refuses. He's furious and too proud and feels it's something he has to do on his own."

I find my voice. "But if we can help him now, he can still do orchestra in the fall."

Ash's laugh is sharp, and I flinch as it cuts through the tension in the car. "He was banking on a scholarship, but how could he ever go back?" He finally looks over at me. "Not one person, even in his own band, was willing to speak up against those players."

His gaze has me rooted to my seat, and my insides are a snarl of hot, angry feelings. I wish we'd never gone to the school. I wish I could reconcile all these pieces of Josh into something that makes sense.

"You believe me, right?"

I want to wipe the doubt off Ash's face, because even after just a few weeks, I know he wouldn't lie to me.

"I do," I say softly. The crease between his eyebrows smooths out and I know he wants me to say the plan is off, but I need time to process. I murmur a soft "Bye" and slide out of the car before I can see his disappointment.

Poppy's right where we left her, surrounded by a small stack of books.

Odette drops her bag in a chair and swears loudly. An older woman who I'm certain knows my mother turns toward us with a shocked expression.

"Let's keep Jesus and the rest of River Haven out of this," I say. "Unless you want me dragged to church a little extra this week."

"Get *this,* Pops." Odette leans across the table. "That insufferable turnip told Ash to stay away from her and helped these football douchebags bully Spence out of marching band."

Poppy's nose scrunches up, and the judgment on her face makes me itch to defend Josh. But I don't. I *can't.* His words constrict around me a little more.

Odette crosses her arms. "Be honest, Lo. Is that who you want to be with?"

What do you want, Marlowe?

I shake my head. Nobody is just one thing, and Josh is not *only* that smug and terrible boy from the hallway, but I need to sit down and look at all the pieces. I need all the data to help me figure this out.

"I have to think" is all I'm able to say.

She smiles, the angle punishing. "You should really raise his blood pressure. Post a picture of you and Ash holding hands, or a close-up of his face and the caption *I'll be his Renfield any day.*"

"How is every sentence out of your mouth somehow worse?"

"Just talent, I guess."

My phone meows, and we all freeze. I pull it out and the timing makes me feel sick. I open Josh's chat to: Been thinking about you a lot recently. Let's catch up soon?

If this had come even an hour earlier, I would have been over the moon, thanking my lucky stars and Ash and every romance novel under the sun. Now, I'm just flat.

The bubbles pop up again and spit out: Also, I wouldn't believe everything Hayes tells you.

Poppy and Odette lean over to read, and Poppy pulls back as if stung. "That's very suspicious timing."

"I know." I close the screen and toss my phone back in my bag. I wrap my arms around myself, wishing I were back on my couch and buried under three weighted blankets.

"Are you okay?" Odette asks, concern written across her face. I don't move when she steps forward, but I sag when she folds me into a tight hug.

Odette's arms squeeze tighter. "Just breathe, Marlowe."

A laugh wheezes out of me and into her hair when Poppy joins from behind and whispers, "Why are we hugging?"

Fourteen

I don't know which is worse—knowing that I might actually hate *Wuthering Heights,* or the fact that I am solely responsible for bringing it into my life. I toss the book onto the kitchen island and place my forehead on the cool marble. I'm pretty sure Heathcliff just murdered a dog, and I'm equally sure I might not make it through the rest of this book.

"Oh, *Wuthering Heights,*" Momma says, walking in with a cloud of Guerlain and an armful of purple hydrangeas.

"I see you're familiar with my nemesis," I murmur, cheek squished into the stone.

She purses lips painted a dusty rose. "You don't like it? It was one of my favorites when I was your age." She places the flowers in the sink and pulls her shears out of the junk drawer. "I thought Heathcliff was so moody and romantic."

I snap upright. "Romantic? He just murdered a puppy, and word on the street is that he might have dug Catherine's body up, but I haven't got to that point yet." I hear the echo of my earlier conversation with Ash, and I blush at the memory of his face as I was waxing on about soul mates and the power of their love. This love doesn't feel like it's conquering all, it feels toxic. Like a tree that looks healthy and beautiful until you peel back the bark to reveal the rot underneath.

She pauses, snipping the ends off the stalks. "Does he murder a puppy? I don't know if I remember all that, I just remember him being tortured by his love for Catherine. Poor lamb." She shrugs, the flowers going one by one into a heavy crystal vase that belonged to my great-grandmother.

Her words sit uncomfortably with me. Maybe I would be looking at *Wuthering Heights* differently if I hadn't been ingesting other examples of romance at an increasingly alarming rate. Heathcliff's dark tempers weren't sexy, they were self-indulgent and toxic. Catherine's actions weren't based in love; she was a petulant child who might have died simply to spite everyone else. You want romance? I can name you a dozen other couples that would put these two to shame, and I would enjoy doing it. It's like I've become addicted. I can't *stop* myself. I want all the stories, all the tropes, and every happy ending I can get my hands on.

I don't even want to bother Ash for more recommendations beyond the one a week he's giving me, so Sloane and I have become fast friends. I just finished a story with passionate, but slightly murderous, fairies, followed by a sweet but slow-burn contemporary between a sports journalist and a minor-league baseball player. I even squeezed in a novella involving a Mafia don with a heart of gold that was a little too tortured for me, but at least he didn't harm any animals.

"We're going to have to agree to disagree on this one," I finally tell Momma as she turns the vase, looking for gaps.

"There's two-thirds of my girls!" Stu's personality enters the room almost before he does, and he's all blinding smiles, kisses for

Momma, and a wink in my direction. "Did you like that, Lo? I added that fraction in just for you."

I roll my eyes, but he gets a smile out of me anyway. He spins Momma in his arms, and in seconds they're moving across the kitchen floor, bodies in sync and never missing a beat. I watch them dance and wait for that old pang. The one telling me that one of these things is not like the other. A square peg looking at nothing but round holes.

But that feeling never rises to the surface. All I can hear is Ash asking me why I never bothered to learn. Telling me that dancing is not genetically passed down and looking at me as if I'd purposefully set myself apart from something I'd decided wasn't for me.

And the most annoying thing is that he might be right. I could decide that I didn't *want* to learn to dance, and that would be fine, but I'm capable of doing hard things. Unexpected things.

I might even be good at them.

Or not, and that would be okay too.

I resist the urge to put my forehead back on the island, and instead say, "Do you think you could teach me that sometime?"

They slow, looking back at me with twin expressions of surprise. Stu recovers first. "Get over here, girl. Let's see what you got!"

I shake my head, face already burning from this small step. "Not right now. I just might want to learn at some point."

Momma smiles, gold hoops shining as he spins her one last time for good measure. "Of course, honey, all you have to do is ask."

The door to the living room creaks open, and Blue marches in. My other nemesis stares at me from her arms.

"What is *that* doing in here?"

"Don't be mean to Snow White."

I pause and count to ten under my breath while the fat old duck molts onto the floor. "We eat in here, Blue. Get her out of here."

"She's perfectly clean."

"She's a duck. She's not house-trained."

"She has *never* pooped in my room."

"A statistical anomaly she will soon correct."

She scowls, and I hate the distance that has been growing between us with every year. The way she doesn't want to spend time with her boring older sister anymore when there are parties, cheerleading practice, and makeup tutorials instead. She gets up two hours early every day to do her hair before school and finds reasons to go by Josh's table during lunch. How can I compete with the *popular* crowd? I never looked the part quite as well as she does, but I can't deny a tiny, vain part of me didn't enjoy it. After more than one tearful night over slumber parties or birthdays or movie nights I didn't get invited to, it was nice to have every door open for once.

"Ladies," Stu says, gently stepping in. "Bluebell, baby, let's get Her Majesty back to her little hutch. She's probably ready to turn in for the night."

"*Fine,*" Blue says, tossing blond hair over her shoulder and stalking out.

"You know, I kept waiting for her to stop naming all her pets Snow White, but she never did," Stu says.

"The lizard was a choice," I agree.

"Rest in peace, lizard Snow White. His poor untimely end," Momma says reverently.

"Cat Snow White who helped him shuffle off this mortal coil didn't help," Stu adds.

My phone explodes in a flurry of jangles. Incoming video call from Odette and Poppy. "And on that note," I say, heading to my room and leaving sounds of whispered laughter and two-stepping behind me.

"Long time no see." I answer the call and flop onto my bed. The floral duvet is soft as butter, the pale blue almost faded to white.

"Have you seen what's happening on Gabber?" Odette's grin fills the entire screen.

I sit up. "Not since yesterday."

"Pull it up!"

I sprint to my desktop, fingers flying. There on my home screen are thousands and thousands of posts about Never Mind the Monsters. People from school asking, "Isn't this Ash Hayes's band?" Local clubs and radio stations with shout-outs asking the band to reach out. And at the center of the storm is a repost from one of my little monsters: a snippet of their song "Divine Inter-ference" along with the picture I took of Ash in that graveyard. Shirt off, the hint of that leather harness over lean muscles, his hair wild around his shoulders and the dim light almost washing it all away. @GuitarTodayMagazine reposted it with the comment, "They're growing some talent down in Georgia these days."

I pull up the band's website. I'm not done yet, but at least I have the new framework in place, their contact info for bookings, and a few of the new photos. All in a clean, modern black-and-white design. I pull up the engagement numbers, and freeze.

"Holy shit," I breathe.

"What's happening?" Poppy asks.

"I think we've officially gone viral," I say, my chest tight with a kaleidoscope of feelings. I never imagined this response. I'd felt like I was a burden, and like Ash wasn't getting nearly enough out of this. Especially after the run-in with Josh. But this? This makes us partners. Or at least puts us on equal footing.

Odette whoops through the phone, her grin eating up most of my screen. "I gotta call Hazel, she's going to *die*."

"Are we on a daily calling schedule now?"

She winks. "Maybe. Wish me luck." She kisses the camera before winking into darkness.

I smile at Poppy, still riding high. "Do you want to come over? We can continue the cake-mug experiments."

She shakes her head. "Sorry, but I'm deep in *The Reunion*. I barely had time for this phone call, but Odette said it was important."

"Is that the book Sloane helped you pick out?"

"Garrett and Rebecca just had their first night together, but her ex called the next morning and Garrett left thinking she's not over him."

"Oh wow, you're really moving through it—"

"Got to go, bye."

The screen goes dark, and I lean back from the whiplash of it all. I've never heard Poppy express any interest in romance, or dating, or anything other than puzzles and robotics. I set aside two more books Ash had lent me to pass along to her.

I scroll through my feed, liking and resharing some of the more clever comments, but I feel restless. Like we just pulled off something huge. I have no idea if it's going to make a difference or lead to any gigs or sales of their single, but we got the band out of Ash's tastefully decorated basement and into the public eye.

I pull out my phone and stare at his number—which I'm sure he shared only for logistical reasons. For example, if he had plans to meet me and literally anything better came up, he could text me, *Hey, can't make it, work on your own pathetic love letter by yourself*. But he hasn't, and nothing has seemed like a good enough excuse.

Until now.

I type and delete about five times, before finally settling on a very casual Looks like you're famous now.

I see the dots almost instantly, and I'm smiling until: Sorry, who's this?

I toss down my phone, heat flooding my face.

He must not have saved my number. I guess we're not really friends, and I just forced an admission out of him during a dance-floor hostage situation. I should delete his number too. I'll wait and tell him in person the next time I see him that the online strategy is working well—

My phone rings. I stare at it in betrayal. What if I don't answer it? No, then it'll go to my voicemail. What if I just answer and then immediately hang up? No, what if he does need to call me at some point and realizes I was the phantom weirdo who refused to talk to him? I take a deep breath and answer.

"Hey, sorry—"

"Meadows, I was joking."

My mouth snaps shut.

"I could hear you overthinking from here. Sorry, the joke didn't land."

I clear my throat, desperate to move on. "I just wanted to tell you about the online response to the streaming song and photos."

"You mean the reason our band email is full of requests to play parties and car dealership openings, and some very awkward sugar mama offers?"

His voice is deep and rich, filling my little bedroom. His amusement trickles down the phone.

"*What?*"

"They were very generous, Marlowe. One woman is willing to set me up in a nice apartment and take care of me, so at least I don't have to worry about school anymore."

"Ash!" I say, shocked, but also not shocked. I mean, I saw that photo. I took it.

He laughs. "Relax. Hearing your outraged response is infinitely more enjoyable than becoming Martha from Statesville's mistress. Mastress?"

His teasing shocks another laugh out of me. "We're definitely going with mistress."

"I can't promise Mateo won't take some of them up on their offers, though."

"Well, he's still deeply in debt to his little brother, he needs help pulling himself out of this financial hole."

"It's true, twelve rides to the mall don't just grow on trees."

I smile, walking back to my bed and flopping down. I was worried the conversation would be stilted, that I would panic and try to fill every spare second with mushroom facts, but here we are. This is actually . . . nice.

My door slams shut. I don't even look up, the words coming out automatically. "Hey, Meemaw."

"Is your grandmother there?"

"Well, in a matter of speaking."

He pauses. "What does that mean?"

"She died about ten years ago, but still likes to visit."

"Are you telling me that your grandmother is haunting you?"

"Only a little bit, and to be fair, it was her room a lot longer than it's been mine."

"Do you need me to find a priest? I'm sure we can order an exorcism online."

"Ashton Rasputin Hayes, we take care of our elders in this family. We do not just ship them off to another dimension. If she wants to slam my door and kill every plant I bring into this room, that's her prerogative."

"I stand corrected," he says. Is he smiling? It sounds like he's smiling.

"Why didn't you just text me?" I ask, clearing my throat.

"When?" He sounds off-kilter for once.

"Five minutes ago? Why did you call instead?"

"Why wouldn't I call? I like talking on the phone."

"You *like* talking on the phone?" I shudder.

"Yeah, what's wrong with that?"

"Don't worry, I know some very good therapists, we'll get you sorted in no time."

He chuckles. The sound crawls inside my brain and carves out a little home there. I label it "Ash finding me amusing" and promise myself I'll replay it later.

"I'm almost through *Wuthering Heights* and things are not going well." I flop on my belly, my pillow muffling the words.

"Well, it's not a comedy, Meadows."

"No kidding. Why didn't you tell me to shut up when I was going on and on about love conquering all?"

"Because I imagined we'd be having this conversation at some point. What did it? The dog?"

"The dog," I confirm. "Our thesis can be a thorough analysis of how Heathcliff sucks."

"What about . . ." His voice is hesitant in my ear. "What about the destructive effects of toxic love? Or maybe the impact Heathcliff's toxic masculinity had on the lives of those around him?"

"Toxic masculinity?" I wince as Josh and the football team

shove themselves into the forefront of my brain. This new Josh continues to haunt me, better than Meemaw has ever been able to. "Those seem like two different papers."

"Not if we combine them to focus on the Heathcliff character specifically."

"I like it," I say, sitting up. "I'll try to power through the rest of the book, and we can work on an outline."

"Okay," he says, and I sit up, ready to begin the dance of two almost strangers getting off a call neither one of them expected to be on.

"Want to watch a movie?" Not a single syllable is hurried.

"A movie?" I look at my bedside clock. "I don't think anything is playing anymore."

"At home, on the phone together," he says, gentle enough that I flush. I have *got* to find an opportunity to do some math in front of him soon.

I pick up my laptop and sit against my headboard. "We just watch it together and talk?"

"Well, that depends on how interesting the movie is," he says, as if he's just suggested the most natural thing in the world. "What do you think? Rom-com? Documentary? Deep dive into the predatory world of mom leggings?"

I pull up Netflix, sinking down into the pillows, and scroll through the choices. We could do a rom-com, and it could count as his fieldwork this week. He might want to free up his plans this weekend. On the other hand, the idea of watching two people fall in love, in the darkness, with Ash's thoughts and breath in my ear, is something that might take my anxiety level from its current low simmer to Instant Pot kitchen bomb.

In the end, my people-pleasing tendencies rise to the top, like always.

"You did say we needed to watch a rom-com soon, so now you're off the hook for the fieldwork this week."

His silence wraps around me. "I guess we could count it if you want. I did have something else planned, but whatever you prefer."

"No," I say, a little too quickly. "I think we should do whatever you've already planned." I take a deep breath. "Since you've already gone to the trouble of coming up with it."

I don't care if Josh thinks I should stay away from Ash, or how breathless or ridiculous I look to Meemaw's ghost. I can't even explain it to myself, but I want to see whatever he wants to show me.

What do you want, Marlowe?

"Okay then," he says, pleased. "In that case, let's stick to microdosing romance, and watch something different tonight."

"Let's do a documentary," I say. "I don't know how much talking I should or shouldn't be doing while watching a movie on the phone with someone. At least this way I won't miss anything."

He laughs, and my honesty feels less like an apology. "Okay, let's see what we got. I'll admit the leggings don't sound very interesting to me. Here's one about animals in the ocean, a few serial-killer options, and . . . wait . . . oh, this is the one."

"Which one?"

"Oh, you're going to love this."

"Ash, tell me." I scroll through, trying to find one that stands out.

"How do you feel about mushrooms?"

My heart swells inside my chest and I swallow down the words that want to bubble out of me. He knows exactly how I feel about them, and that I'm going to talk the entire time, and that this is a gift just for me.

I clear my throat. "They're okay, I guess."

He laughs. "Come on, Meadows, let's learn about mushrooms. Click on *Fungi of the Forest*."

I want to make it weird. I want to tell him that if he only wants to be casual friends, or people who are helping each other out only for the mutual benefit of separate goals, this is not the way to do it. That he's being too nice to me. That my head and my heart are going to assign importance to him that he might not be ready or willing to accept.

But I don't say anything, because a lion's mane cascades down the screen and my words are caught in my throat.

I try to let the narrator do her job, but little snippets leak out of me. A fun fact here, a personal anecdote there, and he laughs twice more before I realize it's not because the puffball's pollination process is so personally enjoyable to him.

It's shaping up to be one of the better evenings I've had in a long time when my Gabber tab dings. I click over and pull up my direct messages. I sit up straight when I see Josh's profile. The pillows, the mushrooms, Ash's voice in the dark are instantly forgotten, and I'm opening it like this message will hold the secrets to the universe.

All it says is: You never responded to me. That's not like you. Why are you still spending time with him?

The air whooshes out of me and down the line.

"Meadows? Is the bleeding tooth too much for you?"

"Josh," I say, pushing the word out.

"What about him?"

The question is sharp, and I flinch even as my fingers are flying over the keys.

Ash and I are friends. I hesitate for only a moment before adding: Did you lie about Spencer's uniform?

"He messaged me," I say, eyeing the dots as Josh continues typing. My brain spins, juggling both conversations.

"About what?" Easygoing Ash, friend to the mushrooms, is gone, and the sullen, reluctant Ash of before has come to the phone.

I clear my throat. "He wants to know why we're hanging out."

Ash swears softly. "What did you tell him?"

"That we're friends," I say, eyeing the little bubble indicating Josh has more to say. I don't have to wait long.

> I knew he would bring that up. I swear I didn't have any-
> thing to do with that, Lo. I can't testify to something I didn't
> see.

"Is that it?"

I hear the question underneath. The one that's asking if I'm going to let Josh slide. On the bullying. On the ugly comments in the hallway. On the way he broke my heart and now he's back, rattling the pieces around.

"He says he didn't see anything that night," I say softly. It's not an excuse, but it's an important data point. I need to see the full picture to understand.

He laughs, but it's brittle and wrong. "You honestly believe that he didn't know about it beforehand?"

I sigh, because I don't know anything for certain.

"Well, let me hang up so you can get back to him."

I frown; the movie has another forty minutes to go. "We don't have to do that—"

"No, it's best you devote all your attention to him. Night, Meadows."

He's gone before I can even process my next thought, but then Josh's message pops up and my brain blanks.

> You know me. We were together for two years. You're really going to believe a stranger over me?
> You should stay away from him. I care about you, Lo. I just want you to be safe.

He still cares about me? I *mean* something to him, despite weeks of him ghosting me and a new Mr. Hyde side of him that I was unaware of. *But he's also the Josh from your second letter. The one who cherishes his grandparents and always brought you flowers.*

I sit there, torn between wanting to message him back and wishing for a sign that will tell me what to do.

"Am I still in love with Josh?" I ask my inbox, half agonized, half desperate, and fully confused.

The door flings open and crashes into the wall. My framed National Honor Society certificate flies off and into my dirty laundry basket.

I sigh. "Thanks, Meemaw."

Fifteen

"I wasn't sure what we were going to be doing, but I brought some running shoes just in case."

Ash's car always reminds me of a cave. Not one of those creepy damp places where translucent monsters live and you get dripped on the entire time, but somewhere cozy and safe. Warm seats, the bracing October night kept at bay, and Ash's breathing slow and steady in the dark.

"What did you think we'd be doing?" Ash's voice rumbles over the engine. "Chasing people through the streets and demanding they tell us about their relationships?"

"I don't know, Ash, because you've been extremely tight-lipped about this week's excursion." My tone is flippant, as if it hasn't been noticeable that Ash has been tight-lipped about everything this week.

"I'm just trying to build a little suspense." He matches me, measure for measure, and we both ignore the ravine inching wider between us.

"And *I'm* just trying to be well-prepared." He's lucky I didn't pack a carry-on to account for all possibilities. "My book this past week was about two spies who fell in love. What if you were planning on having us infiltrate a crime ring?"

"A crime ring? In River Haven?"

I lean closer. "I don't like to gossip, but Brian Poole once said you could buy weed through the Chicken Shack's drive-through if you ordered a seven-piece, extra crispy."

He leans in too, and the car defies physics and shrinks a little bit. "I think we'll just let that one slide."

I nod, because the spies from my book weren't busting small-time pot dealers. They were stealing back nuclear codes, kicking ass, yelling (and then kissing), and having an amazing time doing it. I sit up straighter. "A karate class then."

"Nope," he says, cracking a smile.

"We're going to case a bank?"

"Based on the enthusiasm with which you just asked that question, I'm never going into any government buildings with you. My parents travel too much to post my bail within a reasonable time period."

The joke falls flat, memories of his big, empty house looming between us.

"Don't worry, my parents will bust us both out." I want to reach out and touch his arm, but the abrupt way he got off the phone the other night keeps my hands by my sides.

"I thought they wouldn't accept someone like me."

The words slice into me, and I hate the stiff set to his mouth. The fake little smile trying to pretend that it's all a joke, and he doesn't care. I'm not sure what's worse—that Josh believes my parents are that judgmental (they're not), or that he knows they aren't and said it just to hurt Ash.

I haven't even been able to write the third letter, and it's eating me up. Every time I sit down, ready to write about *body,* the words dry up. Not a single thought about Josh's beautiful face or the way his kisses used to light me on fire. All I can think about is that angry voice in the hallway. Him telling me that Spencer wasn't his fault. The way he dropped me like I was nothing, only to turn around and say I still mean something to him.

What do you want, Marlowe?

I keep my voice light. "My parents would love you. Momma would want to talk your ear off about books, and Stu would be thankful that someone else is willing to hear about mushrooms."

He snorts, his fingers gently tapping the wheel to the quiet strains of music filling the pauses between us. "You know, it's not the first time I've heard that about parents?" He looks over briefly. "About me not being an ideal choice?"

"You mean with Brandon or Rebecca's parents?"

He raises an eyebrow, and I realize it's clear how much I've paid attention to his love life.

"Not exactly," he says, letting it slide. "My dad was very similar to Josh when he was younger. Football, prom, court shit." He waves his hand. "President of his frat, and you can probably assume how surprised he was to have a son like me."

"I love surprises," I say, barely loud enough to be heard above the music. I'm lying through my teeth, because surprises are terrible, and I want to know everything at all times. Ash *was* a surprise, though. A good one. An exception to the rule.

I don't say anything more because I'm afraid my response will ruin this. I want every scrap he's willing to share until I have enough clues to piece together the entirety of him.

"Of course, they love me, we just clash," he says, eyes fixed straight ahead. "It's not like I need them around, anyway. I'm more than old enough."

"Need" is a loaded word, but the slope of his mouth sets off alarms that we've dipped our toes into this particular pool long enough for tonight.

"Hold on," I say, unlocking my phone. "Just going to share my location with Odette and Poppy, because it seems like we're going to encounter murderers tonight, and I want to make sure someone finds my body."

"It's laser tag." The words come out sheepish, and I squint at his profile.

"Laser tag?" I repeat, trying out the words and the idea.

"They're shooting stuff in the book," he says, almost defensive. "Plus, it's still fieldwork, because we can observe all the couples."

"The couples at the laser tag?"

"It's BOGO tonight, Marlowe. Plenty of couples show up."

"Wait," I say, swallowing down the laughter that is rising dangerously fast. "Not *only* are we going to laser tag, but we're going to a laser tag place that you are extremely familiar with?"

"I don't know if I would say *extremely*—"

I don't hold back this time, and my delight rings through the car. "How did you know tonight was BOGO?"

"A lucky guess."

"You're on an email list, aren't you?"

He coughs. "I don't know what you're talking about."

"Am I interrupting your regularly scheduled laser tag night?" I laugh as his affronted expression grows.

"I stand by my decision that this is a perfectly acceptable place for fieldwork."

I'm hit with such a jolt of fondness that my stomach aches. "The spy novel was a nice segue."

He turns and grins at me, his lip ring glinting in the darkness. "Wasn't it?"

My insides twist again, and everything feels messy and overwhelming. I don't want to be watching Ash smile at me in a car and immediately thinking about whether he's hot or wondering if he'd be horrified or ambivalent about accidentally starring in a dream I had last night. It was easier when we were strangers carefully and separately celebrating the small wins of our contract. Now we're dancing at harvest festivals, watching mushroom documentaries, and I'm not sure what box to put him in anymore.

Sure, Marlowe. We're friends.

My face burns and I grab for something to squash the tension snapping through this dark, quiet car.

"We need to work on the next letter." The words leave me in a rush, and I stare straight ahead. We've been tiptoeing around the topic of Josh, and Ash has resolutely refused to ask me any more questions about whether or not he's still reaching out. He's *not,* which would be frustrating enough, but it feels like we're just treading water as the semester continues to slip by. We need to get back on track, otherwise what are we even doing here?

What do you want, Marlowe?

I want to scream, *I don't know! I don't know what the right choice is!* But until I do, I am going to keep going down the path I've already committed to.

I see him shift in my periphery, and he finally asks, "Any ideas?"

"No," I admit. Because it's true. A wall has come up and bricked over the connection between my heart and my brain. I remember these snapshots of sweet moments with Josh and it's like watching a movie, like it happened to someone else.

"That's okay," he says, and the lack of judgment feels like a hand in the dark. I can't seem to find the words or moments, and all that's left are snarled feelings and intrusive thoughts.

"Let's talk about your book this week, *Secrets in the City*. What did you like about it?" he asks, breaking through the gloom.

I lean back into the warm leather, grateful for the change in subject. "I liked Agent McGuire. I liked how she moved through the world without hesitation." I look at him, and he's nodding. "I liked that she made the other agent earn her time and her love." I blaze forward, but the devil is in the details, and I don't know what's important. "I liked that there was only one tent when they were running for their lives from the Marino Group." I rush ahead so we don't linger on that part. "I liked the banter, and how they argued so much at first, but it turned into affection and respect."

"I'm glad you liked it, Marlowe." I shiver at my name again.

We pull into the parking lot next to a squat, unassuming building. STATESVILLE LASER TAG blinks across the top in neon lights, and color creeps into the car and washes over us both. "You're right, this looks like a romantic dream."

"You laugh, but wait until you see the inside," he says, getting out of the car.

"The strobe lights? The middle schoolers on first dates?" I step out, following him. "The sexy plastic vests?"

"I'm trying to remember if I liked it more back when you were content to ignore me." He opens the door to a lobby whose dinginess they tried to disguise with neon paint.

I look up. His words are teasing, but I hate the picture they paint. "I never ignored you."

He lifts one dark brow. "We went to the same school for over a year, and you never spoke to me until that day in English." He leans down, his mouth curving. "And then the first time you did, you accused me of trying to slack off."

I'm locked in place, but he's right. I had Josh, and Odette and

Poppy, so I kept my world small. I made no effort to get to know him when he moved here, and that had been my loss.

"I'm sorry." He shrugs, but I poke him in the ribs, hard. "You never spoke to me either."

He laughs, acknowledging the point. "Fine, but I noticed you."

"Well, maybe I noticed you too."

He nods once, his faint smile draining the tension out of me. "Okay, Marlowe, if you say so." He smiles wider at my scowl. "Let's go in."

Black lights, fake graffiti, and bored cashiers greet us inside, and we pay and move through the orientation process fast. We're asked for our player names, and I blurt out "Catherine and Heathcliff" before Ash can say anything. He gives me his exasperated face, so it's worth it.

Our hard plastic vests are locked in place, and I hold my gun awkwardly as he tightens the straps against his chest.

I frown, looking down at my outfit. "I'm going to be a pretty easy target." My white T-shirt lights up the area around us. "Look, I'm glowing."

He tightens his last strap and makes a funny face I can't read. "I know." His smile dips sideways. "Don't worry, Heathcliff, I'll protect you."

I pull myself up to my full, and impressive, five feet eleven inches. "I don't need any help, and why do *I* have to be Heathcliff?"

"Sorry, too late." He grins and shoves me into the maze.

I was right about the middle schoolers; kids half our age (and height) jump out from behind walls and run across our path, and I'm shooting wildly at anything that comes near. Ash backs us into a corner and, at some point, squishes me into the wall, trying to hide my Day-Glo shine from our tiny enemies.

I take a deep breath in, the rough denim of his jacket brushing my cheek. "What do you say we make a stand here, Catherine?"

I feel the rumble of his chest more than I can hear it over the loud house music piped in from all around. "Whatever you say."

I step out from behind him and wince at the embarrassingly high number of hits flashing across my chest. He's doing a little better, but neither one of us is winning any trophies tonight.

"What do you think?" he yells to be heard over the music. "What were the three things you learned from *Secrets in the City*?"

"Hmm," I say, scanning the dark spots of the maze for ambitious players. "I learned that you can stab someone with just about anything if you have a can-do attitude and just believe in yourself."

He nods. "A valid observation."

I continue, encouraged. "I also never considered Belgrade to be one of the most romantic backdrops in the world, but I stand corrected."

He laughs, and I feel fifteen feet taller.

"And lastly . . ." I say, mulling it over.

He leans in, just as a wiry eighth grader jumps out and shoots him square in the chest before running away.

I smile at the thunderous look on his face, and I know if it weren't for me, he would be deep in the maze and running after anything that moved. "The last thing I learned was one of Agent McGuire's favorite lessons."

His brow furrows as the countdown on his chest blinks until he's ready to be shot again.

"The last thing I learned is that you always shoot a man when he's down." If he's not going to allow himself to have fun, I'm going to help him along.

Surprise flickers across his face, but he doesn't register my meaning until my gun comes up between us. The lights flashing across his chest dim, and I fire.

I race into the maze, legs eating up every one of those five seconds before he's back in play. I zig and zag, bursting through groups of kids, and move into the upper level.

My ankles burn as my loafers slide across the floor, and I regret not putting on my sneakers before coming inside. The burn is good, though. This is how I imagine Agent McGuire feels when she's racing through rainy Serbian streets to underground poker games or meatpacking plants. I'm *in* the game this time.

If I were with Josh, I would probably be trailing along after him, helping him by being a lookout, and letting him protect me. I would be on the sidelines, in a place that I carved out for myself. Hobbled by my own hand.

I lean against the wall, wedging myself into a corner, so my beacon of a shirt can't attract any more attention. I'm out of breath, a little sweaty under my collar, and suddenly angrier than I have any right to be.

Can I even blame Josh for this? That I spent two years determined not to make any waves? That it was so easy to go with the flow, and yes, maybe even let someone tell me what the right decision was. What the best thing to order at the steakhouse was, and how *this* day we had to do this, and on *that* day we had to do that. Blah blah blah.

The laughter leaks out, but it's jagged and harsh.

I *let* him make me like this.

I slide down the wall, tucked away in my corner, and my breathing slows.

What do you want, Marlowe?

I know I want to be like Agent McGuire. I want to be in

charge and to make my own crazy plan. I want to be the main character for once.

I want to figure out what to say to Josh. *Body* should have been the easiest letter of all, but any attempt to describe the intimacy I used to crave has dried to dust. Disco cats now contains pages of crossed-out snippets where I can't even *imagine* kissing him anymore.

I get back on my feet and step out from my corner. The words will come back; they have to. I ignore the anxiety shooting down my limbs like electricity, but the heavy beats of the music amplify it with every chord change. I'm scanning left and right, but Ash is in all black, and a lot better prepared for this than I am. I move quietly along the back wall of the upper level, and dart across a dark hallway.

Ash jumps out, his gun raised, but a kid slides in from behind him and shoots us both before he can pull the trigger. He laughs, but the sound dies when he looks at me.

"The words won't come," I say, the words rushing out. "That's the problem. *I'm* the problem."

I'm standing here in a laser tag of all places, and I finally feel it all. I'm simmering with anger and hurt and things I want to rub in Josh's face, but I'm also trying to win him back so we can deal with all of this together. I don't have the slightest clue how to navigate this.

"I'm reading all these books, and they're filling my brain with these passionate declarations, big romantic gestures, and descriptions of kissing that go on for pages, and I've got nothing."

He rolls his eyes. "You could write him three pages about kissing if you wanted to."

"No, I couldn't," I yell, my voice carrying above the beat. The gun hangs limp by my side. "I have writer's block. *Kisser's* block. I tried. There's nothing there. I don't know if I even remember it."

"Come on, Marlowe."

"I'm serious. I don't remember the last time we kissed. I don't remember ever critically thinking about it when it was happening. I didn't catalogue the feelings or sensation. I don't know if I've ever felt the world just melt away like how they're describing. My brain is broken. Maybe *I'm* broken." That old, familiar fear rises up in the darkness.

"There's nothing broken about you."

"Prove it," I say. The words are a plea, dug up deep from the most scared parts of me.

"I am. We're here. We're working on it."

"No, help me prove I can feel it. I *want* to feel it." I step forward, the solution crystallizing. "Kiss me."

He steps back, and it takes him a minute to formulate a response. "I'm *not* going to kiss you."

"Ash, it's not like I have poor hygiene or anything. Ten seconds tops." My brain latches on to the idea like a life raft.

"No." His face is stony, betraying nothing.

"This is fieldwork! Help me make some real-time observations!"

He starts walking away, and I panic.

"Please."

He stops, and I keep talking.

"I don't know if I'm blocked, or angry, or *not built for this,* but I need you to help me answer that. Right now."

He turns, and his eyes look nearly black. They slide over my face, but I don't waver, and I can see the moment he decides.

He drops his gun, and it swings limply by his knees. His chest is rising rapidly with every breath. "I'm not going to kiss you just so you can think of him the entire time."

My watch vibrates, letting me know my heart rate has tripped up into an alarming range. I can hear my pulse roaring in my ears as his words sink in. The ones that suggest his only objection would be me thinking about Josh.

"I won't be thinking about Josh," I say, the words sticking in my throat. "I know who I'm asking."

He takes two careful steps toward me, and I already feel like I've lost control of the situation. "It'll be an experiment of sorts."

He closes the distance between us, and his heat wraps around me. I'm already cataloguing what I need to keep track of. Heads, hands, noses, his chest, my chest, locating lips, tongue. Do I go right or left? Do I start this?

All of my prior confidence abandons me, but I find one last sliver to look up. His expression is unreadable, and his pupils are so blown out I could fall into them and drown. "How do you feel about tongue?" I murmur as he leans down.

"Jesus *Christ*." He looks at the ceiling, his throat bobbing.

"Ash, I'm trying to organize this moment to be as convenient to you as possible."

My brain stutters as he yanks on my vest, and I'm pulled into his personal space. The hard plastic of our vests clacks together, the air is close and warm, and he's approximately three inches from my face. My order of operations and list of romantic-but-poetic adjectives are exhaled along with my last brain cell.

His hands tangle in my hair, and his breath skates across my jaw before the soft press of his lips and the cold bite of his lip ring shove me back into reality.

He *moves,* and I want to hit pause because I'm being swept

along on a current, but also never stop because I *am* built for this.

My back is pressed against the wall, and I briefly slip beyond the laws of physics. Am I still on the ground? Am I still in a laser tag maze? The only things I can keep track of are hands, teeth, and Ash's lips and blinking vest lighting up my world.

The words slip through me like water and when I bite down and swallow the little groan that bubbles out of him, I stop caring.

What do you want, Marlowe?

I don't know. I am too many big feelings, but right now the focus of all that is targeted at the boy panting against my mouth in the dark.

I barely register when he pulls back, but the pressure of his forehead against mine brings me back to the ground. His hands stay buried in the straps of my vest, anchoring me in place.

I'm still on fire. I want to drive to Odette's door and yell, "Fine, Ash is hot, and I hope you're *happy*."

Then I want to drive home and write every single second of this kiss down so I can remember it, reference it, and analyze it.

It helped. I remember the moves, the cadence of it all, but it also wasn't the same.

Josh and I had a well-worn path. A familiar route that we moved along to the inevitable in the back of his truck or his basement game room. It was familiar, it was the same, and I was fine with it, because it made me feel close to someone.

This kiss was like a free fall that gave no hint of the crash ahead. I am wrecked, and I have no idea what to say to the sort-of friend that let you put your tongue in his mouth in the service of helping you win back another guy.

I lean back and paste on a lopsided smile. "Thank you," I say, as if I'm not rattled to my core.

He shakes his head, and I would give all the cash in my possession to read his thoughts.

He nudges me toward the exit, and I keep looking back, hoping for a sign or a hint to let me know that wasn't the worst thing to have ever happened to him. The second time I trip, he grips one of my vest straps and pulls me in closer. When he finally speaks, he's laughing a little.

"You're welcome."

Sixteen

"I read the wildest post ever this weekend," Odette says, leaning against my locker, not a care in the world. "This woman asks this dude to watch her fiddle-leaf fig while she's out of town. It's not the neediest of plants, and they'd been dating for nine months, so she thought it wouldn't be a big ask."

"They require at least weekly watering," Poppy says from my other elbow.

Odette waves her hands. "*Still*. She's not asking for the world, and this dude agrees, but then he ignores all her instructions and murders this plant in cold blood."

Poppy gasps, her reaction enough to keep Odette going. I pull my notebooks out of my locker, trying to focus on not vomiting when I see Ash again in approximately seven minutes.

"I know!" Odette says, swiveling to Poppy. "He kills it, and then when she comes back a month later to its desiccated corpse, she's pissed. She asks him to replace it, because it's an expensive shrub."

"Tree," I say, my underarms getting a little sticky.

"Tree, shrub, plant, whatever. *Anyway,* he refuses because he says it's a used plant, and he's not going to buy her a new one to replace something that's old."

I slam the door and tune back in. "He said what?"

She grins, basking in our undivided attention. "Oh, yes. This man was asking the internet if he really is an asshole for saying she only deserved a used plant at best."

"Well, how old are we talking? Did anybody do the math on the actual depreciation?" Poppy asks.

Odette scoffs. "And what model are we using for that? I would assume, if anything, a plant you've invested time and energy in that's bigger than when you bought it would be worth *more*."

My skin buzzes, and I know I should participate in this conversation, or wait for a transition, but it builds to a fever pitch, and I'm helpless to stop the words from coming out.

"Ash kissed me."

Two heads snap in my direction, and I panic in the spotlight.

"Well, it was my idea. I may have even *insisted* on it."

Odette chokes on her gum. "*Excuse me?*"

"Probably a mutual decision if you're going to be picky. There was at least a consensus at the end there."

"I swear to God, Lo, I will *scream* if you don't start from the top."

Poppy looks as lost as I feel. "Was this a book thing?"

I shrug, ignoring Odette's rapidly reddening face. "Kind of? More of an experiment. Maybe even a pity kiss." My left eye twitches, *Nope, don't like that.* "Let's just call it an attempt to kick-start my memory?"

Poppy nods slowly. "Oh, okay."

Odette explodes, and I struggle to keep up with the movements, hands, and facial expressions. "*Oh, okay*? That's it? Am I the only one listening to this? How about *Oh, okay,* that's a hell of a thing to drop on us five seconds before the first bell. Or even *Oh, okay,* that's a big jump from someone who's supposedly trying to get Josh back."

"I *am* trying to get Josh back!" I say defensively. The words feel wrong on my tongue.

"Or even better: *Oh, okay,* but what does Ash's lip ring taste like?"

Poppy raises her hand. "I would like to change my response. I want to go with that one."

I cover my face and hope the bell inexplicably rings several minutes early.

"Marlowe Meadows, stop hiding behind your hands. We're still standing here, and all you're going to do is clog your pores," Odette says.

I sigh and whisper through my fingers, "It tasted . . . cold. Like the sharp bite of metal with a sting of spearmint gum."

I drop my palms and face the music. Poppy is nodding, but the disappointment in her face has me opening my big mouth again.

"Fine." I roll my eyes. "And the sharper bite of his actual teeth when he shoved me up against the wall."

Poppy's face lights up like a Savannah sunrise, and Odette's shriek echoes off the lockers, down the hall, and probably all the way to Hertford High the next county over.

I grin because I can't help it. It was a stupid request, one that caused no fewer than two sleepless nights, and a very awkward car ride home from laser tag. But in that moment? When his lips moved against mine, and my body remembered absolutely *everything*? I had no regrets.

I tried to reason away the way my fingers curled into his soft cotton shirt, tangling us closer together. The way the house music drowned out everything, and how I felt, and swallowed his groan into my mouth.

I feel prickly all over and shake out my hands. I had no regrets in the moment, but I know I've made things more complicated, and I'm pretty sure normal people don't ask their friends to take one for the team and kiss them.

Odette steps closer, drinking up whatever is broadcasting from my face to the rest of the student body. "*Oh, okay,*" she says softly. "Now this is a development I can get behind."

I shake my head, feeling sick with big feelings. "The third letter is a bit of a struggle. I wanted to be able to describe something less sweet." I clear my throat. "More physical. And I felt too disconnected to find my voice, or the words. Ash was just willing."

"Willing to help you find his tongue," Poppy says.

"These romance novels are a delightful influence on you," Odette adds after a beat.

I laugh, but it feels wrong. Like I'm making fun of the fact that I'm supposed to be in love with Josh, and what I convinced Ash to do in the dark. I don't want any of this to go past these lockers. I don't want anyone thinking this is more than it is.

"Do you think . . ." The words clog in my throat. "Do you think Josh will consider it cheating?" Should I tell him now? Send him a quick text? A little FYI in case I forget it later?

Hey, Josh! Remember when you told me to stay away from Ash? Whoops, I did the exact opposite instead!

My brain assaults me with the memory of a thumb tracing my jaw, and I know I'm not forgetting anything anytime soon.

"I'm not an expert, but I'm pretty sure it's impossible to cheat on someone that dumped you," Poppy says.

"I don't know if that's fair—"

"Incoming." Odette's smile grows and I know exactly who's walking down the hallway.

Poppy clears her throat, her voice too loud to sound natural. "And that's how we decided on our *Cyrano* presentation."

Odette and I nod along, and I can feel Ash looming over my right shoulder. I shake off the urge to lean back and see what he does. Should I get my hormone levels checked? Or my frontal lobe? Maybe I was dropped on my head as a baby and the area in charge of impulse control is damaged.

"What are you doing for the presentation?" Ash asks, like it's a normal Monday and we're all normal people who don't possess *many* adjectives about how each other taste.

"Well," Poppy says, staring at him a little too long. "We're going to present a wood carving of Cyrano's death scene. I'm writing the paper, Billy's doing the carving, and we haven't had to speak since that first day."

"Sounds ideal," Odette mumbles.

Ash looks down at me, worrying his lip ring with his teeth. "We really need to work on our project."

"But there are so many other books and mushroom documentaries."

His crooked smile punches me in the stomach. "And don't forget laser tag."

My face flames, and I don't respond until I make myself name three things I love about Josh. *He challenged me by taking me to do things I wouldn't normally do*. I'm now a girl who knows about football rules. *His easy confidence and the way that confidence spilled over into me*. I try to superimpose nights with Josh in the backseat of his truck over that moment in the laser tag maze. *The way he introduced me to my body*. Josh was my first kiss. My first everything, and you don't just get over that or replace it with something just because it's shiny and new.

"Yeah, I've heard some good things about this laser tag," Odette says, her smile bland, and I make a mental note to murder her later.

I take a step to the side to give myself a little more space. That kiss was an anomaly. It was a one-off experiment, and I dislike the way it erased all the normal boundaries between us. Like I could trip into his personal space, and the chances of us making out against the lockers are exponentially higher because it's already happened. I turn toward him, my words barreling over Odette's. "We can try to figure out some of the project now?"

He nods, nudging me toward the doorway. We take our seats, me settling into the space next to him as if it were the most normal thing in the world.

We work through a writing prompt based on Richard Wright's *Native Son,* and then while the class shuffles around into groups, he opens his laptop and slides a blank Word document over to me.

"Okay, we're doing this." He rubs his hands together. "*Wuthering Heights* time."

"Or we can talk about this week's book assignment? *One for the Money?*"

"No. Behave."

"Ash, you can't assign me a math book, and then get mad when I read it early."

"You're done? It's only Monday!"

"You're right, I need to go to Three Little Words tomorrow to pick up something else."

"I've created a monster." He pulls his hair up out of his face. "And it's not a math book."

"Sophie is a genius at statistics and applies game theory and some light card counting to win a national poker championship." I wave my hands around. "Math."

He sighs. "You know what else is a romance? *Wuthering Heights.*"

"Really?" I'm close to the end, but I don't see any hope for a happy ending in sight.

"Nope, but we're going to work on it anyway." He slides the computer closer to me, and I give in.

"Fine, but I'm going to hope for the best. Maybe Brontë sprinkles in some light necromancy and they all get to ride off happily into the creepy moors."

He hums, the sound noncommittal, but it vibrates down to my bones. "You do that. In the meantime, it's toxic-love time. What do we want to highlight?"

I feel a little lost, like I frequently do in this class, and around him, but I want to pull my weight. "I'm not sure."

"Give it a go, Marlowe. No wrong answers."

I find more confidence in the easy silence. "We can highlight how this is the only book where I'm going to advocate for the blond love interest."

"Okay, maybe there's one wrong answer." He looks up from his laptop, his smug face knocking me flat. "You like dark hair, huh?"

I briefly calculate the chances of spontaneous human combustion and barrel forward. "We want to make Heathcliff the romantic hero, because he's moody and wild, and it's thrilling to think of a love that all-consuming." He leans forward. "But it's not about love in the end, is it? It's about . . ." I grasp for the word, just outside my reach.

"Possession," he finishes quietly. "Power. Both Catherine and Heathcliff spent so much time on power struggles and mind games that they missed the opportunity to love each other or anybody else."

"Yes." I nod, his face closer than I remember. "You're good at this, you know."

He leans back, clearing his throat. "I've written a bunch of papers."

"So have I, but you're extra good at this." If I didn't know better, I would think he was embarrassed. "I haven't asked before. What are you planning to do with your life?"

"The same as everyone else. Rock band on the weekend, and a little card counting during the week to supplement my income."

"Oh, sure, the usual." I pull his laptop toward me and start a list of Heathcliff's most toxic moments. "What's our fieldwork going to be this week? Are we going to count cards in a casino, and then go on a shopping spree with our winnings?"

"I really feel like *One for the Money* should have made it more clear to you that card counting is illegal. I wouldn't even trust you at a bingo hall."

"You shouldn't, I'm ruthless. I have my own dauber and am not unknown to the Wednesday night group at the Methodist on Main."

His lip twitches. "Why am I not surprised?"

The bell jangles—the hour disappearing in an instant. I hurry to pull my things together, and he waits by my chair.

"I've been thinking. Maybe we can combine the fieldwork and the band practice this weekend."

I look up from arranging my three separate pencil cases in my backpack. "Combine them?" I can hear the hurt in my voice. I don't know if it's from concern that we won't do as much work as we would normally do, or me worried that I'm eating up too much of his time and he's trying to get rid of me.

He tilts his head. "Unwrinkle your forehead, Meadows. This is a good thing. Hazel's having a birthday party. The band is going to play, and a party is the perfect place for fieldwork."

"Perfect, we're really making progress. I even finished the

third letter last night." The words fall out, and I can feel them re-draw some of the boundaries between us. I watch his face, need-ing the reminder.

"Right." His shifts the bag on his shoulder. "And how did the ode to Josh's body go?"

"So great," I say, easy and breezy. It wasn't, though. It felt too sticky and wrong to reference any of the things Ash's kiss inspired in a letter I was going to send to someone else. Even picking up a pen felt like a betrayal.

"I'm so glad to hear that." We're having a contest on who can maintain the blandest smile the longest—he's winning.

In the end, I'd only managed one sentence. I wrote *you're beautiful in a way that made it easier to ignore more than I should have*, and sealed it this morning.

I give Ash another tight smile, and move down the hallway to physics. I pause briefly, slipping the third letter into the slots of Josh's locker as I move past in the crowd. A sleight of hand that would make *One for the Money* proud.

It was the only way I could be truthful, because every scorch-ing, passionate word that's rattling around in my brain now has Ash's name tattooed on it. I squeeze my eyes tight, hoping I can reboot my entire system.

Josh *is* beautiful. Of course he is. You only have to look at him to see the truth in that. And maybe I was willfully blind, because I spent two entire years by his side and thought I knew every-thing about him. I romanticized our love story, and his sweet gestures, and maybe he was right when he questioned if I really loved him. Maybe I didn't know him at all.

Seventeen

I zip past side roads that I know as well as the lines on my own palms and pull out onto Main Street. The cobblestones, towering live oaks, magnolias, and crepe myrtles are big sellers on the small-southern-town postcards we sell to tourists traipsing in from Atlanta. In October, once most of the greenery and life has withered away, they're less of a draw.

Not to me, though. The naked limbs stretch up to an overcast sky, and it feels like the world is being honest for once. *Here I am. No embellishments*.

Blue shifts in the seat next to me; no matter how much I try to lint-roll it, or vacuum, or sanitize, my passenger seat has a permanent layer of glitter and vanilla body spray. She slouches down farther, and I picture the plastic flakes digging deeper and deeper into the fabric.

"You're going the wrong way," Blue says as we turn onto West Church.

"No, I'm not." I roll my eyes so hard I almost sideswipe old

Mr. Martin's Cadillac, which is only held together with the power of optimism and Jesus.

"I'm too tired for any errands."

"Then you can wait in the car." I pull up in front of Three Little Words and its very new and very prominent window display. A life-sized cutout of Elphaba from *Wicked* glares out on River Haven, dusty-pink paper flowers unfurling around her like a throne. Elphaba stands on a matching cobblestone road of yellow books, and my fingers itch to text Ash. To prod him about his flower-folding skills. To ask him how long it took to lay the patchwork book floor. I want to gobble up his inevitable exasperated response, but that charged conversation we had after class has my stomach still in knots. The placid curve of his lips had yelled *lie* as I smiled and blustered, keeping us firmly on this course. We're playing chicken and watching to see who swerves first.

I stomp down the feeling that things are shifting under my feet and reach for the door handle.

"A bookstore isn't urgent. You can do that after you take me home."

You're older. Be better. I dutifully recite Stu's mantra from my childhood and let the door fall closed behind me. "Sounds like you prefer to wait in the car."

The passenger side opens before I even reach the front door, and I hold it for her with much more patience than I naturally possess.

She's pricklier than she used to be as she continues her campaign to be noticed at school, and I'm finding it harder to *be* better. She wants the friends, the homecoming crowns, the adoration, and she wants it bad enough to smile at the boy who broke my heart and pretend that I'm a minor detail.

A rush of warmth and dopamine floods me as I step inside. Stacks and stacks of books full of new characters, meet-cutes, and kisses glitter from every surface. I feel desperate and greedy; I want to own them all. Hoard them all. I want to immerse myself in a Scrooge McDuck vault of paperbacks until I'm less Marlowe and more like the main character of somebody else's life.

Sloane's grin widens when they see me, and the collar of their Hawaiian shirt desperately fights against gravity as a dozen enamel pins glitter around their neck. "What did I do to get so lucky as to have Marlowe Meadows walk into my humble establishment on a *Monday*?"

I grin back, because how could I not? "I ran out of books."

They gasp, and I relax a fraction. There's no fifty questions about where Ash is or why he isn't recommending my next book. And it's not like I don't *want* to ask him. I've typed out and deleted a dozen messages, but lines feel a little too fluid right now, so I'm playing it safe. I'm losing at chicken.

"And who do you have here with you?" they ask, turning to Blue. "I'm Sloane."

"I'm hungry," Blue mumbles.

I snap a look in her direction that was copy-and-pasted from every female ancestor in our bloodline. Momma and Meemaw would have stood up and clapped, and I feel briefly possessed by my great-aunt Eula.

Blue stands up straight and clears her throat. "I'm Blue."

I turn back to Sloane, my smile fixed in place. "Bluebell, my little sister." I find a half-smooshed energy bar in my bag and thrust it in her direction.

"Well, I'm glad you're here. Both of you," they say, correcting themselves, and smiling at Blue with a lot more grace than she deserves. "Is there a specific book you came in for?"

Blue shoves the entire bar in her mouth, and I wince through the smack and smell of peanut butter. Her chewing gets louder, undoubtedly for my benefit, and I power through the noise to focus on my question.

Misophonia. When someone is hypersensitive to ambient noise, especially chewing. We've come a long way from me tearfully yelling that I couldn't let Blue sleep in my room because the sound of her breathing had crawled into my ears and wouldn't let go.

She clears her throat again, the sensation of food wrapping around me.

We've come far, but not completely beyond.

I step up to the counter. "I was hoping you'd help me pick something out?" I feel shy, like my cannonball into the romance pool has become weirdly personal.

Sloane does a little shoulder shimmy. "I know Ash has been your tour guide so far, but I'm so selfishly excited to help."

"Who's Ash?" Blue asks, stepping closer.

I don't want to get into it, but my mouth is unable to say *nobody* in the place that he works, in front of his boss, and in the company of all the magic he's given me access to.

I settle for a half-truth. "He's a bookseller." Sloane looks as if they're waiting for me to add more, so I compromise. "Here."

Six months ago, I might have told her more. I might have shown her a picture from NMTM's website and told her about how his singing makes my hands sweat. How he's considerate, and quietly hilarious.

Blue's teeth scrape a smear of energy bar off her lip, a little divot appearing between her eyebrows. "Isn't he that mean kid from school?"

"I don't think 'mean' is really—"

"He told Jeremy Johnson that nobody cared about his fantasy football team."

I wait for more, but that was apparently the extent of his crimes. "Do you have any evidence that anybody *does* care about Jeremy Johnson's fantasy football team?" I ignore the choke from Sloane. "Any signed affidavits we can reference? If not, we'll just have to consider the matter between them."

Blue rolls her eyes and picks up a stack positioned next to the cash register. The display promises paranormal romances to heat up your Halloween, and I slide out a book with a purple cover that promises "A wicked good time!" Two women in pointy hats embrace on the front, and the back says that "Adelaide Conners can turn a person into a toad, but can she let Sabine Rothschild transform her heart?" I'm willing to bet yes, and I pull it over to the side into a pile I am designating "keep."

Blue flips over a book with a shirtless vampire on it. "So, what? These books are all about sex?"

"No," Sloane and I say in unison.

"But sometimes, yes," they clarify, without a hint of reproach.

Blue narrows her eyes. "What's up with the sudden interest in romance? You'd rather replace Josh with fake book boyfriends instead of the real thing?"

The accusation crawls under my skin like a splinter and lodges there. I want to yell that not everything is about boyfriends, but she's not wrong that my motivations were not as pure as I wanted them to be. It wasn't about Josh, but it had started with Josh. And here I am, still trying to patch myself together into something lovable with the words and stories of characters that don't exist.

"It's not about book boyfriends," I say, unclenching my jaw. "These are stories I enjoy." I wave my hand around. "I enjoy this store, and Sloane, and *yes,* Ash."

Her chin juts out. "I've heard some things about him." She steps closer, as if it's an illicit secret. "And about you and him. You shouldn't be spending time with people like that."

Sloane clears their throat and moves out from behind the counter to tidy up a nearby display.

My face flushes, and I pitch my voice low. "People like what?" The words whip out, tight as a bowstring, but she doesn't heed the warning.

"Like some freak."

I hear Josh's ugly words come out of her mouth, and I want to throttle them both. I want to lock her in her bedroom and not let her leave until her frontal lobe develops more. She has all these gifts, and I'm choked by the fear she's going to waste them trying to make herself small and mean. Something more palatable for the masses.

"You say that like you know anything about him."

She rolls her eyes. "I don't have to—"

"Careful, Bluebell."

She tries to bluster her way out of it. "Just stop being dumb and give Josh a call."

I'm tired, and it goes beyond our usual snapping and martyred patience. Blue gets to skip through life with a brain that doesn't actively sabotage her. She gets to navigate everything from friendships to family to ordering coffee at an unknown café where she wouldn't once worry if she was going to misunderstand the ordering protocol.

"And what am I supposed to do, Blue?" My tone is sharp, but we aren't being gentle with each other today. "Handcuff Josh to the front porch until he wants me again? Apologize to the boy I loved, who told me I was *bad* at it, and wait patiently for him to hopefully want me again?"

She steps back as if she's been slapped, but she's been careless with her words, and I'm not going to hold back now.

"Or should I try to be proactive, like always?" I wave my hand at the tables of books next to me. "Find a way to meet the world halfway, and maybe fix what's broken?"

She's rooted in place. Blue, who has never once thought that she wasn't enough, looks so flummoxed at the idea that other people might have a different outlook.

I smile over at Sloane, frozen at a werewolf-romance display. Their expression is a little too raw for me to hold, but I breathe deeply until my voice is steady. I hold up the sapphic witch book. "Have you heard good things about this one?"

"I think that's a great choice, Marlowe," they say, so kindly that it's like a different sort of knife twisting in my gut. They turn to Blue. "What books do you like?"

Blue shrugs, her voice smaller than before. "I don't really read."

"That's okay. Are there any types of stories or hobbies you're interested in?"

She shrugs again. "I don't know. I guess I like cheerleading."

Sloane beams and says, "I have just the thing," with enough mystery that Blue follows them to the far side of the store.

I take the moment to myself. It's not quite a meltdown, but I feel as lost as I did when Josh first ripped me off like a Band-Aid. The letters haven't miraculously fixed this, or me, and I've been leaning on Ash a little too much. This is a problem that has a solution, *every problem does,* but I don't have the right equation, or all the data points, or a single brain cell that isn't already overheated by working on this for almost three months.

Sloane comes back, but Blue is still crouched down, pawing at slim volumes on a bottom shelf.

"What's got her so interested?" I smile, cheeks tight, trying to sweep away the embarrassment. "A book on why ducks aren't good indoor pets?"

"I don't think we need an entire book to realize *that,*" Sloane says, leaning across the counter. "But I was able to offer her some zombie cheerleader graphic novels."

"A romance?" I pivot to see Blue sitting cross-legged, poring over open pages.

"Oh yeah, they're eating brains, but two of the cheerleaders have a surprisingly sweet love arc."

The snort wriggles out of me, and Sloane clears their throat. *Here it comes.*

"I didn't realize what was at the core of your interest in romance."

I shove my normal human face firmly in place. "I may have had some unusual motivation to start, but I'm enjoying them for very selfish reasons now."

Sloane's lips tighten a little. "I'm so glad to hear that. I just feel like I have to speak my piece here. I know it's none of my business, but somebody has to say it."

I brace for impact.

"Nobody is inherently *bad* at love. Sure, people have different communication styles and love languages, and we might not all be on the same page at all times. Those challenges can require work, sometimes professional work, but your instincts aren't *wrong* just because they're not *his* instincts. And anybody who would make you think or feel that way is not someone worth fighting for."

I squeeze my eyes tight, the meltdown edging closer, and all the coefficients still dancing outside my reach. Maybe they're right. God, am I *Isabella Linton*? Am I so defiantly determined to stick to this path and this boy that I will ignore anything and everything just to get back into his arms?

I open watery eyes, but I'm at my limit. "Thank you, truly, but I think this will be all for me today. Blue?" I call, trying to sound as unbothered as I can.

Blue shuffles up to the counter, two thin books in hand. "Can you get these for me? There's brains, and kissing, but they also go to Nationals."

I slide the books toward Sloane and swipe my card without any more eye contact. They bag up our purchases, and I'm leading Blue out the door before anything more can be said.

I put the Volvo in reverse and inch down the street to home.

We pull up to the curb, and she's out of the car and up the porch stairs before I even have a moment to turn it all over in my brain.

I'm reaching for the phone, and when his voice fills the car, the tension starts to bleed out of me.

"Hey, Dad."

"There's my girl." Ten years in Colorado has done nothing to dull the smooth current of his southern accent. "I was just thinking about you."

"Was dating hard for you?" I don't bother with a segue, but neither does he.

I hear the faint sound of chewing, probably graham crackers he swiped from the doctors' lounge. "I think it's hard for everyone, darlin'."

"You know what I mean. For *us*."

"Virgos?"

"*Dad*." I drag the word into three syllables.

"Why don't you tell me what this is about, kiddo?"

I lean back against the headrest. I want to ask him about Momma, and where it all went wrong. If things broke down because he didn't try hard enough or didn't act a certain way. All I know is that people have spent a lifetime telling me I'm just like Dad with one breath and whispering about how the divorce was all his fault with the next. The fear that I'm too broken, too awkward, too autistic to love rears its head, smothering me.

"I don't think I'm very good at it."

"Is this about that Jason kid?" he asks after a pause.

I don't bother to correct him, because he knows Josh's name. He's met him over a few holidays, and I thought Josh's charisma and med school plans would have them getting along like a house on fire. Instead, he looked at me after Josh left and said, "Maybe he grows on you."

"I thought you two had broken up?" he continues, when I let the silence drag out a little too long.

"We have, but I'm a Meadows, and we're not quitters."

He coughs, and I don't think it's the graham cracker. "Baby girl, let me tell you something from experience. Things just don't work out sometimes, and that's okay. It's not always a matter of effort or determination but recognizing that changes happen, and it can be for the best."

"You hate change," I say, my voice sullen.

His laughter rings down the phone. "Now, I'm not going to deny I hate it when my favorite restaurant changes their menu, or when my cases get shuffled around after I've already prepared myself for a certain kind of day, but there's nothing wrong with trying something new." His voice lowers. "Or letting something go."

"Who are you? What has Denver done to you?"

He laughs again, and the block of ice in my chest thaws a little.

"Only good things, baby girl. Now, back to your previous question, I think your old man is pretty good at dating."

"Really?" I don't bother to hide my disbelief. I want to ask about Momma, but he's laughing and enjoying his graham crackers, and it feels wrong to ruin his day just because mine has sucked.

Someone on an intercom drowns out his reply.

"My next case is ready for me, sweetheart. Talk soon?"

"Sure," I say, but he's already gone. I kill the engine and sit long enough for a chill to seep into the car.

Eighteen

My fight with Blue hangs heavy over us at dinner that night, poisoning every course. The polite clatter of silverware against porcelain fills the silence, and I push green beans around with my fork until I can finally escape to my room.

"I saw Grandpa today," Momma says, valiantly trying to carry the conversation. "I'll have y'all know that they've made a new CSI—I think it's in Montana or one of those square states, and I'm now aware of every single case during the first season."

I look up, throwing her a bone. "Montana? Is it all horse-smuggling rings, and oil-millionaire murders?" I grasp for another option. "What's in Montana, again?"

Momma shrugs. "I think they're banking on none of us really knowing."

"Fancy that." Blue smiles between bites of mashed potatoes. "We've found something that Marlowe doesn't know."

"I don't know why you're being so nasty today," I retort.

"*You're* being nasty." She scowls, a smear of potato collecting in the corner of her mouth.

"Girls," Momma warns, eyes narrowing between us both. "What is going on with you two tonight?"

I smile back, a blank slate. "Nothing."

Stu coughs, trying to resuscitate the conversation. "Anyone have any fun plans this weekend?"

Blue sits up straighter. "I was hoping to go to Becca Hightower's cabin in the mountain this weekend. We're going to bake, do puzzles, hike, and—"

"—and hang out with boys," I finish for her.

Her face purples and she chokes on a green bean.

"Is that true?" Stu asks. "Are her parents going to be there?"

"Yes," she says quickly. Her expression is thunderous, and she tells me with her eyebrows that I better shut my mouth.

"Nope," I say blandly, cutting another piece of chicken.

"You think you're so smart," she hisses across the table. "You think you know everything, but you *don't,* and you just want to make everyone as miserable as you are."

I'm fully aware that snitches get stitches, and the venom in her voice means that she thinks I ratted her out over jealousy and not concern. *You're older. Be better.* I'm so tired of this anger settling between us, and I'm starting to worry it's going to become permanent.

"I went to this party last year," I say slowly, keeping my gaze steady on hers. "I know what goes on there, and that there wasn't a single parent or rule to be found." I blush a little, turning to Momma and Stu. "You can ground me if you like, and I should have called when I saw how bad it could get, but I spent most of the weekend taking care of more than one person who was flirting with alcohol poisoning."

I grimace, turning back to Blue. "You want to talk miserable? Try spending the weekend in rubber gloves. I'm not your enemy here. That cabin is bad news, and I'm always going to try to protect you."

"I don't need your protection," she grinds out. Her face is flushed, and she refuses to look at me. "May I be excused?"

"No," Stu says, looking between the two of us. "Y'all are on kitchen cleanup until you can work out whatever this hatefulness is between you both." He pushes his plate toward Blue. "You should listen to your sister; she has a good head on her shoulders."

I sigh, leaning forward and collecting his plate and mine. He gives me an encouraging nod, but he's already made it ten times worse.

We barely make it through the door to the kitchen before she lets loose.

"You can't even help yourself, can you? You always have to be so smart, and so perfect, and you can't leave *anything* for me." She dumps her plates in the sink and spins around, her cheeks wet.

I'm stunned. I'm so far from perfect, it's a joke. In fact, I narrow my eyes at her, looking for the irony. The insult hidden beneath. "Are you making fun of me?"

"What?" Her voice wavers, and I catch her so off guard, she forgets to yell.

"There is not a single thing about me that's perfect," I say flatly. My brain, my relationships, my mismatched-size feet, or anything in between.

"Poor Marlowe," she says, finding her second wind. "Perfect grades, perfect skin, perfect fancy college that you're going to get into and leave all of us behind. Boo-hoo."

"You want to talk about perfect?" I meet her volume, our angry words ricocheting across cabinets. "You're Momma 2.0! How am I supposed to compete with *that*? They never even bothered to ask if I wanted to do pageants or equestrian camp."

I absolutely did not, I think I'm allergic to hairspray, and horses will literally bite you in the face, but that's beside the point. "You're the perfect daughter she always wanted; one *exactly* like her. You're probably going to be prom queen, and I can't believe you have the balls to pretend you're jealous about anything that I have."

I'm angry, and hurt, and my breath is so rapid and shallow I feel lightheaded. I wait for the next volley of abuse from her side of the island, but she deflates. And when she starts to cry in earnest, I feel my own eyes start to well.

"What's wrong?" My voice catches. "Bluebell?"

She shakes her head, and slides to the floor, and it takes me about ten seconds to join her on the black-and-white marble.

"Hey," I say, softly. "Talk to me."

"I don't even *care* about pageants," she wails.

I scoot closer, massively out of my depth. "Okay? That's fine."

She hiccups. "I don't even know if I want to cheer anymore." She swipes at blotchy cheeks and refuses to look at me. "What if I want to play soccer?"

I have whiplash from this entire conversation, but I manage another "Okay?" I brave the likely rejection and wrap an arm around her. "So quit the squad and play soccer. I promise I'll come to your games."

She pulls in a ragged breath. "And tell Momma that I want to quit? She was *captain* of the squad."

I feel a few tears drop against my arm and pull her closer. I'm not a smart girl. If I were smart, I would have seen my baby sister getting smothered under all these expectations I'd so readily refused to carry. These characteristics and talents that I thought made her a perfect River Haven girl, and all the while a small part of me had resented her for it and never bothered to ask if she even *liked* it.

"Momma would understand," I say, firmly. "She just wants you to be happy."

"I'm not good at anything else, though." She sniffs, rubbing her face on her sleeve. "My grades are average, and nobody's going to care if I'm just *me*."

That pitiful "*me*" almost sends me over the edge, but I squeeze her until she looks up at me. "I'm sorry," I say, voice wobbling. "I should have checked in with you more. I thought all of this was effortless to you, and that you loved it." I shake my head. "You're so talented and strong, it's hard to remember sometimes that you're just fourteen."

"Almost fifteen," she says, narrowing her eyes. Her bottom lip starts to wobble again. "*And* I think I'm failing geometry."

"That's an easy fix," I say, pulling her to her feet. "I'll tutor you. You're going to pass geometry, you're going to find a hobby that makes you happy, and *you* are enough without any of these other clubs or medals or trophies."

"Easy for you to say." She looks down, her sock tracing the edge of the tiles. "I'm sorry too, about Josh. All my friends want to hang out with his group, and I didn't think you would care." She finally meets my gaze. "I promise they're not talking bad about you or anything, you know I would tell you. It's just that I couldn't really choose—"

I wave her off. "I don't care about that. I don't want my breakup to force you into anything, I just want you to be careful. When he dumped me, every single one of those people just went back to pretending I didn't exist. I want you to ask yourself if that's the type of friends you want. If those are the type of people you want to surround yourself with."

She nods, looking uncertain for the first time, and I can't help remembering how easily she used the word "freak" only hours before. How some, or all, of those people stepped on Spencer so easily, and his only crime was being good at something he loved.

"I want you to promise me that if you ever see something that feels wrong to you, that you won't sit on the sidelines and pretend it's not happening. That you will say something or do something."

I don't expect a blood oath, or her to really listen to my warning, but when she finally speaks, I believe her. She doesn't blink, and slips her sticky hand into mine. "I promise, Marlowe."

Nineteen

Odette, Poppy, and I stand outside a massive brick house nestled deep in a polished neighborhood with old oaks, carefully manicured lawns, and signs urging us to drive like our children live here.

"I can't believe I was worried we'd have trouble finding it," I say. The house in front of us is doing its very best to mimic a Spirit Halloween.

"Aren't they Catholic?" Poppy asks as a zombie butler draped in tattered rags shrieks at us.

"Sure, but isn't that the most dramatic of all the Christian flavors?" Odette straightens her black turtleneck and knocks on the door.

"Is it?" Poppy asks. She opens an umbrella with dangling luminescent strands glued to the edges. "Aren't there some that speak in tongues?"

"A fair point," I say, hiding my smile as Odette checks her hair in the reflection of the door. Strobe lights on the lawn wash dancing black cats over us and I sigh. "Is it too late to remind y'all that I don't love Halloween, or costumes, or things randomly shrieking at me?"

The door swings open, and "Monster Mash" leaks out onto the stoop. Hazel steps out in ripped fishnets and a red leather romper, looking every inch a rock star.

"Probably a little late," Poppy murmurs.

Hazel grins, the slash of black lipstick stretching wide, as she obliterates any space between her and Odette. "Let me guess— Steve Jobs?"

"I even exerted some effort. Would you believe I didn't own a black turtleneck?" Odette's fingers trace the silver spiked cuff on Hazel's wrist.

Poppy meets my eyes, and one of her eyebrows notches upward.

"Are you going to go around firing people?" Hazel asks, her voice teasing.

"Absolutely, especially if they're not in costume. Rules are rules."

Then Hazel's pulling her inside, and her smile is warm enough to include us too.

I relax a fraction, but I'm wearing synthetic material that might burst into flames if I get too close to any real heat source, and the lace eroding the skin on my neck is making it impossible to focus on any conversation.

Not that many people are going to be trying to talk to me, I remind myself. This is Hazel's birthday—her friends, her turf— and there are very few familiar faces in her foyer.

I walk around a lumberjack and a sexy dogwalker, gently pulling one of Poppy's tentacles after me. We lose Odette about three steps in as Hazel sets about introducing her to everyone she knows. We push past the crowd, and don't stop until we collapse on the couch in a dark corner of the living room.

I wiggle in place, yanking on the collar of my dress again.

"Stop fussing," Poppy says, her lip twitching. "The dress is very pretty."

I roll my eyes, because it's easy for her to say while she's sitting there in black overalls, but the deep bloodred color of my dress and its Empire waist *did* make me feel like a Victorian heroine for a moment. One with the guts to step into a ballroom—or a South Georgia rec room—full of strangers and dare them not to take her seriously.

"Clothes have power," Momma always used to say with a secret smile, when me and Blue would pile into her bedroom and watch her get ready to go out. She'd curl her hair and drape herself in satin and silks while we'd stick footie pajamas into heels too big for us. The polyester material wrapped around me is not quite the same thing, but the full skirt has me standing up a little bit straighter.

"And you are an extremely accurate jellyfish," I tell Poppy, brushing the curling silver ribbons that spill over her shoulders. "These are very pretty tentacles."

"Oral arms, Lo, be serious."

The laugh is startled out of me, and the Velcro breakaway dress is momentarily forgotten. "Not all of us are jellyfish experts, especially when there are a million other things to read about."

"Like mushrooms?"

"Correct." I look around, squinting in the dim light. *I can't even imagine what costume Ash would pick.*

"Or that really spicy scene in the fourth Lady Jessica book? The one with Lord Arlo?"

My saliva goes down the wrong pipe. "That beats the jelly-fish."

She twirls the umbrella, silver slivers of material catching in the ropes of orange twinkle lights taped across the ceiling and the mantel next to us.

"I don't know, the high-stakes world of jellyfish is extremely sexy. I could tell you a little bit about them if you like?" She shrugs, as if she's not dying to sit me down and give me the entire TED talk.

"Or you could volunteer an analysis on the historical accuracy and legality of what Arlo and Vanessa get up to in that chapter."

"Don't tempt me." She closes the umbrella with a snap. "How are the little monsters doing? Is engagement continuing to grow on the band's platforms?"

"Get this." I lean closer as the first bars of "Li'l Red Riding Hood" play overhead. "They've booked three gigs so far. *Paying* ones, and I'm seeing more and more traffic on their website every day."

"Ash must be thrilled he agreed to help you. He gets to see his band blow up, and you get . . ."

"Josh." His name hits me like a brick, and I produce a shaky smile. "Sure."

What do you want, Marlowe?

I see Ash coming a mile away, and it's both relief and execution. He fills the doorway—looming over knights, Red Riding Hoods, and one jarringly sexy Care Bear. He's just *himself*. Same black jeans, boots, and black long-sleeved shirt shoved up over elbows. His head swivels, as if he's looking for someone, and I shiver at the smile that tugs on his lips when he finds me in the corner and slips through the crowd toward us.

"Great look, Poppy, you should stick with this," he says.

I'm grateful for the moment to pull myself together. The effort it's taking to pretend that everything is normal has drained me. Sure, we're still texting back and forth as we finish outlining our paper. I even sent him a breakdown on *Hexes and Happily-Ever-Afters,* thrilled to be able to recommend a book to him for once. But I can't shake the sense that space continues to creep in, inch by inch, and letter by letter.

"Jellyfish eat and poop out of the same orifice," she replies with a smile.

I blink and she shrugs.

"High-stakes, right?"

"You're right, I was warned," I say, eyes skating over Ash, looking for a sign that he didn't just roll out of bed, throw on some clothes, and accidentally attend a Halloween party. He lets me look my fill, his attention heavy as hands on my shoulders. "Very disappointing," I say eventually. "Hazel's going to have you bounced from the party for not wearing a costume."

He rolls his eyes, all-suffering, before peeling back his lips to reveal pointed teeth.

"A vampire? You're just barely cosplaying yourself."

"As opposed to Lady Jessica in the flesh?" He steps back to better see the dress.

I stand up, moving a step closer to him, and stuff my hands in the pockets. "It's red, and it swishes when I walk."

"Good to know." The tiny points of his fangs peek out from his lips.

Poppy leans in and Ash jerks back before an umbrella prong skewers him in the eyeball. "Jellyfish have no brain or heart." Her voice is low and conspiratorial.

"Relatable." Ash clears his throat, and nods toward the kitchen. "I feel obligated to warn you that if you wanted one of the cupcakes Hazel made, there's only three left. She *will* ask you if you tried one."

That doesn't mean anything, he's probably asking everyone. I try to be sensible, but I can't help feeling special. "I'd better grab one then, wouldn't want to disappoint her."

"They have candy fingers sticking out of them," he says, smiling down on me.

"I want one less so now, but am still willing to consider it," I say as Poppy wrinkles her nose.

"I'll grab them," he says quickly. He points at Poppy, shuffling back toward the door, until she nods.

"Whether or not I'm going to be able to eat this is still up in the air," she says.

I flop back down next to her. "That was really nice of him." *Too nice? Normal friend nice?* I sigh, sinking deeper into the cushions. This wasn't one of the caveats of the contract: fill the hole in your heart and your brain (that apparently jellyfish don't have to worry about) with a new guy who will sing you songs over the phone and bring you cupcakes until you're completely turned around.

My phone meows loudly, and Poppy's head whips toward me, her eyes wide.

I scramble for my dress pocket, and Poppy leans in.

"*What are you up to tonight?*" she reads.

I slump back. *Just like that?* Josh has decided we're casually texting back and forth again and get to check in like everything's regular-degular? *He's* the one who wants to know what *I'm* up to tonight?

"Are you going to respond?" Poppy pulls her legs up onto the couch and under her.

I *shouldn't,* but he's opened a door, and curiosity is one of my

219 THE CALCULATION OF YOU AND ME » 219

fatal flaws. I would always rather know, even if the knowing kills the cat, me, and burns everything else to the ground.

At a party, I type back, like it's the most natural thing in the world. Look at me, being social without you.

The dots are immediate. Where? With who?

You wouldn't know it, I text back with massive satisfaction. With Odette and Poppy.

It feels a little deceitful. Ash invited me, and is off fighting for cupcakes on my behalf, even if I *did* come with the girls. I should have added his name on the end there, but I wanted Josh to focus on me. On *why* he's texting me, instead of pivoting to tell me all the reasons I shouldn't hang out with Ash.

The dots appear slower this time.

"*Cool have fun,*" I read to Poppy, and look up. "That's it?"

She shrugs. "Lo, we've proven beyond a shadow of a doubt that none of us have any idea what Josh is thinking."

Her grin returns as Ash fills the doorway again, cupcakes in hand.

He holds one out, and I take it. The gummy severed finger sticking out of toxic green icing has my stomach doing backflips.

"Wow, you weren't kidding." I lick some of the icing off my finger, and only manners drilled into me over seventeen years of life prevent me from spitting it out. "What *is* that?"

Ash grins, and my stomach flips again. Poppy carefully sets her cupcake down on the coffee table.

"I believe she said it was licorice icing on a mango chili cake."

"*Why?*" I wail, willing the taste to evaporate out of my mouth.

"It's a Halloween party, and she wanted the taste to be scary too." His delight is completely disarming.

"You could have warned me."

His smile grows, the teeth ridiculous. "Nah, you're cute when you sputter."

My stomach moves beyond flips. It does a perfect dismount off the vault, and a 10/10 on its floor routine. It's on its way to the Olympics, and I'm frozen until my phone meows again.

"What does he want now?" Poppy asks, rolling her eyes.

"Who?" Ash frowns at my phone.

I clear my throat, which is sticky from licorice and Ash casually throwing the word "cute" at me like a grenade. "Just Josh," I say, reaching for nonchalant and failing miserably.

His eyebrows shoot up, and his mouth snaps shut. The points of his bulky teeth poke out a little. "I didn't realize you were texting again," he says eventually. "Congratulations."

The words fall flatly between us. "It's not very consistent," I say weakly. I pull open the chat: See you at school. It's a message that tells me nothing except that this conversation is over.

Ash takes a step back. "You'll probably be back together in no time. Congratulations."

Every congratulations is like a punch in the stomach. I shake my head, jumping to my feet. "No, it's not like that—"

"And then this will all be over, huh?" He gestures between us.

"Say cheese!" Hazel runs up, a Polaroid camera in her hands. Odette's face is pink, and her dimples and shining eyes hit me like another punch to the gut.

Hazel leans forward, grasping my shoulder, and the space between me and Ash disappears as we're squished together.

"Close your mouth, Lo," Odette says, laughing. "And Ash, put your arm around her. It's a party, you're supposed to look like you're having fun."

I should protest. I should say, *No, he doesn't need to do that, just take the picture.*

But I don't.

What do you want, Marlowe?

That question at the root of everything beats me in the head again.

And then his arm settles over me, like a weighted blanket draped across my shoulders. Warm, steady, and perfectly Ash.

"Take the picture." The words rumble in his chest, and I can't tell what my face is doing.

Hazel's camera shoots up and she snaps. She pulls the picture out and hands it to Ash.

"Hold on to this for me, will you?" Her smile hints at insider secrets.

He slips it into his pocket, and the weight of his arm disappears. I feel impossibly light, like I could float up to the rafters.

"I'm going to go make sure the equipment is all set up for later," Ash says, making space between us. I feel him slipping away, in every sense, and I hate it.

"I checked it earlier," Hazel says, waving him off.

He acts like he doesn't hear her. "I'll see you all later," he says, heading back toward the kitchen.

Hazel frowns at me, like this is somehow my fault, before following him.

"Try to have fun, Lo," Odette says, stepping forward and giving my braid a tug. She waits for my small nod before going after Hazel.

Poppy moves in front of me, her eyes vaguely pitying. "Jellyfish are adapting well to climate change."

"Excellent," I manage.

She opens her umbrella and drags me away from the dark corner where I had planned to grow roots the rest of the night, surrounded by the dulcet tones of howling werewolves spilling out of a sound system that works a little too well. We find some Rice Krispies treats with witch hat sprinkles and no surprising flavors. We also find Odette clinging to Hazel by the patio doors, stretched up on her tiptoes and kissing her with the intensity of some of the older romance novels that Ash declares "potentially iffy."

Not that it's a surprise they're kissing; I've seen the evidence across Odette's neck and in a bra that was not her size in her backseat. The surprise is in the whites of her knuckles as they clasp Hazel to her. The oblivion of the audience they have, from the girl who notices everything.

I snap my eyes to the ceiling. "Well, we might not need to worry about giving Odette a ride home." Poppy continues to stare until I elbow her in the kidney. "I don't think we should be watching this."

"She's really crazy about her, huh?"

I spin her back toward the snacks. "Let's pretend we don't know until she does."

We crowd back into the kitchen, and Poppy gives up on her umbrella, snapping it closed with a billow of tinsel and ribbons. We lean against quartz counters, neither one of us truly skilled in the art of small talk, and smile blandly at strangers. Poppy drops a few more jellyfish fun facts on a group of Minions, and two Greek goddesses who get a little too close.

I kill some time with a trip to a bathroom that has not held up well against a handful of teenagers, and when I get back to Poppy, her shoulders are set in determination.

"Hey, my mom's outside, I'm going home."

"What? Poppy, I *drove,* we could have just left if you wanted to go."

"You didn't say you wanted to go, how was I supposed to

know?" She waves her hand. "I didn't want to ruin your time, but I've hit my limit and I've run out of jellyfish facts."

"Poppy!" I look around for Odette. "If I knew you were uncomfortable, of course we would have left."

She shakes out her arms, like she's trying to expel an excess of energy, or a demon. "My overstimulation shouldn't impact your night. Plus, I thought you liked parties. You used to go to them all the time."

Her comment completely deflates me. I can't explain that I only liked them when they were easy, and there was someone holding my hand through it.

I smile instead, wanting to smooth out the worry lines that have prickled across her forehead. "You're right! Tell your mom I said hi, and I'll see you later."

Her forehead smooths, and she grabs her umbrella full of arms. "Plus, it might be a good time to fix whatever weirdness is going on with you and Ash."

"He's always weird, Poppy."

"You know what I mean. Even *I* felt awkward back there."

My face flames hot, and I'm just a tower of different shades of red. Hair, face, dress, not an inch of me cool and collected. "I don't know—"

"I think you should talk." Her tone allows no room for disagreement. "Just think how all these books would wrap up one hundred pages sooner if these people just *talked*."

"I guess that's true," I say, dazed.

She just smiles as if she's finally enjoying herself and muscles her way to the front door.

I grip the cool stone of the countertop, and debate making a break for it. Giving Poppy a five-minute head start, ripping this dress off on the front lawn, and heading home to crawl under my comforter. I go so far as to text Odette we're heading out, have so much funnnnn. I add an extra *n* until I've reached what I assume is a very sexy number of *n*'s, and that's that.

But.

I release my grip on the counter.

But.

What if he does want to talk? What if the new weirdness is completely my fault, and I ruined everything, ruined *us,* by insisting on that kiss? A kiss he thinks I described to another boy. Maybe I can just say, *Hey, what's going on? I don't understand and don't like this.* Maybe I can just stop pretending that I'm happy and easygoing and on the same page as everybody else? Wouldn't it be worth it if I could fix something on my own this time?

I pull on the front of the dress, and the Velcro back splits open. I yank it off and shove it into the overflowing trash can under the sink. My black bike shorts and loose tank top settle against my skin in a way that doesn't yell *hey you, you have clothing on* until I can't think about anything else. All the sensors that were previously screaming WARNING: WEIRD MATERIAL over and over again fade away. Now it's just me and a mission. A Lady Jessica–level mission. I may not be wearing a gown, but I have a tank top that says Y'ALL NEED SCIENCE, and I'm going to march through a ball (party) and demand something from someone.

I stalk through the living room, and the sunroom, before opening the door to a room with a washer, a dryer, and a half-dressed pirate tangled up with an astronaut.

"Mateo? What the hell!"

"Sorry, Lo," he says, not sorry at all. "Mind locking that on your way out?"

"Laundry rooms do not typically need locking doors," I say, eyes on the ceiling.

"That's a pity."

I backtrack, continuing my search into the backyard, until I finally find him. It shouldn't have been hard. Even in his black not-costume, his outline stands out against the velvet night. He's sitting alone by the pool, legs dangling off the diving board, and I make a beeline for him, trying to outrun my common sense.

I see the AirPods in his ears and realize bleating his name from dry land isn't getting me anywhere. I step onto the board, and Ash dips a little more dramatically than I expected.

"*Shit!*" He lies flat, his hand grabbing behind him for extra purchase, and I drop to my knees as we continue to sway. "What the hell, Marlowe?"

"Sorry, sorry!" I babble, the fiberglass biting through my skin.

He scoots up to the middle of the board and eyes me warily. "Were you trying to dunk me?"

"No!" I say, all high ground lost. "You couldn't hear me, and I really overestimated how sturdy this was."

He spreads his arms out. "Well, I'm here, still miraculously dry. What can I help you with?"

I shift onto my butt, goose bumps spreading across my arms and legs. I settle in place, mind spinning. My pathological people pleasing wants to fix whatever is happening between us. I want to make him laugh with some stupid mushroom joke. I want to tell him that I'm being haunted (by my brain, or heart, and sometimes Meemaw's ghost) by the question of what it is that I want, but I'm paralyzed by the fear of taking the wrong step. Most of all, I want to make him promise we'll always be friends.

"Are you avoiding me?" I mean to sound casual, but I fail miserably. "I thought tonight was for fieldwork, but I've barely seen you since the cupcakes."

He sighs, and the sound settles around us until everything is as still as the water below. "I know a lot of people here, I had to make some rounds."

"Says the vampire alone on the diving board."

"Vampires are solitary creatures."

"Ash, be serious."

He ignores my question. "And you ditched your ball gown for another weather-inappropriate outfit." He moves to take off his jacket, but I hold my hand up. I don't want it. I don't want to ask him why he's not spending time with me, and then have him explain it while I'm wearing his clothes.

He doesn't say more, so I poke him back in the right direction. "You made your rounds with all the people you needed to check in with?"

He nods. "Yeah, we're going to play a few songs later, and I needed to check the setup. Mateo was—"

"—a bit busy?"

"I guess, I haven't been able to find him. I think he's a pirate."

I flush. "Yeah, I ran into him."

"Are you having fun?" he asks finally. The silence settles between us again.

"No." I think of Poppy, and the guilt slides between my ribs. "Wait. Yes. I learned a staggering amount about jellyfish, but I don't really do well at parties like this."

He's silent for a moment, and I consider repeating myself, but he speaks first.

"I'm avoiding you."

I flinch, but his tone is gentle, and it hurts a little less than I expect. A little less now that it's out in the open.

"Why?" I don't really want to know, because if he tells me I'm just not built for friendship I will toss myself into this salt-water pool and haunt it for the rest of time.

"You and Josh are talking again, and I figured you didn't need my help anymore." He laughs, but the sound is rough along the edges. "You must have really nailed the *body* letter."

The memory of our kiss hangs between us for a moment.

"I heard you went to the store, and Sloane helped you pick some books out, so you don't need me for that either."

"And the fieldwork?" I ask, the words thick in my throat. "We were supposed to hang out tonight, and you were going to walk me through some romantic party montages. We haven't even begun to discuss *A Wicked Blade* and—"

"Why are you pushing this, Marlowe? It was always going to be a temporary thing, right?" He sounds as tired as I feel.

I shift, weighing the likelihood of pitching into the pool while trying to crawl off this diving board. "I thought we were friends," I say, when I can't take the silence anymore.

"Sure, friends." The word drops between us like an anchor.

I wiggle again and the board dips us low enough that Ash has to raise up his legs.

"At least until that dipshit comes crawling back and decides me being your friend isn't going to work for him," he murmurs.

I don't even blink at the derogatory term anymore. Instead, I jump headfirst into the conversation we've been dancing around for weeks.

"I don't care! Do you think I have so many friends that I won't notice if one disappears?" Does he think I would leave him behind without a second glance? That I could do that knowing what I know about his parents? That I would do that to *anyone* after Josh did that to me?

"And if he insists?"

I shake my head. "I don't even know why we're discussing this. It was just a couple of text messages."

"But you *do* still want to get back together with him?"

I open my mouth, but the words wedge at the back of my throat. I can't pull them out or arrange them in any way that will slip off my tongue. I'm frozen. *Terrified* that my plan to win Josh back was a mistake, or that calling it off would be an even bigger one.

Do you still want to get back together with him?

I allow myself a teaspoon of honesty. A tiny whisper from the deepest wrinkles of my brain admits *maybe not.*

I stuff this thought inside a box and seal it up tight until I can organize it all in a way that makes sense. Not here, under moonlight, with this boy.

I smile tightly and scoot in closer. "What would you say if I told you that the real ship in *It Happened One Evening* is Felicity and Brandon?"

He stills, eyes narrowing as I sidestep around his question, but he doesn't push it. The crushing vise around my heart loosens a smidge.

I swing my legs, all false bravado. "Sure, Roberto is hot and confident, and brings her orchids, but Brandon? Brandon understands her in a way nobody does."

He shifts to face me, and I fall against him. "He's not even on the table as a love interest! He's just a random shop owner, and I'm pretty sure he only loves his cat."

I grin, my goose bumps exploding (proliferating?) despite the heat coming off him. Why is it so satisfying to needle him?

"You're joking," he says, narrowing his eyes at what he sees on my face.

"I never joke about cat men. I trust them implicitly," I say.

He turns his head, but I see the quirk of his lips that he's trying to hide. I poke him in the side because I deserve to see the fruits of my labors, and when he looks at me it's like the space between us has evaporated. The air is now our air. His thigh is pressed so tightly against mine, it's practically my thigh. All the normal systems of stops and checks are no longer in place, and I belatedly realize that it's becoming harder to not lean a fraction forward and press my lips against his.

I wonder if his lip ring is still cold.

What do you want, Marlowe?

I jerk back, the movement causing Ash to swear again as the board dips beneath us. I turn back on my knees and crawl to the lawn, each movement like knives against my skin. When I get up, he's clutching the board with both hands.

"A little warning would be nice."

"Say we're still going to be friends." The words burst out of me, pressure-cooked and determined for release.

He doesn't respond, crawling to the middle of the board before pulling himself to his feet.

"Is it so awful to agree to?" I didn't think it was that dire.

He sighs and steps down onto the lawn in front of me. "It isn't." I consider my previous plan of throwing myself in the pool, but his voice dips lower. "It isn't. We're friends."

"Like before?" I'm suspicious, but I can't tell if he's lying.

"Like before."

I hold up my pinkie finger. "Promise me."

I want to see him agree to it, but I also want him to see that I'm serious.

He lifts his pinkie, but the challenge on his face tells me he doesn't really believe me.

I squeeze until my knuckle blanches, and it's almost painful, but this moment is carved into my brain.

"Deal," he says, and I take a step back.

I take another step back. The effects of being out in the cold the past few minutes have my body feeling like a Mentos somebody dropped in a bottle of soda, and I'm minutes from rocketing into the stratosphere.

"Are you going to accept my jacket now?" His voice is dry, and we're back on solid ground—where he's exasperated at me but trying to pretend he's not amused.

"No," I say, but I smile so he knows I appreciate the offer. "I'm solving my own problems these days."

Twenty

I pause outside the door, hand poised to knock. I didn't need more band-practice content this week, and the website is completely up and running. The format is simple (goodbye Papyrus font) but professional. All of the songs they've recorded up to this point have been uploaded with easily sharable links, and I made a press kit full of the graveyard photos and a bio on every member. Hazel even told Odette they have two more gigs lined up: playing at a club next week with two other bands, and a birthday party for someone at Hazel's school.

The faint sounds of music leak through the heavy wood, and I lean in a little, resting my forehead on the door. *Just admit it. You want to see him.* Things are normal-ish at school, and we're texting about the project, but it's been more than a week since the party. There hasn't been a single book recommendation or plan for more fieldwork, and I think I might *miss* him.

I wait another minute, but if they're already playing, they'll never hear me out here. I jiggle the knob and it turns easily.

Are we "just walk into each other's houses"–type friends?

Odette and Poppy and I passed that mark ages ago, the cadence and schedules of each other's families now as ingrained as our own. I know better than to drop by Odette's on a Sunday night. It's her mom's one day off, and between cleaning houses and night school, not a single thing is going to come between her and dinner with her kids. Poppy's house has a very vigorous Wednesday game night. They don't necessarily hate visitors at that time, but if you do show up, you will be conscripted into playing, and they're all terrible losers. The point is, I know them well enough to know that when I'm walking through that door, it's the right moment, because I know when all the wrong ones are.

What if I walk through this door and Ash's parents are finally home?

I crack my knuckles until I can feel my pulse in my fingertips, then stick my head over the threshold.

"Hello?"

The distant rise and fall of what I think might be "Not Tonight, Never Tomorrow" is my only answer.

"I promise I'm not an intruder," I call out as I close the door, sealing myself and this awkward step in our friendship inside.

I slip my shoes off and race to the stairwell.

I take the basement steps two at a time, only to stop short when I see the band is down one very important monster.

"Ash isn't here," I announce as the music sputters to a halt.

Hazel just raises one eyebrow.

I try again. "I'm here to work on the website and socials."

"I gathered." She bends and twists some knobs on a glitter green pedal.

"Is he . . . home?" I look toward the stairs, but I can't remember if I saw his car in the driveway.

"Nope." She slides her fingers along the neck of her guitar, and an angry yowl explodes from the speaker behind her.

"He'll probably be here later," Mateo says, putting me out of my misery, and reminding me of the fact that I'm pretty sure I saw his bare ass at Hazel's party.

"Hi, Marlowe!" Julian waves vigorously in my direction.

I feel waterlogged with disappointment. I should have called first, but Tuesday is always band practice day, and there have been enough half smiles and eye rolls in class that I felt us settling back into a routine. He didn't mention he wouldn't be here. I grip my bag tight.

"Where is he?" Look at me, easy-breezy Marlowe.

"He's—"

"Maybe you should ask him that yourself," Hazel says, cutting off Mateo.

"Okay, I will," I say, cracking my knuckles again. "Does he have a laptop around here? I'll just get to work."

"There's one in his room," Julian supplies, and I'm up the stairs before anyone can say anything else.

I have promoted myself from "walk into your house"–level friends to "spend time alone in your room" friends, and the level-jumping I'm doing is drastic, even for me. Both Meemaws, the alive *and* the dead one, would swat my knuckles and tell me to have a little shame. But I don't. I've committed to being here, and seeing him, and taking a thorough litmus test to make sure we're back to normal. I have thrown myself so far down this path that there's no escaping now.

The pale gray walls and rows of bookshelves in Ash's room soothe me like slipping into a warm bath or putting on noise-canceling headphones. Every cell quiets.

I take my time, brushing fingertips against the spines of old friends, and making note of colors and titles that pop out and yell *take me home*.

He reads more widely than I thought. Horror, mystery, some nonfiction, and several well-worn graphic novels riddled with dog-ears. I float along, heady with all these little snippets of insight, and his desk advertises the potential for more details. His bullet-gray laptop sits right in the middle, and the surface is littered with guitar picks and scraps of paper covered in lines and chord progressions in deep forest-green ink. I hold up my phone and take a picture. It's the perfect tableau for their socials. Snippets of the process, but not too personal. I caption it: Musical genius at work, or absolute chaos—the desk of our lead singer, Ash Hayes. I post it straight to the band's Gabber, and make myself at home. I do promise the universe, and the deceased Meemaw, that if the laptop is password protected or looks personal, I will acknowledge that it isn't meant to be used.

I lift the screen up, and I'm immediately in. There's no password and there are no questionable tabs; it's worse. His desktop is a mosaic of every assignment, saved document, and single thought he's ever had. I can barely see through all the files, just stacked on top of each other. I'd almost prefer porn virus pop-ups.

The urge to put everything neatly into folders grips me so hard I'm almost breathless, but I find my one sliver of self-restraint left and just pull up the band website. I filter through and delete the spam comments on pictures and old posts, and question whether some of the more sexual comments are bots or just weirdly honest members of this community who deserve to shoot their shot.

I play the latest streaming track, "My Dear Abigail," as I upload it to the New Music tab, and my foot taps to the melody and my own nerves.

"I was told I'd find you in here."

I swivel in his chair like a mastermind villain, smiling as hard as I can. My foot vibrates harder. "I'm sorry. I hope this is okay. You weren't here." I was aiming for breezy, but it comes out solidly accusatory.

"Yes, I know."

"I came into your house, and then your room, and I know that's indicative of a really deep friendship, and I totally understand if you don't feel that way." My crimes spill out of me, unprompted. "I get it if you'd like to establish some boundaries, but I panicked in the moment and—"

He leans over me and taps on the laptop, silencing the music.

"I'm sorry," I say. Again. Just in case that didn't translate.

"I don't mind that you're here," he says, dropping his backpack on his beige linen duvet.

No, not beige. Ecru? The pale cream color on the inside of an eggshell. A made bed, and a desktop in shambles.

"Marlowe?"

I snap back into the present. "Yes? Here."

"I asked how the website is going."

I swivel hard, back toward the laptop. "Really well! Your engagement has steadily climbed since the graveyard pics, and I've added this sliding header at the top, so the pictures can just rotate, and we give the people what they want."

"Looks great," he says. Reaching from behind me, he moves his long fingers across the trackpad. His forearm tenses with the movement, and my eyes trace the delicate network of veins lying under his skin.

Odette's words ring in my ears. *Hot.* Yes, and yes. Josh was hot in a way that the sun is—all in your face, almost blinding, and sometimes burning you to nothing in its wake. Ash is less

obvious, with asymmetric angles, and the distraction of his pierc-
ings and loose clothes. Like moonlight. Softer, slower to realize,
but it can still make your head spin.

"Where were you? On a date?"

He pulls back, and suddenly he's across the room, dropping
rings and a spiked ear cuff on top of his dresser. "That's a weirdly
specific question."

I wait, because it was, and I hope if I imitate a lamp, no sudden movement or sound, he might just answer me anyway.

"And if I was?" he continues, which is still not an answer. His
black-and-white-striped button-down goes next, and he's left
with the white T-shirt below.

"That would be amazing," I say, the world's most enthusiastic
lamp, with a leg that's bouncing so hard it's likely to rocket to the
moon. "They would be a very lucky girl, or guy. Or person."

He nods, unclipping a chain from his belt. "And how do you
think they would feel about my good friend Marlowe, who spon-
taneously pops up in my bedroom? Do I need to start checking
for you under my bed at night before I fall asleep?"

I flush, and I hate it when he's so right, and I'm again display-
ing such a lack of common sense it's shocking I can function in
the world at all. "I'm more of a back-of-the-closet kind of girl."

He smiles a little at that. Like I'm funnier than he wants to
admit. "I was at the dentist."

"Oh." *Oh.* I stand up, not sure if I'm supposed to leave at this
point, or what direction to put my body in. "Dental hygiene is
important."

"Extremely."

"Combating that plaque buildup, and flossing? Don't even get
me started on flossing." For the love of God, will somebody just
push me out the window.

He just looks at me expectantly.

I'm not ready to go, or for him to go downstairs and get wrapped into a sea of sounds. I'm embarrassingly needy and starved for his attention after days and days of surface-level smiles.

"Teach me to put on eyeliner," I blurt into the space between us.

"Marlowe—what?"

He has whiplash, and I know it's my fault, but I push forward. "I've been meaning to learn, and you . . ." I wave toward the smudges around his eyes. "You're good at it."

"I don't think this is the technique you're looking for."

"Is too."

Laughter creaks out of him, and my veins are full of bubbles. I'm a soda someone shook too hard. I walk over to his dresser. Sunscreen and a few telltale sticks of liner are stacked carefully in a pencil cup shaped like a cactus. I pull out a purple one and hold it out.

"What is with you today?"

"I don't know." I don't bother to hide that I've gone off the deep end. I'm so tired. I'm so tired of pretending I don't want to be here.

What do you want, Marlowe?

He pulls me over to his bed and we sit on the edge. He pulls off my glasses. "I would, again, like to go on the record that I don't really know how to do this the fancy clean way. I'm more of the messy, smudged, most-likely-to-play-you-a-little-metal-if-you-get-too-close style."

I breathe through my nose as he tilts my jaw to the side. "You just like the look of it?"

He exhales and I can feel it. It's all faint toothpaste, and cedar, and leather cuffs. "I liked how annoyed my dad was when I started wearing it. Look up."

A light brush of pressure skates the underside of my eye. "Are your parents off on another work trip?"

He grunts, and I think that's a yes. "Two weeks," he says shortly.

It's a long time to come home to an empty house. My heart spasms. I can't imagine what project would make them think they can just drop everything. Drop the company of their son. "Does it still annoy him? The eyeliner?"

"I couldn't tell you, but now I like it regardless of him. Close your eyes."

I oblige, and the pressure of his fingertips sears my face.

He slides the liner across my lash line. "That's what it's all about, right? Figuring out who we are and what we like and trying everything until we find the answers? Stop trying to blink."

I hold my face as still as possible, as if I'd ever tried to be in charge of my eyelids before.

"Perfect."

I blink.

"Or terrible," he says after a beat. "It could go either way."

I jump off the bed and run to the mirror hanging over his dresser. He's right: it's not the knife-sharp precise lines that swish along the eyelids of the girls at school. Purple is slowly spreading away from my eyes like a bruise, and it's both terrible and perfect. I smile at the bunched muscles between his eyebrows as he waits for my verdict.

"Do you think anyone will wonder if I'll play them some metal if they get too close?"

"Only if they're smart."

My phone meows. There he is, texting more and more. Picking up right where he left off—two years full of plans, I-love-yous, and more than one picture I would die if my momma saw, and Josh is just strolling back in to say: Why are you in a picture on Hayes's desk?

The words are a jumble. I read them again, the meaning slipping away from me.

"Bad news?"

I look up, and Ash's eyes are wary. I wonder what my face is doing.

"It's . . . um . . . it's Josh. Again."

"Oh, really?" The end of that sentence asks for more information, but I have nothing to give.

I text back a ?.

Dots appear immediately, and then disappear. Ash is looking at me like my phone is going to bite us both, but then a message pops up and it's a shared picture from NMTM's Gabber. The latest one that I just took of his desk.

Why is there a picture of you on Hayes's desk?

I zoom in, and then look up at the source material. A Polaroid I missed. Carefully leaning against a framed picture of the band is the picture Hazel took of us at her party. My smile is strained, his is nonexistent, but our faces are close.

"I shared a picture of your desk." I nod over at it, as if he wouldn't be able to follow my train of thought. "I'm sorry, I was just trying to think of something for the band socials." I clear my throat. "Josh is asking me why you have a picture of us on it."

"And what did you tell him?" His voice is soft.

"I . . . I don't know."

He steps closer, and the heat from his chest wraps around me. "Well, I'm going to go practice. You're a smart girl, Marlowe, I'm sure you can figure out why I would have a picture of us on my desk." He's out the door before I can respond, and I'm left holding my phone like a bomb.

I wobble as his words sink into my skin. I do not feel like a very smart girl right now, and the possibilities threaten to shift things so drastically, we won't be able to come back from it.

I type out the words even though they may make me a coward.

I don't know.

Dots appear, and then disappear for good.

Twenty-One

I stab my fork into mug cake, the lumpy mixture deflating a little. Just like me, when Ash called off our fieldwork after it took me over a week to get him to commit to one. We were supposed to go to the drive-in movie, and I'd put on a *dress*. I'd been so ready to watch Kate Hudson and her abs somehow lose a guy in ten days.

The cake sags a little in the middle, making me second-guess my decision to pour in maple syrup instead of sugar.

"Do I smell chocolate?" Momma blows into the kitchen, hurricane style, and drops her bag and mail on the countertop. "Look at my sweet girl in this dress!"

I let her wrap me up, hairspray and peony-pink lipstick pressing into my cheeks.

"Where are you off to?"

"Nowhere," I mumble, and stab my cake again.

She purses her lips before sliding my mug across the island toward her. She eats a forkful and looks how I feel. "Well, this isn't going to solve anything." She drops the fork and leans in. "Hit me with it. Fight with the girls? AP assignment holding you up? Something to do with Josh?"

I don't bother to bring Ash into the mix, because it's clear she can't imagine anyone but Josh even being a possibility.

I shrug and keep my voice light enough to give her an out. "No, just plans changing, no big deal." Maybe his parents came back into town and decided a family dinner out was what they needed to make up for weeks away.

"So definitely boy problems," she says, her smile knowing. It makes me want to sink into the floor. "I had a feeling we hadn't seen the last of you and Josh."

I'm sure that's what she's been hoping for, her and Stu both. My return to the parties, and football games, and phone calls and invitations—all things that reassured them *yes, don't worry, everything over here is completely normal.* All green flags.

"This doesn't look like *Wuthering Heights.*" She grabs my latest paperback romance off the counter, and I frown as my attempts at a pity party continue to be interrupted.

She flips it over, eyes skimming the back, and there's no hiding what it is. A foulmouthed bartender and a librarian hatch a plan to help her save face when she's invited to her ex-fiancé's wedding (although seriously, who would do that), but the more time they spend together, the harder it is to pretend it's all make-believe.

I watch Momma's face: the slight arch in her eyebrows, the twitch at her lip, and finally her small nod.

"I didn't know you liked romance." She slides it back to me, and I shrug.

"I may have started picking a few of them up."

She walks to the bar and pours a glass of wine, the rich purple swirling into a glass. She sits down, and I realize we're in for the long haul.

"It started with your book *Lady Jessica Conquers a Duke*," I volunteer. "I kind of got hooked."

She laughs, and it lights up her entire face. Some crinkles pinch the outer edge of her eyes, and even though I see her frown at them in the mirror, I know she's come by them honestly. They map out a woman who loves to laugh.

"Dear Lord, I forgot about that one." She shakes her head. "That ball, the scandal with her—"

"—sister?" I finish. "I thought I would scream when that happened."

"I did scream," she laughs. "Your meemaw almost swerved into a light pole! She didn't talk to me for a week."

I smile, because it was just like Meemaw to hold a grudge and then forgive you when the spite was too inconvenient to maintain.

Momma's smile turns a little wistful. "I suppose I was your age when I started reading them too. I would steal them from the library and return them with an extremely earnest apology letter tucked inside the cover."

"You didn't!"

"Oh, yes. Even if it wasn't the sort of book your meemaw would have approved of, she at least taught me the importance of a nice note when someone does you a favor."

I dissolve into giggles. "I'm sure they knew exactly who was stealing them."

She sips her wine. "Oh, one thousand percent. Old Ms. McCreary would glare at me in church, and I know she knew. Still, that woman wasn't going to get in the way of reading, no matter the cost."

"I just can't imagine you shoving a paperback under your shirt and running out the door."

"It was a large purse, I'll have you know, and what can I say?" She shakes her head. "I would sneak all my momma's *Redbooks* and pore over every article in the bathroom. I just wanted to know everything. I wanted to hear everything there was to hear about love—" She drops her voice. "—and sex, and relationships, and how people connect with each other."

I nod because I feel it too. *One more page and I'll understand this thing that grows between people. I'll understand it enough that it will make sense.*

She takes another sip of wine. "No more mug cake, let's watch a movie!"

"A movie?"

"Don't sound so thrilled," she says, laughing. "Just the two of us. Stu will be in a little later, Blue's at Hailey's, and I just found out my daughter loves love stories. Watch a rom-com with me."

I hesitate, inclined to say no and wallow in my room, but I'm physically incapable of disappointing the woman in front of me. "Is there a good one that you have in mind?"

She grins and grabs my hand, the wine sloshing a little over the rim. She drags me into the den and is scrolling through titles before my butt hits the couch. "There was this one that looked so cute the other day. Wait, here it is!"

"*Portland Promise,*" I read, as a beautiful woman with dark hair and a streak of blue paint on her chin fills the screen. "*When Katie Bell gets dumped by her husband of five years out of nowhere, she decides to start over at an artists' residency in Portland. Soon, this children's book illustrator and a grumpy widower who makes incredible pottery are spending more and more time in the studio. Can Katie find inspiration and love in the overcast streets of the Pacific Northwest?*"

"I bet she can!" Momma says, tucking a blanket around her legs.

I press play, and we're immediately sucked into Katie's life. Her third-floor walk-up in Brooklyn (so chic, Momma declares), the implosion of her life following the breakup, and her tumultuous first meeting with Bryant, the potter who's trying to mend his own broken heart.

"It looks like his nose has been broken in a few bar fights," Momma says, before eventually deciding, "I like it."

Their fights mellow into conversations and then kisses, and soon Christopher the ex is knocking on her door filled to the brim with excuses and apologies.

"Kick him to the curb," Momma yells from her blanket nest.

"Yeah," I echo. "Send him and those old bowls back to Chicago!"

"Wait!" Momma lurches up, pressing pause. "Are you rooting for the *ex*?"

"Christopher? The love of her life? Of course I am."

"The one who broke her heart?"

"For which he has already apologized! People make mistakes."

She shakes her head, mystified. "Baby girl, he's the bad guy."

"Why? Because he made a stupid mistake, which he quickly realized? Does that mean it's over forever?"

"Oh, honey." I hate the way she's looking at me, like she can just pull up the hood and see all the ugly and damaged pieces rattling around inside.

All the fun and lightheartedness is sucked out of the room in a moment. "If we spend so much time and effort on something, aren't we supposed to try to save it?"

"Is that what you're doing? Trying to save things with Josh?"

"I don't know. Maybe?" I confess to my lap, unable to look her in the eye. "That's part of the reason I've gotten interested in romance novels. I'm trying to learn to be a more romantic girl-friend."

"A more romantic girlfriend? What does that even mean?" Momma's sitting up now too, and we're perched on the edge of the couch, all hint of relaxation gone.

I'm sick to death of explaining this, but it rolls off my tongue with minimal stomach pangs this time. "That's the reason Josh ended things. I wasn't romantic enough, or 'good'"—I throw up air quotes—"at love. But that's something I can fix."

"He said you weren't *good* at love?"

"To paraphrase, yes."

She rockets to her feet, pacing around the coffee table. "Mar-lowe Amelia Meadows, if I *ever* see that boy again, he better start running immediately, because if I catch him—"

"Momma!"

"Don't you bring him into this house again. How *dare* he say that to you!"

I'm up and shouting to be heard over her. "What if it's true? Isn't it healthy that he realized his needs weren't being met and shared that with me?"

"*Healthy?*" She laughs, but it's an outraged sound that rings hollow through the den. She grabs my hand and pulls us both down onto the couch. "You listen to me right now. This boy does not deserve this level of effort from you."

I pull my clammy hand out of hers. "Why can't I want to be better? Do you think it's preferable to just drift along and end up like Dad? Having lost the love of his life and all alone?"

She sits back, her heart on her sleeve and all over her face. "Marlowe, I don't know why you would think that, but I'm *not* the love of your dad's life."

I snort, picking at the tassels of Blue's favorite throw pillow.

"I'm not," she insists. "That's you, and his patients." She takes my hand again, trying to anchor me to her. "I'm so proud of him, and so grateful for the time we had together, but sometimes pride, family, and the sheer want of something are not enough."

My response is caught in my throat.

"I needed someone to come home every night and fight me for the covers and fill out the morning crossword with—and let me keep pretending I'm a good speller. I wanted sweet words, and surprise takeout, and a man who makes me belly-laugh just to hear me make that sound." She sighs, looking more drawn than I've seen her in years. "Your dad's the most brilliant man I've ever met, and dear God, I made him my entire existence. And when he would wake up and drive off in the middle of the night, I would feel so thankful that he walked this earth and was able to help people."

Tears leak out of the corner of her eyes, and everything rises to the surface. A teakettle pressurized with two decades of hurt.

"But after four years?" She swipes at the tears forming. "Four years of marriage, with a sweet girl in my arms, a million things to do, and me fighting tooth and nail just to capture a few seconds with the man I chose to spend the rest of my life with?" She shakes her head. "After too many of those moments slipped by, and too many promises were broken, I realized I was never going to be his priority. We couldn't just go on like we were— him turning gray from the stress of trying to make me feel loved, and me wasting away in front of him and trying to pretend it was working."

Her beautiful face blurs and hot tears track down my cheeks.

"I had to cut us loose to save us both. Oh, he fought it for sure. Your dad has never failed at a single thing in his life, but he couldn't see it was my failure too. I couldn't be what he needed—someone strong and independent enough to build a separate life. Family was all I knew, all I wanted to know, and I just wanted to sit in this room with the wallpaper my grandmother hung and always be surrounded by my favorite people."

"It felt like you rejected him, and we're so similar in so many ways." My face and neck are slick, and everything rushes out in the deluge. "I know the autism can be—"

"Marlowe!" Her face is stricken, her words rapid and frantic. "Don't you ever say that. How could you think that?"

"How could I not? What if I fixate on the wrong priorities too? Or can't see or understand what the person I love needs until our relationship has withered away?"

"Your father is a workaholic, Marlowe. Yes, he's also autistic, but do not reduce him to just one thing. He deserves more than that. He's also a Virgo, but we're not even going to touch that."

A jagged laugh rips out of me.

"You see the world and navigate it a little differently from me, and I hate that I don't have the ability to give you a road map to make it any easier, but I'm so grateful that every day I get to try."

My glasses are fogged, I'm producing snot at a truly alarming rate, and I wipe my hands in the skirts of my dress. "I thought you'd be happy about Josh," I say. "I thought you were relieved by how normal it was when I was with him. I thought you and Stu found it easier to relate to me—"

"Lord have mercy, we hated him."

"What?" I fall back onto the pillows. "No, we're talking about *Josh*."

"*Hated* him, Marlowe." She's dabbing the corner of her eyes with the throw, and still manages to look glamorously misty, while I'm a mucus monster. "He would strut around here, try and shoot the shit with Stu, and every sentence out of his mouth was 'Marlowe should really get an organizer' or 'Marlowe's going to need a navy prom dress to match my pocket square.' He was so bossy, and full of himself, and we couldn't stand him."

With that, I burst into tears again. "How am I so *bad* at this? I can't read anything right."

She tucks me into her arms and the pressure around me eases the ache. "I'm southern born and bred. Nobody was going to know how little I cared for that peacock until I told them, but I was hoping you'd move on from him sooner or later."

"And if I decide I want him back?" The words taste strange in my mouth.

What do you want, Marlowe?

I feel her sigh in my bones, and she smooths my hair back from my forehead. "It's your life, Marlowe, and I'm not my mother. I don't believe in forcing my opinions on my children, but don't expect me to let him inside the house anytime soon."

Twenty-Two

"I don't think," I say, and suck in a deep breath. "I don't think Josh and I had the best relationship."

The words fall like stones and shatter the sleepy silence in Odette's room.

"What?" Odette drops her bottle of water, and it rolls under her desk into a maze of servers.

"It's just something I've been thinking." I wave her off. "Forget I said anything."

"Absolutely not." She squeezes an arm between computers, and the bottle comes out covered in a mixture of condensation and grime.

"You should stick a Swiffer back there every now and then," Poppy says. "Better yet, just swipe it all around the room."

Poppy and I are draped across Odette's bed, her SpongeBob socks perilously close to my face. Odette is parked in front of her computers, as always, her mind half in our conversation and half chronically online. The hum and heat of her machines has prickles of sweat beading across my chest and hairline.

"Poppy, let's try to focus on the present issue." Odette cuts her eyes to me. "Like Lo having a breakthrough."

"Like I said, it's nothing. Are you done being mean to people on the internet yet?"

"No, no, lean into that truth."

I stick out my tongue. "Maybe if you turn off one—"

"—or two—"

"—or two, thank you Poppy, monitors, we wouldn't be melting into your Lord of the Rings bedspread."

"This just guarantees that we'll continue our tradition of always getting milkshakes when you come to my house."

"I don't need to steam like a pot of crabs to agree to that."

"At least open the door," Poppy says, undoing her purple denim vest with a collar she personally bedazzled.

"And let my weasel brother ruin anything with his eyeballs or greasy little fingers? No, I'd prefer the melted human remains." She points accusingly at me. "What made you finally see the light about Josh?"

I sit up on my elbows, peeling myself off of Aragorn son of Arathorn's face. "There was no lightning strike." I feel shy, like the words are important. Like finally looking at all my twisted feelings and acknowledging them makes them real. "I'm just realizing that in hindsight the relationship may not have been as healthy as it should have been."

"Fucking *finally*!" Odette whoops, spinning in her chair.

I blush. "I wasn't dragging my feet on purpose; I just needed a little time to work through it all." I flop back and try to ignore their attention aimed at me like a laser beam. "As long as we're all sharing revelations, anything you want to add about Hazel? We want to know everything about your love life too."

Odette rolls her eyes. "Yes, I'm familiar with your greedy

brain, and we haven't had this conversation yet because . . ." Her mouth twists as she struggles for words. "I don't know. I'm just seeing what feels right, and labeling every feeling and relationship made it too serious."

"Oh no, not *serious,*" Poppy whispers.

"Shut up, you. Don't think I haven't noticed you mainlining romance novels and not volunteering a single peep on your own thoughts."

Poppy sighs. "They're just books, Odette. We're all allowed a good story now and then." She has a point, and a silence settles in the close, sticky air. "Plus, I'm pretty sure I'm on the ace spectrum, but Sloane is giving me recs and I'm still feeling it out."

"Look at you, such an overachiever you had to collect two spectrums."

I snort, and Poppy elbows me in the calf. Her skin sticks against mine.

"Where does our hot, grumpy goth fit into all this?" Odette grins, oblivious to the swamp ecosystem she has created.

"We're friends." Even I can hear the uncertainty in my voice.

"And that's it?" Poppy's voice is soft and slow, and we're probably ten minutes away from her passing out on us. She's like a shark or a toddler—if she stops moving, it's lights out.

I shrug, although only Aragorn and I can tell. "Things have been strained, and he's gotten more distant as we get closer to the last letter." I feel like there's an anvil on my chest. "I don't think I want to give it to Josh anymore anyway."

"Nothing left to say?" Odette rolls closer to me, as Poppy softly snores.

"More like *too much* to say," I murmur, choking on a rising tide of anger and hurt and regret, the pieces finally sharpening into focus.

"Let's finish it then." Odette rolls across the room, digging for a pen under the haphazard stacks on her desk. "Let's do it together right now."

"Now?"

"Yes, now. I can help." Odette grabs a sheet of paper off the printer and rolls back. "I'm something of a romance expert too, you know. I've had many dates, many sexy moments—"

"—almost zero relationships beyond a month." I yelp as she pinches my armpit.

"As I was saying, I'm well on my way to a serious relationship."

I study her face, looking for signs that she's joking.

She grimaces a little, but nods. "Yes, I'm serious, yes, I'm more surprised than you, and yes, you should apologize to me." She lets the news settle before hitting us with: "I don't know, I think I might . . . love her."

I gasp and shove a still-snoring Poppy until she sits up. "What?"

"Odette loves Hazel!"

"What?"

"Calm down, both of you. You're disturbing Legolas."

Poppy's hands unclench from the bedding. "Did I miss anything else?"

"Yeah, we're going to help Marlowe write her last letter, so she can put this all behind her," Odette says.

"Or I can just stop responding to Josh's messages and fade into the ether?" I protest.

"Don't you want him to know how much he hurt you? How much his little games have sucked?" Poppy wipes sleep out of her eyes, but the question hits me square in the chest, poking and prodding at my already badly bruised heart. It gives a heavy thump, and I feel the answer in my bones.

Yeah, I kinda do.

"I'll deliver this last letter in person," I say, making up my mind and announcing it to the universe before I can take it back.

Odette whistles low. "Well, let's get cracking then. Should it just be a page or two of roasting him? At least you don't have to try to wax poetic about his *soul,* which I think is only made up of football and cheese fries."

I nibble on my lip because I've been asking myself the same thing. "It's almost too big a topic. How do I describe everything I've felt over the last few months? All the questions I still have?" I sigh, flopping back on the bed.

"What is it that you need him to know? What just made you tell me, Pops, and all my servers that you think things weren't healthy? That his soul is kind of a dick, and that dumping you before first bell in a freshman lab does *not* make him Mr. Darcy?"

"It should have at least been the fancy new chem lab," Poppy says.

I smile at the joke, but my head feels stuffed with cotton. Why couldn't I be honest? Why shouldn't he know what the last few months have cost me?

I pull disco cats out of my bag and flip through my prior attempts. The failed letters where my hurt would bleed onto the page, and I scrapped them for not being lighthearted or lovey enough.

> *What happened to "me and you forever baby," as your face lit up from my lips and the dashboard light.*

I rip it out and keep flipping.

> *I want to dig my fingernails into you until you stop that distant pitying smile, as if I'm just something unfortunate you're hearing about secondhand.*

Rip.

*Do you check my activity on socials to see if my schedule has
been disrupted too? Are you also scrolling through strangers'
babies and recipes at 3am because my face is what you see
when you close your eyes?*

Rip.

I miss you.

Rip.

*Sometimes I want to apologize for not being enough, and
sometimes I remember your faraway stare and disinterest in
the things that matter to me. And I wonder if maybe it was
you who were not enough?*

Rip.

I'm panting, and every wound from the past four months
is spread across Odette's bed in a sea of scribbles and paper
scraps.

Wordlessly, Poppy and Odette sift through the wreckage, my
feelings leaping from the pages, and my face burns.

"Yes," Odette says, clearing her throat. "This is what the fourth
letter needs to be. *Your* soul."

I pull out another pink envelope, too aggressively optimistic
for these contents, and stuff the papers inside.

"When are you going to do it?" Poppy asks.

I have the good sense not to pull anything like this at school,
and I would never recover if I showed up at his house and his

mom told me to go home. "Tomorrow. Derrick is having his annual ugly-sweater party. I'll do it then."

My invitation must have mysteriously gotten lost in the mail this year, but no matter. I will get in, say what I need to say, and then listen to my mother. I'm not chasing Josh Stallings any longer.

"And with all of this settled," Poppy starts, "are we crystal clear, hypothesis proven without a shadow of a doubt, could take it all the way to the bank, *sure* . . . that we don't want to make a new plan for Ash?"

"How about we press pause on any more plans for a while." My stomach cramps, but I deflect, deflect, deflect, and hope the ache will go away.

She scoots closer to me on the bed, sticky limbs and stickier thoughts crowding me. "Look me in the eye and swear on all that is holy—the *Entoloma hochstetteri* mushroom—that you haven't thought about Ash kissing you every day since it happened."

"Analyzing the mechanics of it is hardly—"

"Marlowe. You want to insist on Josh being honest about the breakup, your relationship, the ways you both fell short? At least be honest with yourself first," Odette says, sliding closer in her rolling chair.

The fuzz clears a little, and I hate it. I hate the messiness of this more than I did when I only had my snarled tangle of Josh to unravel. "It's just a crush. What am I supposed to do with that? Tell him I want him to kiss me again, and this time Josh has nothing to do with it?"

"Yes," Odette and Poppy say in unison.

WHAT DO YOU WANT, MARLOWE?

Odette rolls closer still, her knees knocking against mine. "It's okay to just jump and see what happens. Maybe nothing! Maybe something! Take a risk, Lo!"

I shake my head, even less inclined to respond to this intervention than the one about *The Sims*. I shiver as I remember Ash stepping closer and closer in his room. *You're a smart girl, Marlowe, I'm sure you can figure out why I would have a picture of us on my desk.*

But what if I'm wrong? What if it blows up in my face and it's too awkward for us to carry on? I don't want to lose the books or teasing or weird adventures. I can't lose *him*.

"I don't know. I just want to focus on one thing at a time."

Odette slides away, and I can tell that they're sharing knowing looks over my shoulder, and that I have failed some epic character test. But I am not a jump, then fall, then flourish type of person. I want a ladder, a survey team on the bottom, and a slow descent into friendly territory.

I shove the envelope in my bag and force every ounce of normal to the forefront.

"So, is it milkshake time?"

Twenty-Three

I almost wear my hair down for once. Josh would always go on about how you *have* to look your best for a party. I even almost wear a dress, old habits dying slowly, so he could smile all slow and molasses-sweet and say it was a good choice.

But I don't.

Because tonight isn't about him. Tonight is about broken hearts and promises; about the end of an era. About getting some answers.

So, I come as me. Jeans, freckles, questionable social graces, and a T-shirt that says ENTROPY? IN THIS ECONOMY?

A cow moos, and I yank my phone out of my pocket. I'm breathless when I answer, and my words tumble over each other. "Ash? Hey, I didn't think I'd hear from you tonight. What's up?"

"Hey." His voice is cautious, and the tiny pause makes something flutter inside my chest. "I heard about this great sushi place over in Statesville, and I was wondering if you wanted to go?"

The flutter turns into a swarm. "More fieldwork?"

"No," he says firmly. "I want us to go. Just me and you."

"Oh. *Oh.*" My voice is reed thin. "I—I wish I could, but I'm at . . ." I trail off, staring at Derrick's door. What *am* I doing?

"It's okay." His words are hurried. "I know it's last-minute. Are you out with the girls?"

I shift my bag on my shoulder, the letter burning a hole in the bottom. "Actually, no." I pick my next words carefully. "It's the fourth letter. I'm going to deliver it in person tonight—"

"Got it." His voice scrapes over me like sandpaper. "Never mind, forget I said anything."

"Wait, no! I just wanted to give this last one to him to—"

"You don't have to explain, Marlowe. I guess this is the end of the contract, huh?"

It's as if some higher power has reached down and pressed pause and all my systems power down.

He continues, despite my silence. "I really appreciate every-thing you did on your end. The band is really starting to take off."

His voice wraps around me, and I thaw enough to squeak out, "Ash, wait—"

"Good luck, Marlowe."

I blink as the call dies.

Shit.

Did Ash just ask me out? Does he think I'm still trying to give Josh a *love* letter?

I consider sticking the letter in this topiary and calling Ash back, but I can't bring myself to do it. I *need* this. I need to finish this. Full circle, beginning to end, a real resolution.

I don't bother knocking. Sorry, ancestors, and Derrick—although I don't really mean it with you, because you're a fake friend who'll smile at me one day and pretend I don't exist the next.

The house is starting to fill up with ugly Christmas sweaters, and I'm just grateful I didn't have to pull out the monstrosity that lives in the back of my closet. The tinsel around the collar makes me want to peel my skin off.

That's *another* thing. I'll no longer be entertaining suggestions on dress codes from anyone—not for dates, parties, dances, or anything else. I may not always read the vibe right, but if I misstep, at least I'll be doing it in clothes that I like.

"What are you doing here?"

Tiffany's in rare form tonight. Her face is as red as her sweater with Santa holding a six-pack.

"Tiffany. Always a delight." I shift my bag, waiting for her to get it out of her system.

"You're not supposed to be here," she says, her objection duly noted.

"I don't intend to stay long."

"Did *he* invite you here?" She imparts so much emphasis on that pronoun it almost sounds italic. Or capitalized. Or akin to God.

"No, he didn't."

Her lips twist into a smile, and the transition is jarring. "Well, you should go see him. I'm sure he'll be *thrilled* you're here."

My head spins and even though my brain is yelling *Danger, Will Robinson,* I can't tell where it's coming from. "You *want* me to find him?"

"Absolutely. He's up the stairs, second door on your left." Her tone has slid into a sweetness that makes my teeth hurt. Full of something bad for you, but you can't identify it through the sugar.

I don't want to spend any more time with her or trying to puzzle it all out. I head for the stairs, avoiding the banister that's already sticky from Fireball and whiskey Cokes that have sloshed onto it from overfilled red Solo cups and flasks.

I'm about to go up when I see a familiar blond head, wearing a familiar red headband that I saw at breakfast this morning.

My come-to-Jesus with Josh can wait a moment.

I walk up behind Blue and tap her on the shoulder, and her brilliant smile deflates at the sight of my face.

"This doesn't look like Whitney's house."

"We're only stopping by for a moment!" Her cherry-red lips press into a thin line. "Are you going to bust me?"

"Are you doing anything I would need to bust you for?" I ask with a raised eyebrow.

"No," she says, a little too quickly. "What's going on? I thought you didn't come to these parties anymore." She doesn't say *since the breakup,* but I hear it anyway.

"I don't." I look up the stairs. "I just have a little unfinished business." Her eyebrows bunch together, but I jump in to avoid any more questions. "I'm going to go take care of something. Will you promise me you'll be safe?"

She nods, concern still written across her forehead. I know she wants to ask more, but I'm already heading back toward the stairs.

Sometimes when these parties were still finding their momentum, the boys would go upstairs and play video games until things reached a fever pitch. I'd stay downstairs, helping set out cups, tidying up messes, and playing house—a role I realized too late I didn't want.

I pause outside the door. That's *another* thing. I like video games, and I would have really liked to sit out a few parties. I'm not going to become one of those couples again who can't do anything apart, like the terrible Mr. and Mrs. Fitzgerald in *A Rake for the Holidays*. Separate interests are *healthy*. All my spare threads and puzzle pieces are finally laid out in front of me. I can see the big picture.

I take a deep breath, and just marvel at the air in my lungs (not yet tainted by Marlboro Reds, or booze, or sweat), and the peace I have, arriving at this point.

I reach for the knob, but I can't bring myself to turn it.

I don't know why, after all this time, I'm almost inclined to leave the door closed. How the ache from our breakup has faded into something that barely registers anymore.

I shake the thought loose and flex my fingers. *Closure is important. He should get this last letter, if anything to know that there are no more coming.*

I push open the door.

It's dark, and there's no glow from the TV to light the way. Something scratches at the periphery of my brain, some realization I can't even process.

I hear the rustling, and the breathing, and I know I'm not alone. I scramble for the switch, and I light it all up at the same time a female voice says:

"Get out of here!"

And then there's no denying it, and it's Josh who's swearing "Marlowe," as if it's my fault he's mostly naked with a sophomore underneath him.

Isabel, I think her name is. She's on the squad with Blue.

I'm stock-still, envelope clutched in my hand, brain unable to send any commands to my limbs or mouth while it processes everything else.

It's not until Josh says "It's not what it looks like" that I start to laugh.

And laugh.

And laugh.

"What has gotten into you?" Josh asks finally. He's turning an ugly mottled red, and finally I pull enough air back into my lungs.

"It's not what it *looks* like?" He scowls as a few errant, unhinged giggles fall out again. "Of all the *stupid* things to say to me."

He gives me a look as if to say *That's enough,* and I almost start laughing again because I do not care. He has cut all the ties between us, and nothing he says can touch me at all anymore.

"Did you think I would say, *Oh, gee, Josh, it must be another one of those Marlowe misunderstandings. Let me just pop out to the hall while you put on some pants, and I'd love to listen?*" I grab a plastic water bottle off the dresser next to me and hurl it at his head.

He deflects with his forearm, his face an open book of confusion. "Marlowe, what the hell has gotten into you?"

"God, you really *are* a dipshit."

Blue bursts through the door. "I thought I heard yelling." She takes in the scene in one blink. "Oh shit."

"Can everyone get the hell out?" Isabel scowls, straightening her clothes.

"I swear I didn't know," Blue says, eyes roving my face. "I knew Isabel was sniffing around him, but I didn't think she was dumb enough to try to hook up with him."

"*Hey.*"

Blue grabs a second bottle off the floor and chucks it at him, hitting center mass. "That's for being such an asshole to my *sister.*"

My eyes water a little, because she made a choice, and this time it was me.

Josh stands up, trying valiantly to pull his own clothes into place, and maintain the high ground. "Marlowe, let's talk outside."

"I don't want to talk to you." The words come out so easy. His shirt is on backward, and he looks so put out that I almost start laughing again. "You know what's really funny? I think out of the two of us, I was way more romantic."

I take a step closer to him. "Because I romanticized everything about you. The way you would keep me in this little box, and I didn't realize how small you made everything in my world until you set me free."

His jaw tightens, and he can't meet my eyes for a minute. "You don't mean that." He nods toward the door. "Let's go talk—"

"No." I fling the last letter at his feet, relishing the surprise that ripples across his face. "That's the last one. Feel free to choke on it." I brush the hair out of Blue's face, and smile until she believes it. "I'll see you at home, Blue."

"Look, Marlowe," Josh says, raking his hair with his fingers. "This whole thing with Isabel is nothing."

Isabel storms out, but I'm locked in place by the twinge of desperation in his voice.

"Sometimes guys just need to sow some wild oats. I was going to ask you out again at the end of the year." He raises his eyebrows like I'm a naughty child who's forgotten something important. "You know? For Clemson?"

Us going to the same school. The apartment together junior year. Him going off to med school, and me inventing grafts he can use in surgery until we're both shining. Or at least, he is.

I smile again, but he doesn't look deep enough to see it's not happiness, but satisfaction. I know what I want. His expression smooths over, and the lines of his body relax.

"I'm not dating you again, Josh." There's no anger in my voice, although there probably should be. There's just the relief of having escaped such a narrow life. "I don't love you, and I'm not even sure I like you as a person anymore."

He rocks back as if struck.

"There'll be no apartment at Clemson, and I'm not even all that sure about biomedical engineering anymore." I spin for the door and toss over my shoulder, "I might want to teach math. Or become a mycologist."

I'm texting my lifeline before I even hit the first landing, and by the time I get to the front door the reply says, ten minutes.

I walk down to the mailbox, and suck in air in cloudy, puffy gulps. I start counting, and by the time I reach one hundred and twenty-eight, I see headlights. Josh calls, and I immediately send him to voicemail. He tries again, and then the phone goes silent.

Odette and Poppy bundle me into Odette's car, and after briefly asking me if I want to go home—*absolutely not*—we head south to Poppy's house.

I sit numb and white-hot furious, and let it wrap around me like a little shell. His stupid face, his stupider comment, and me—the most stupid of them all. Because the second I saw his shocked (but still perfectly perfect) face, I had already realized my mistake.

I *had* opened the wrong door. I didn't need to hold up all my feelings to him like some pitiful show-and-tell. I'd already moved on.

They lead me inside, gently push me into a seat at the kitchen table, and slide a full glass of water in front of me.

"Marlowe, come back to real life," Odette whispers.

I throw back the glass, water leaking out of the corners of my mouth and down my shirt. "Fire, I need a fire."

They exchange a look and sit down as a unit.

"Marlowe, sweetheart, what's this about a fire?" Odette trips a little over the endearment.

"Set a fire. A trash can or a bonfire." I wave my hand, the options numerous and irrelevant. "Maybe something in the cul-de-sac. I think I have some matches." I dig in my bag.

"Well, you heard her."

Poppy glares. "I am not starting a trash-can fire in the cul-de-sac, Odette. If I knew we were summoning demons or something, I would have driven to your house."

"I need to burn it."

"Josh's car?" Odette hazards.

"Disco cats." I want to get rid of it; its continued existence on this plane makes my skin crawl. I don't want to inhabit the same space and time as my pathetic little scribblings about love, and tropes, and lessons. I want it to be as charred and nonexistent as every scrap of feeling I ever had for Josh Stallings.

Odette chews on her lip. "The grill?"

Poppy rolls her eyes but leads us to the deck. We get it turned on, managing not to blow the doors off or lose any eyebrows. Odette pulls up one of the grates to access the flames below.

"Are we thinking medium rare, or more of a well-done situation?" Poppy asks. I hand her the notebook, and she hesitates.

"Are you sure? This was for you more than it was ever for him. Don't you want to look through it first?"

I shake my head. "I'm not losing the books I loved, I'm just killing the evidence that they came into my life because I let someone convince me I wasn't enough. That I needed to learn something that I didn't feel."

"Fair enough," Poppy says, and she snatches it up and tosses it into the flames. The pages curl, retracting into the cover like a turtle, and slowly each cat winks out of existence and crumbles to ash.

Odette collapses into a deck chair, the orange glow from the grill bathing us in a warm light. "Are you going to tell us more about what happened? Did he blame all y'all's problems on you, high-five his douchebag friends, and then do a keg stand?"

I'm emptied out, and only have the energy for the TL;DR. "Pants gone. Isabel Sawyer under him. He told me it wasn't what it looked like."

Odette lunges out of her chair with an outraged pterodactyl shriek. "He is the *worst*."

Poppy pulls in a shaky breath. "Okay, did you murder him? Is there a body back there that we need to take care of? I don't know if I can get my hands on that much lye, but I'll try."

I'm pretty sure she's joking, so I just shake my head. "Witnesses."

"Ah, yes, the sophomore."

It's not what it looks like.

I bury my face in my hands. "I can't believe he thought I would listen to him. I can't believe I spent months trying to get back with him. I *am* that stupid."

Poppy makes soothing noises and pats my lumpy bun, stuffed full of pencils for stability. "I've seen you do Pythagorean triples; you're going to have to come up with a better defense."

Odette circles us, her face beet red. "That absolute himbo asshole, I'm going to—" She paces the deck, muttering under her breath.

I sigh. "Is this just a testament to how messed up I am? That I hated the idea of change, and was so scared I couldn't be someone that anyone else could love, that I convinced myself *this* was the pinnacle?" I slump back in the chair, my chin tipped up into the sky. "Oh, God, Momma was right. Christopher *was* the bad guy."

"So where do you go from here?" Poppy asks, scooting her chair closer.

"Where is there to go? I get to spend the rest of senior year thinking about things that actually matter."

"And Ash?"

A deep ache pulses through me. I can't face that part yet. His voice on the phone, and what hit me as soon as I opened that door, before I even knew how little Josh deserved any of what I had been so determined to give him: *I am head over heels for Ashton Hayes*.

"That's a whole different mess," I say. Odette stomps back and I point at her chair. "Sit, I'm too tired to keep watching you."

She slides against the gray vinyl, her anger popping like a balloon. She doesn't say anything, just reaches over and grabs my hand so tight it goes numb.

We sit there in the cold until my face and limbs get heavy, and I can't feel anything at all.

Twenty-Four

"What do you think: sapphic flower farmers, or second-chance holiday book with surprise baby?" Poppy holds up two cheerful paperbacks.

"My instinct is flower farmers, but the holidays are approaching, and that one could be a nice little gateway drug to all the holiday movies starting to trickle onto the streaming platforms."

Poppy frowns, pulling out a notebook and starting a good old-fashioned pros and cons list.

God, I love her. I take a sip of a disgusting latte that Ash clearly did not make. (Sloane, bless their heart.) Darcy perches in my lap, his bulk wobbling as he kneads biscuits into my knees. I give him a little scritch behind the ears as Poppy lists things like *pro: would like to learn more about flowers*. And *lesbianism. Cons: might not be in the mood for fighting*.

"How's that latte?" Sloane walks up, looking like a proud parent watching their children start to stumble around. They lean over, nodding at Poppy's list. "Yes to the bickering, but the slow burn is worth it, and no third-act breakup."

Poppy lights up, gay gardens steadily moving into the lead.

Sloane pulls up a chair and shines their *how-are-you-my-poor-lamb* smile at me. "Speaking of third-act breakups, how are you holding up?"

"Very funny," I say. Darcy bites me for not patting his head correctly.

"You haven't happened to mention to Ash that you're not even interested in Josh anymore?"

"And how would that work, Obi-Wan? Any books on the shelves back there about a girl realizing she was chasing the wrong guy too late, and then asking her unwilling helper to just slide into his place instead?"

"Actually—" Sloane leans back, craning their head to look out at the room.

"I want that one," Poppy says.

Sloane spins back around. "It's not rocket science, right? You can't just tell him that over the past few months, you fell out of love with Josh?"

"No, I can't." I push my feline companion to the floor and suppress the urge to down an entire bottle of Tums. "Because he wouldn't believe it. I barely realized it myself until the last minute."

Sloane slides my mug closer to me, their primary method of comforting. I let it warm my hands and thaw the block inside my chest.

"And at the core of it, there was no devastating sadness or sense of betrayal. It was . . . relief." The words bubble to the surface and pop out of me in a rush. A pressurized release that's been building inside since Josh looked at me and told me that *not everyone's built for it*.

Sloane raises their coffee mug. "A toast then. To *growth*. To realizing we deserve more. To wanting more out of the people we let love us."

I weakly raise mine, and they crack theirs against my mug and Poppy's juice until I can feel the reverberations in my bones.

"I guess I just don't know why it took me so long."

"You got there in the end," Poppy says.

"You've read the scriptures," Sloane says, waving a lazy hand at the shelves. "Anyone who always knows exactly what they want, and makes the healthy choice at page one, is probably fictional." They evaluate me over the rim of their cup. "That is not most of our journeys."

"I thought I was a smart person who's supposed to have at least one brain cell working."

"You're a real-life human who's barely through the first act of her own story and hit a bit of a rough patch. That doesn't mean you just throw away everything good in your life."

The acid bubbles up again and I push away the cup. "This isn't about Ash," I say, settling for the simplest truth.

"I'm not attributing transformative life experiences to anyone but you," Sloane says with a scoff.

"But you're the one who keeps bringing him up," Poppy says in a stage whisper that rattles through me.

"I can't just trade guys," I argue, feeling like the worst caricature.

Sloane laughs, and I press my sweaty face into the tabletop.

"Again, who said anything about *trades*? You're here wilting in my café because you miss someone who's become important to you. You want to spend more time with him. You want to kiss his grumpy face again—"

"I should *not* have told you that."

"The point is, sometimes we believe things—relationships,

moments—are all or nothing. You've spent months planning everything out to the nth degree with only one possible end point. Why don't you try just seeing where things go this time? See if Ash wants to hang out in more graveyards? Maybe you'll even *hate* the next kiss—"

"If you keep bringing up kissing, I will not be able to come back in here."

They gasp, clutching their jean jacket. "But kissing is what ninety percent of my conversations are about!"

"*Sloane.*"

"Fine," they say, standing up, their smile spreading from dimple to dimple. "I will let you wallow all you want, but when you want recs on books with big romantic gestures, I will be over there restacking the hockey romances."

Poppy's eyes are wide, and I can see this coming from a mile away. "No," I warn, heading her off.

"A *grand* romantic gesture!"

"Nope."

"It's *perfect*."

"It's impossible, and I'm going to do both me and Ash a favor and just lie low."

Then the bell jangles and a winter rush blows cold air and a tall, raven-haired, sullen boy inside the store.

Poppy's face lights up like it's Christmas, and I wish for the ability to melt into linoleum.

Ash pauses, frozen under the fluorescent lights, and I can see it play across his face. The quick calculation when he wonders what would happen if he just . . . didn't come over here. That moment, that consideration hiding in the twist of his lips and the bunching of his eyebrows, hits me harder than anything Josh could have done in that guest room. I want to rise up out of my chair and lecture him until he sees the picture crystal clear. My TED talk about how I was blinded by my own hyperfixation, and how I have never felt more unraveled.

He rolls back on his heels before slowly making his way over to us. Each step feels like an accusation, slow and reluctant and pointed.

I dig deep and produce a smile that hopefully hides all the feelings I'm worried my face is shouting at him. I beam up at him like a sunflower.

"Hey, stranger."

He nods at me, and smiles at Poppy. "Hey, Pops."

"Good to see you, Ash." She's gone stock-still in her seat, her eyes looking everywhere but at us, then finally pushes back in her chair and shoots over to the YA section.

I pull my smile wider. Something happy and carefree, and with teeth. Teeth that say *I'm doing just fine,* and *I am extremely fond of that peacoat.* I know he's not going to sit down, that he's moments from devising a hasty exit, but I give my lungs a second to expand and, for the first time since I started spending time with him, I give myself a moment.

To look.

To marvel.

To recognize that my chest tightens when he looks at me, and it's not anxiety or indigestion, or a misfire in my brain. It's because the idea of him *not* looking at me causes such a rush of unhappiness that it nearly brings me to my knees.

I dwell on the curve of his neck, the divot of his upper lip, and the cowlick with several unruly strands spinning off in a different direction along his hairline. Everything stills and all I can say is:

"I feel like I haven't seen you much." I sink everything into that one sentence.

His mouth tightens, and he sidesteps it. "I'm almost done with the paper. How is the presentation coming along?"

I can talk business first. It's important. The presentation is practically on our doorstep. "It's good," I say, my voice uneven. "It's good," I try again, hoping to sound like someone who has thought about this for more than five seconds in the past few days.

"Are you going to tell me what it is?"

"And ruin the surprise? Never."

"Marlowe." My name sounds like it's being pulled out of him kicking and screaming.

"Don't worry, Ash," I say. "Don't you trust me?"

He takes a deep breath in through his nose, and his throat bobs with words I know he would prefer to spill at my feet than swallow. "I would like to not be steamrolled in front of the entire class."

"No steamrolling," I say, my voice softening. "It'll be great, and I'll send it over to you the night before."

He nods and walks back behind the café counter without another word. I can feel my pulse in my toes, and my heart lodged in my esophagus. He's upset and I don't even know where to begin to fix it.

Poppy walks back over with two more books for the pros and cons list, and I hope my face has returned to some semblance of normal. The door swings wide, and another gust rattles through the aisles. Two bundled-up figures wedge through the door, and that coat . . . I know that coat. I rise out of my chair as Momma and Blue make a beeline for me.

"I *told* you that was her car." Blue is victorious, piling her pom-pom hat and pink wool mittens in the middle of the table. "Hey, Pops," she says, before leaning over and taking a swig of my latte. I feel a little less annoyed at the ripple of disgust that flashes across her face.

"What are y'all doing here?"

Momma pulls off her cream cashmere duster and drapes it across my chair. "We were down the street at the dry cleaner and Blue said this is the bookstore you've been raving about." She looks around in wonder, and I feel a twinge of guilt for not bringing her here sooner. She spins back around to me. "This is all *romance*?"

Her expression has me producing my first real smile in days. "Every. Single. Last. One."

She takes off for the closest display table, and Blue heads straight for Sloane and more zombie cheerleaders. I watch their progress and can't help feeling the heavy presence at my back. I don't even know if I should march them up to the counter and introduce them to Ashton Hayes—the one responsible for all of this. I don't know if he wants to meet my people or if he's too busy trying to make space and extricate himself from my life.

But I *want* to. I want him to know me, and I want the people I love to know *him*.

Momma stops at every single shelf, and the stack in her arms grows as she waltzes throughs genres and displays. Blue heads back first, her microscopic attention span already ready for the next sparkling thing to snag her interest. Momma's slower to return, only stopping with her inability to carry anything else. She spreads her books out on the table and marvels at them.

"This one," she says, holding up a cover with a woman in a purple Victorian ball gown smiling mysteriously out at us. "This was the first romance I ever read, and I can't believe it's here." She traces the cover with her finger. "God knows, this book got me through a lot."

Her smile, soft and secret, is the same as mine when I look at my Lady Jessica collector's edition. You never forget your first.

I clear my throat, jumping all the way in. "I'd like to introduce you to someone."

She looks up, slightly dazed. I nudge her toward the counter, where Ash is trying to rub another nonexistent stain off the Formica.

I hold her by the elbow and pull her in front of him. "Momma, this is Ash. Ash, this is my momma, Bunny Thompson."

He doesn't even blink over her name. He just nods, gravely. "Nice to meet you."

Momma smiles perfectly, a whirlwind of manners and questions about school and the bookstore.

He answers thoughtfully, matching her manner for manner, although glancing at me more than once. I can taste his confusion in the air. I beam, feeling my heart grow a little just by putting them in each other's orbit.

Ash asks Blue if she'd like a coffee, and her nose wrinkles as she sneaks a look back at my cup. "Hard pass."

His lip twitches, but he doesn't press her.

Momma eventually exhausts all her questions, and I walk her, Blue, and two new tote bags stuffed to the brim all the way to the car. I help her put her bags in the trunk, and when I slam the door, she's looking at me with a twist of her perfectly peony lips.

"So, Ash, is it?"

I flush head to toe, and don't bother to conjure up a defense.

She shrugs, the movement fluid as she opens the driver's-side door. "The eyeliner looks good on him."

Twenty-Five

My leg jiggles under the desk. I dig my fingers into my knee and will myself to stop. To find a way to stim that doesn't include parts of my body violently shaking and alerting my classmates, my parents, the local media that I am *stressed*.

Ash glances over, and I don't blame him for the less-than-enthusiastic greeting. "What happened to letting me know the night before what we were doing?"

"Didn't you get my email?" I ask, eyebrows so high they're in another time zone. I blink until he looks away, stone-faced and counting down the minutes until he is free of me.

I was going to send it; I was going to make a straightforward Victoria sponge cake. I was going to bring in samples and review the highs and lows of cake during the 1840s. I'd had weeks of poor mug-cake outcomes and practice, and it would be a nice little end to all of this. A bow to tie everything up with.

But *no*. I couldn't have just texted Ash a picture of rows of mini sponges and promised him an enthusiastic class response and a bland but comprehensive history of yeast in baked goods.

I had to go searching for references to food in the book. I'd sat there in the kitchen, surrounded by genoise, and gotten swept up in Emily Brontë's prose, and all I could think about was how Cathy and Heathcliff poisoned everything around them.

"Class, let's give a big round of applause for Poppy and Billy as they present a wood carving from the final scene in *Cyrano de Bergerac*." Ms. Chris claps enthusiastically. Poppy smiles blandly in a yellow dress impersonating a tablecloth and a headband with plastic ants glued to it. She makes no effort to contribute as Billy rattles away about Cyrano's great love and unmatched wit. His enthusiasm has her face souring a little, but his carving is objectively skilled.

"*Please* tell me you have something prepared."

I blink. Ash's lack of faith is surprising me. My love life may have fully descended into chaos, but I've never just *not* done an assignment. My skin pebbles at the sheer audacity. "Ash, of course I do."

He exhales in a rush and his words spill out. "I think I have cause to be a little concerned because you never *texted me back*."

I try not to wear every single thought on my face, but it takes considerable work. The truth is his impersonal and solitary ? felt foreign and ugly in our chat, so I just ignored it. I hadn't decided what to do at that point, and wasn't certain I'd fully given up on the sponges.

But sitting there with all my notes and knowing the slant we were taking on toxic love as a theme, I'd wanted to do something more.

I'd wanted to take Cathy's and Heathcliff's hearts, twisted with selfishness, bitterness, and regret, and *fix* them.

So, I did.

Odette and Tiffany move to the front to present *Robinson Crusoe,* each trying her best to pretend the other one isn't there.

I lean in, Ash's heady smell wrapping around me like a vise. "I rewrote one of the scenes to something that wasn't . . . toxic."

His eyes sharpen on my face, zeroing in on my poor attempt at casual. "Which one?"

"The souls one."

He nods, thoughtful. "It's a good companion to our paper." His shoulders relax an inch. "I assume I'm Nelly?"

"You can be Cathy if you prefer."

"No, that's you. The great romantic." The words aren't unkind, but it still feels like the gentlest kiss of a knife.

"Thank you, Odette and Tiffany," Ms. Chris says weakly, as they wrap up and head back to their seats. "Next up, we have Ashton and Marlowe."

Odette whoops loudly and my face feels hot. This was fine when I was scribbling in my kitchen to the soothing hum of my parents' wine fridge, but here on display, it feels like I didn't think this all the way through.

I busy myself moving two chairs front and center. Facing each other. I hand Ash his script and we take our seats, knees brushing.

"Our project was on *Wuthering Heights,"* I say, "and our paper focused on themes of destructive love. *Toxic* love." I almost look at Josh, but don't. "For our presentation, we have adapted one of the more famous scenes to something more modern and healthier."

Ash nods at me and the little nudge helps push me over the edge.

"Nelly, I was hoping to talk to you about something," I begin.

He leans in, like we're a couple of girlfriends out for coffee.

"It won't take too long, but it's a bit serious."

"Not really the vibe I'm looking for," he recites, raising an eyebrow over his script.

Low laughter ripples through the class, and my next words have more power behind them. "I was talking about Heathcliff to my therapist, and how it was a miracle that I'd found him. How being with him was like heaven on earth." I take a deep breath. "But then I realized I don't think I know anything about heaven."

"Probably because you're not fit to go there." His tone is teasing, and he's reading the cues perfectly. The class laughs again, and my brain is shouting *This is actually going well!*

"Very funny. I dreamed about it once. Heaven," I say, clarifying. "What it would be like. Who would be there, and it's *different*. It's different than what has developed between me and Heathcliff."

"Ugh, I hate analyzing dreams. Now if you want to talk enneagrams, I might reconsider." He reads my direction and moves to stand up, but my hand shoots out, his wrist burning my fingertips. I'm supposed to let go, but I don't. I look him right in the face and I don't think I even need my paper for this part.

"Please stay."

He frowns. I'm not reading from the script anymore.

"It's important to me that you know this. That you realize that *I've* realized this. I thought Heathcliff was heaven because he'd been there from the beginning. He'd been as formative to my foundation as orthodontia, and he found me when I was young and clueless and easily swayed by long mysterious hair, moody moors, and pretty words about love."

The class laughs again, and someone whistles that sexy sound. That high-low when something is about to get good.

"But I was wrong." My hand tightens on him. "Just because

something has been present for a long time doesn't mean it has earned the right to stay forever—strangling any hope of growth or happiness. I thought I had no right to look at anyone else, because Heathcliff had brought me so low with his weaponized attention. His whispers that I'm not enough. That I don't deserve *actual* heaven."

I do release him this time, but it doesn't matter. He's frozen in his seat, paper dangling from his hands.

"Heathcliff knew I loved him, and he was right that I wasn't good at it. I let him tell me what I felt and what it meant to be with somebody, but his demands and rules and standards were poisonous. I wasn't myself, and he was never going to help me be anything more than a shadow of that."

I take a deep breath, and it's shaky but grateful all the same. "Whatever our souls are made of, mine is my own. I am not a shared existence—always half and lacking without the other. I'm an entire galaxy, and I need nothing or nobody to orbit."

The silence stretches between us, and Ash flips frantically through his script at my gentle cough. "I'm going to need the name of your therapist."

I laugh, because he sounds more lost than I've ever heard. "Sure, mental health is important. So are books. And friends who are there to remind you what's important." I grin at the back row and my *people,* looking at me like I've done more than just survive.

And then I turn back to Ash.

"Thank you for helping me, Nelly. I thought I lost myself for a while there, but you helped light the way back."

He nods, his throat bobbing.

I stand and give the class a small bow. "Thanks for your attention."

Ms. Chris is beaming. "Thank God someone said the quiet part out loud. I have never forgiven Heathcliff for that puppy." She clasps her hands. "Class? Any questions, comments, cries of protest?"

Josh raises his hand, and I stiffen.

"It was cool, I guess, but I don't know. The original speech has some of the most romantic lines ever written. *Whatever our souls are made of, his and mine are the same.*" He leans back, perfectly confident to share his opinion on anything and anyone. "Kind of sad not to acknowledge that."

I want to tell him that of course he would like the idea that things are fated, and that soul mates exist and it's your duty to sit there and get trampled for *love*. But I know better now. I know a beautiful package, beautiful *words* can sometimes blind you, so you don't see the rot underneath. And I'm pretty sure Emily Brontë would agree.

"You're incorrect," I say simply, and fold my hands in front of me, waiting to be dismissed.

"Excuse me?"

I can taste the indignation radiating off him, and it bursts through me like sunshine and sweet tea.

"You're incorrect," I say again, slower, like he's embarrassed us both by his inability to grasp this. This time I don't wait for the invitation and return to my seat.

Ash folds back into his desk, dwarfing our corner of the room, and I'm too chickenshit to glance his way. To ask him what he saw on my face when I looked at him.

My blood roars in my ears, and I float through five more presentations before the bell releases us.

Ash is transferring papers into his bag, and I hover at his elbow until he faces me. I just want to talk about everything with him.

The weather, the presentation, or how Josh is an empty room where I have shut off the lights, and nothing on this planet could power it up again.

I jump in before I lose this moment. "I gave him the last letter, but it's not what you think." I have his attention, and I barrel forward. "It was a goodbye, Ash. A collection of what I should have known all along." I wait until he meets my eyes, and they darken until I feel like every inch of me is scorched.

I bolt for the door and second period, my courage finally abandoning me. My calves burn and I only allow myself to slow down when my next classroom comes into focus.

It wasn't a *grand* gesture, but it was a start.

Twenty-Six

"What do you think?" I spin in a circle, as if seeing all the angles is required to make a judgment call.

"I think it's so nice for you to make an appearance at the winter formal after coming straight from a funeral." Odette chews on the end of a braid, and her face is not one of rapturous wonder like I'd hoped.

"Odette!" I twirl the black A-line dress again, and the sad cotton skirt briefly curls up like a half-hearted salute before slumping limply at my knees. "It's black. It's the only black dress I have. I was trying to make a point to Ash."

"Did you hear that, Pops? She's trying to tell Ash *something*."

"Did Ash ask you to join his monochromatic lifestyle?" Poppy sits cross-legged on my bed, sewing a fabric cabbage rose to a dress already riddled with sequins and ribbons.

"Of course not."

"Then let's see if we can do a little better than this." Odette yanks open my closet, riffling through sweaters and church clothes.

"You're wearing black," I snap, not annoyed that she, of

course, looks perfect in her black satin jumpsuit, but that I am hopeless and not equipped for grand gestures.

"Yes, and it's working for me," she says, her upper body deep into the section of closet that has evolved into a shrine to my poor middle school choices. "Did you know that you own very few things that are not pants?"

"I have no idea why you're announcing that like it's a surprise."

A soft knock on the door jangles my last nerve, and Momma sticks her head in. "How's it going, girls?" She whistles low at Odette's jumpsuit and gives Poppy a few more suggestions on where she can stick more cabbage roses without toppling over. Then she floats into my orbit. When she raises an eyebrow, I deflate soufflé style.

"Why didn't you ignore me when I said I liked jeans, and buy me a closet full of party dresses?"

She smiles. "Come with me."

I trail after her. "Wait, is there really a party-dress closet?"

She ignores me as we go through her bedroom to the master closet. She walks in and pulls out a garment bag wedged at the back.

"This is old," she says, half apology, half warning. "But it's from once upon a time when I had your figure and your hair color."

I unzip the yellowed plastic and pull out a sage-green tulle dress. It has a corset-style bust, puffed short sleeves, and an Empire waist that would make the dress flare out and hit just above my knees.

"I've never seen this before." I trace the smooth cotton lining and send up several prayers and bless-yous to whoever made it.

"I wore it to my first homecoming in college," she says, voice clogged with nostalgia. "It was the night your father asked me out for the first time."

I look up, my fingers tangled in the skirt.

"I want you to have it."

I pull her into a hug, crushing the dress between us. She helps me pull off the black, and zips me into folds of a green that makes my brain feel like I'm walking through a forest at dusk. Cool and calm and—

"It's perfect." Her eyes are misty, but she's right.

It feels perfect. *I* feel perfect. Even if tonight doesn't end up like I hope, I'll still be standing in a Dress (with a capital D), surrounded by my best friends, and tomorrow I'll wake up and find a different path.

I walk back into my room to squeals and claps, and I do no less than four slow-motion twirls.

I don't attempt Ash's eyeliner tutorial, but I do leave my hair loose and cascading down my back and shoulders like a ginger kudzu. We load into Odette's jeep, and we're almost at the school when Poppy asks, "Do you plan to corner Ash tonight and confess your love to him?"

Never Mind the Monster's newfound popularity has secured them a gig at the formal tonight, and getting to see them perform live again has me straining to speed up the car through sheer force of will.

"I don't have a plan, per se. I just want him to be clear on how I feel," I say, face hot. "And nobody said anything about love."

"Even better, one always appreciates a passionate declaration of friendship."

We pull into the gym parking lot, the night already in full swing. Our school isn't like some of those impressive places in Atlanta or New York with marble floors, mobile coffee carts, or even a paved student parking lot. Our decorating budget allows for fake birch trees and twinkle lights for winter formal, and a prom theme that alternates between *Night in Paris* and *Magic Garden*.

So, when I say they have done the most with so little, I mean it. Swaths of white tulle, like snowbanks in moonlight, drape across the ceiling. The birch trees create a little forest that guides us through the entrance, past a photo station, and then opens up onto the dance floor, complete with refreshment tables and a makeshift stage.

And there he is. Ash is wearing a black suit that hugs every inch of his long limbs, and a snowy white shirt unbuttoned a little too liberally to be socially acceptable in River Haven. Unless you also have studded jewelry and long black hair, and currently have a guitar strapped to your front.

"Hot," Odette says with a sigh.

"Hazel?" I ask, nodding at her girlfriend stacking amps.

"Whichever," she says, leaning into me.

"Tell me," I begin, "would I be super cringe if I tell a guy how I feel about him in a very public way?"

She doesn't answer right away, and my armpits get sticky. "Odette?"

"I'm thinking," she says, without apology. "Are you planning to rush the stage? Stand on the refreshment table and yell about how you want to date the crap out of him? Why does it have to be public?"

I have no plan. I don't know why, but it needs to be *more*.

It's hard to explain. I thought about showing up at his house. Just marching up those stairs and spelling it all out for him with only his guitar amps as a witness. It would be a tidier resolution for sure. Get in, confess big feelings, smoldering kisses, and back home in time to catch a few episodes of my favorite baking show.

"Because he's a big deal to me," I say instead. "And he makes me want to make my feelings about him a big deal to everyone else. Because he's never anyone's first pick. Not with his parents who are gone more than they're not, and before I got to know him and myself better, not even for me. But I see him now. I know him. I want him, and I want there to be no doubt in his mind or anybody else's."

"Again, I'm going to have to say, *hot*."

Poppy holds up her phone. "Can you say that into the microphone again, please?"

I blush. "I'm serious."

The crowd parts, and I see Josh walk in with that sophomore on his arm. I'm perfectly aware of her name, and that none of this is her fault, but it gives me a small wave of nausea to realize that it probably takes someone as young (and gullible) as I was two years ago to not see right through him.

I leave all that in the dust, and we drift over to the stage. Ash is looming over us, his personality almost too big to contain on that stage or in his body. I can't believe I ever thought of him as quiet, or moody. Well, he *is* moody, but he's also electric.

Heavy silver rings wrap around his knuckles, and he grabs the microphone the way he once threaded his fingers through my hair while overcaffeinated middle schoolers with laser tag guns swarmed us. When he leans forward, the deep shadow of his voice plays over every word, every vowel, and I feel my knees go a little weak. Honest to Jesus, like an old-timey Victorian lady about to have a real need for a fainting couch.

Lights slide over all his sharp angles, and I know he can't see me, but it still feels like every song is for me. I move, although I have no idea how to dance to this. No idea how to dance in general, but the three of us knock together—all elbows and laughter—like a trio of loose bottles from my aunt Birdie's wine bag.

"Hot," I agree, sighing.

"Soon, baby," Odette says, twirling and dipping me until my

THE CALCULATION OF YOU AND ME   »   289

back creaks. My hair is damp against my neck, and my limbs are loose and heavy with music.

The crowd moves closer, and my glasses fog until my world shrinks to nothing but Ash's voice in my ears. They hit that last note and I wake as if from hypnosis.

I don't know how long has passed—five songs? Eight? Three years?

The principal, Mr. Weaver, climbs the steps, and I realize we've danced straight through to the announcement of winter court.

"I know you all have been waiting for this!" Mr. Weaver waves a sealed envelope in the air, and the band starts to pack up.

"Maybe I can ask him to dance later," I say, fumbling. "How have I read all these books, and I still don't know how to make a romantic gesture—"

"Can I have everyone's attention, please?"

My head snaps up, as Ash's voice fills the auditorium.

"Ash, we're announcing winter court—"

"This will only take a minute, Mr. Weaver." He cradles the mic, and he's looking right at me.

"Marlowe." He says my name in a way that leaves no confusion to what this speech is going to contain. He pulls out a piece of paper, and my knees wobble.

"I haven't been able to stop thinking about you. Not since I first saw a beautiful, red-haired girl wearing a math pun T-shirt in the hallway on my first day of school last year."

He pauses, looking up from his letter, and the meaning of his words hits me all at once. Odette squeals softly next to me.

"Then when I got a chance to actually spend time with you, I knew I would never recover."

I flush at the murmurs that race through the student body, my face and my brain on fire.

"My point is," he says carefully, slowly. Giving my brain time to catch up. "I want every moment with you. The quiet ones where I'm watching you work on homework, and I can barely keep up with how you process information so quickly. When you're explaining mushrooms and nouns to me in a way that sounds like music. All the loud moments too, where I'm trying to drag out our time together on a stupid hayride, because that's the closest I'd been able to get to you and your smile makes me feel drunk."

I feel like I'm in a sauna, and it's almost unbearable. I race for the stairs, and I'm on the stage in front of him before my brain can catch up. Then it's just the two of us, the spotlight washing everything else away.

"I like it. I like *you*," he says. The whisper of more hangs in the air, unspoken, but I can still feel it. "And I know that every moment with you feels more important than the one before. I want them all. Every laugh, every chaotic thought that runs through your brain, and every facial expression you have—even the one you make where you try to pretend I'm not hilarious. They all just make me want you more."

I'm breathless, like I've finally run the mile that Coach Grubbs swears I'm going to need to be able to graduate.

"That's it," he says, clearing his throat, and shoving the worn paper back in his pocket. "That's all I have to say." I close my eyes as every feeling rolls into a massive, tearful, overwhelming wave, and I feel filled to the brim with everything that is Ashton Hayes. I pray to Jesus that after a lifetime of Sunday school, respecting my elders, and leading grace about twenty percent of the time— the *least* He can do for me right now is not let me faint in this blinding spotlight.

In answer, He sends a cloud across the sun, as Ash moves in front of me. Cool air slides over my face and I let out a small sigh.

His fingers slide through my heavy hair, and the cool kiss of metal rings brings me back to life.

"I thought you deserved your own letter," Ash murmurs.

"I was going to do my *own* grand gesture." I open my eyes and he's blotting out everything else. It's just us, and he's touching me, and I'm wearing a pretty dress, and the slide of his hand against my waist is so gentle I could cry. "I wanted to make sure you know how I feel about you."

"So, tell me," he says, the words washing over me as all the space and air evaporates.

My brain shuts off when I'm reminded of his taste and the feeling of being in his arms and—

"What the *hell* is going on?"

I snap away from Ash as Mr. Weaver's face swings into focus.

"Marlowe Meadows, I am *trying* to just announce these damn winners so I can wrap up this evening and go home to my cat."

"I'm sorry, I—"

"Do you think I get paid enough for this?"

"No, I'm sure—"

"Well, I *don't*. Can I please get *on* with it?"

"We're gone," Ash says, cradling my hand in his and getting us off the stage so fast I almost feel like I dreamed the whole thing.

Mr. Weaver announces the winter court, and it's not me and Ash (because this isn't a teen movie, y'all). This moment is real and it's mine, but not even Ash could have gotten me back up there.

Poppy and Odette tear through the crowd as Josh and Tiffany go up to receive their crowns. Music pumps in from overhead, and Ash leans in and asks, "Want to get out of here?"

I smile up at him, a thousand watts at least, but I shake my head. I came with Poppy and Odette, and there's still a little bit of dance floor that hasn't seen our moves yet. They pull me back into the crowd, and we're jerky movements, instinct, and laughter bubbling up so hard my chest hurts. Hazel joins, and Ash is spinning me and dipping Poppy, and everything is . . . right.

Every coefficient is right. Every variable makes sense. And the answer? It's perfect.

"We're really doing this?" I ask, always needing the box to put things in.

His answer is a soft kiss at the corner of my mouth. "We're going to have to start calling our fieldwork dates."

I grin. "Since you mentioned that, I've been reading a lot of holiday romances, and I think a Christmas-tree farm sounds like an ideal excursion." My brain blanks for a moment at the smile that spreads across his face. "Or ice skating? Or hot chocolate *while* ice skating? Or hot chocolate while ice skating *around* a Christmas-tree farm?"

Long, elegant fingers skim along my jaw. "I can't wait."

I step closer. "Maybe this was my big plan all along. Step one: convince Ashton Hayes to be my romance tutor."

He leans closer until his breath mingles with mine.

I wrap my hand around the back of his neck. "Step two: flood him with mushroom facts and romance tropes until I get him to fall for me." The space shrinks between us even more, and I can feel the smile as he presses his lips against mine.

"Mastermind," he murmurs against my skin. "Lady Jessica would be so proud."

Acknowledgments

A part of me wasn't sure I was ever going to get to this point again, and I can't tell you how grateful I am to be typing this. I sold my first book during the pandemic, but after working on the front lines in an ICU through the worst of it, I felt like I didn't have a sliver of inspiration left. Not a single joke. Not one happy ending. I went a year without writing anything. Then I went two.

Eventually things got better. I got medicated, went back to therapy, and pulled myself out of the dismal place I'd been stuck in. I started reading again, then dreaming, and finally I found my way back to myself. I came up with the premise of this book, and felt cautiously excited for the first time in a long time. The work itself was long, and I was rusty, but I'm so very proud of this book and the journey it took to get back here. This entire experience has been healing in more ways than one.

First of all, a huge thank-you to my wonderful agent, Jim McCarthy. I am forever grateful for your endless support and enthusiasm, and I hope to be filling your inbox with unhinged ideas for years to come.

Thank you to Sarah Grill, my lovely editor extraordinaire. I'm so thankful for your insightful edits, and I know I can always count on you to get my buried Taylor Swift references. Thank you for your patience, and for making the intimidating second book feel a lot less scary.

A huge thank-you to my wonderful publishing team at Wednesday—to the talented team in marketing, publicity, copyedits, and sensitivity reads. To the incredible design team who created the most dreamy, Creamsicle cover design, the perfect complement to my bookshelves. Thank you all so much for helping me polish this book into what it is today.

To the people who supported me, fed my creativity, and just took up every square inch of my heart: Jenna Voris—your talent and speed both humble and inspire me. Thank you for teaching me all the latest Gen Z trends and just being the magical creature that you are. Jo Schulte—your no-nonsense approach to life and unwavering support have been so appreciated these past three years. Thank you for being you, and I can't wait to celebrate all of your upcoming big moments.

Thank you to Mazey Eddings for being the autistic, monster-brained, beautiful friend of my heart. I've known you for a year, but it feels like ten (in the very best way). To Emily Minarik, the other 33.3 percent of the Tism Tro(u)pe Squad—thank you for all the delightfully unhinged things that come out of your brain, and for always being an incredible cheerleader. Can't wait to see you do big things!

To Dehra McGuire for being obnoxiously smart and beautiful, and for always having my back no matter what crazy direction I want to go. I miss your face, and your friendship is massively important to me. To Rose Trotta and Hannah Crosby—I miss *your* faces too and can't wait to celebrate together in London. Love and appreciate you both.

To Paige Ladisic, Katie Perkinson, and Tabby Duckworth—your friendship means the world, and I will forever be grateful to writing for bringing us together. To Caitlin Coons, Megan Puhl, Nirmaliz Colon, Jenna Miller, Allison Saft, Sophie Gonzales, Diya Mishra, Megan Lally, Brian Kennedy, Sasha Peyton Smith, Kaitlyn Hill, Susan Lee, Rachel Moore, Victoria Wlosok, Aaron Scheib, Gaea McCaig, Rayleen Jones, Mel Dixon, Juliet Norman, Allie Sterling, Maria Rapisarda, Courtney Kae, Chloe (theelvenwarrior), and all of the many, many, wonderful readers and authors I have met over the past few years—your talent and support motivate me every single day.

To my Granville and Duke family who preorder my work without hesitation, and act like I am a big enough deal that sometimes I even feel like a real author—you are so kind to me. Thank you.

To my parents and sisters—thank you for all your love and for always cheering on my million hobbies and career pivots. Huge thank-you to the Kaylor clan, and to the Thompsons for just being you.

To Austin—thank you for loving me enough that even when I couldn't write them, I still believed in happy endings.

And to you—the readers. You are the reason I'm able to do this incredible, hard, scary thing. You, who were so kind about *Long Story Short,* and have been so enthusiastic about my sophomore child—thank you. Truly, thank you from the bottom of my heart. I am so grateful for the honor and privilege of this platform, and the ability to send my neurodiverse love stories into the world. All of this is for you, and because of you, and it means more than I can ever express.